Harvest of Dreams

"This is the first time I've read Alison Henderson
but it definitely won't be the last. She writes with a view
that has you inside her stories, living the lives and
feeling the emotions."
~*Happily Ever After Reviews (5 Teacups)*

~~*~~

A Man Like That

"I finished this in one night, because I had to know
what was going to happen. I even cried a few times
along the way as I felt for the characters and what they
were going through."
~*One Hundred Romances Project (5 Stars)*

~~*~~

Unwritten Rules

"Ms. Henderson builds up dramatic suspense along
with mountains of romantic insecurity! …This page-
turner is a true delight. A spicy and fun 'who done it,'
which includes a beautiful love story."
~*In'D Tale Magazine (5 Stars)*

Also by Alison Henderson

Harvest of Dreams
A Man Like That
The Treasure of Como Bluff
Unwritten Rules
Small Town Christmas Tales

Boiling Point

Alison Henderson

BOILING POINT

ISBN-13: 978-153-764-6183
ISBN-10: 1537646184

COVER ART BY CREATIVE AUTHOR SERVICES

PUBLISHED BY ALISON HENDERSON
UNITED STATES OF AMERICA
SEPTEMBER 2016

Dedication

To my sisters Catherine and Eileen, who once again helped bring this story to life.

And to Jannine, whose keen insights and excellent advice keep me on the right track.

Chapter One

Zoë Hargrove jerked the wheel of her red and white Mini Cooper and slammed the heel of her palm into the horn as the rusty brown dump truck clipped her front bumper. She bit off an epithet, downshifted, and glared at the truck's long side view mirror, hoping to meet the driver's gaze. He never glanced over.

Where are the cops when you need them?

She swore again and rammed the horn as the truck lumbered ahead up Lake Shore Drive toward downtown Chicago. Grabbing her phone, she pressed it to the windshield and snapped a quick shot of the license plate. With luck, the picture would be clear enough to read the numbers. When she reached Lake Forest, she could email the photo to Risa back at the Phoenix, Ltd. office. As office manager and all-around go-to person, Risa was a whiz at tracking things down.

If the trucking company refused to pay for the damage to her bumper, Zoë could always file a police report. Her boss, Madelyn Li, had enough connections in the CPD to turn on some serious heat. Heck, she might even call in the FBI.

Zoë relaxed her death grip on the steering wheel and drew a slow, deep breath in an effort to slow her pounding heart.

Nothing like a double shot of adrenaline first thing in the morning to set the tone for the day.

She peered ahead through the damp gray haze of early November drizzle at the usual stack-up as the lanes of traffic neared McCormick Place then flashed the wipers. The clock on the dashboard read seven thirty-two. Even with the rain, she should be able to make it to Lake Forest in an hour, easy. She didn't want to be late the first day of a new assignment.

A loud, whining buzz interrupted her thoughts, and she checked her rear view mirror. Nothing. The high-pitched whine grew louder. When she glanced at the driver's side mirror, she did a quick double take. A motorcyclist in black leathers and a black helmet loomed on her left rear tail. He bent low over a black Japanese crotch rocket like a malevolent wasp.

Where did he come from?

The rider leaned right then disappeared from view. Zoë twisted and located him in her blind spot, keeping a steady pace with her car.

What a moron.

As she turned back, she caught sight of another black-suited cyclist on an identical bike holding steady just off her right rear quarter panel and sucked in a breath through clenched teeth. She was in no mood to play hide-and-seek in rush hour traffic with a couple of kamikaze wannabes.

Up ahead, a rolling wave of brake lights flared. The rust-pitted Toyota in front of her took advantage of a widening space to shoot into the next lane. Zoë had just started to apply more pressure to the gas pedal when a dirty brown tailgate appeared inches in front of her.

It was the same damned dump truck! Had to be. He'd almost changed lanes into her again. What was wrong with the guy?

She downshifted then hit the horn, for all the good it would do. The truck driver was obviously deaf as well as blind.

The whine behind her intensified like a screaming hive of bees on meth. A quick mirror check showed the cyclists bearing down again from both sides, their ugly black machines mere inches from her rear side panels. What were they trying to do? She glanced forward again. The back end of the dump truck filled her windshield. Her pulsed pounded in her ears. If the driver slowed a fraction, she would plow into him.

Just in time, her evasive driving training kicked in and muscled the burgeoning panic aside. Blocked on three sides, she had only one avenue of escape. She glanced in the rear view mirror to gauge her opening then slowed her speed and gave the wheel a quick jerk to the left. The Mini slid sideways into a narrow gap in the neighboring lane, barely missing the back wheel of one of the bikes. Zoë blew out a quick breath and thanked her lucky stars for her car's compact proportions. Horns blared, but the silver Chevy behind her dropped back to give her a few feet of breathing room. The cyclists' black helmets turned toward her in unison before they shot forward on either side of the dump truck and disappeared between the lanes of traffic.

Her hands shook as she gripped the steering wheel. She tried to swallow, but her dry throat balked. When she reached for the bottle of water in her cup holder, a drop of cold perspiration trickled down the inside of her arm.

Great. Just great. Not only had a couple of show-off idiots nearly killed her, but now she had to worry about pit stains when she met her new client. *Real professional.*

Her nerves were already on edge because she'd had so little time to prepare. The client had called yesterday and wanted an agent immediately. She loosened her death-grip on the steering wheel and took a series of deep breaths. She couldn't blow it. This assignment was too important, especially because her boss was in the Bahamas on her honeymoon, and Zoë had taken the initiative to accept the job on her own. She'd only been an operative of the Phoenix, Ltd. Personal Protection Agency for six months, but she wanted to prove she was ready to take on more responsibility. This job could be her ticket.

The client, Lyman Prescott, had been fuzzy about the details of the job when she'd spoken with him on the phone. She'd gotten the basics. He wanted to hire a bodyguard for his wife, someone who could also work undercover as a personal chef. The rest of the conversation had been a bit confusing — something about a person named Watanabe and a grandpa. She would sort everything out when she reached Strathmoor, the Prescott family estate on the western shore of Lake Michigan.

Last night she'd Googled Lyman Prescott and learned he was the grandson of notorious Prohibition-era Chicago bootlegger, Frankie "No Nose" Prescott. According to the articles, Lyman was some sort of inventor. Apparently, he was also a bit of a recluse, since none of the articles included a photo. She pictured a short, bald man with thick, round glasses, rattling around in a laboratory full of mysterious gadgets. This could be a fun assignment...if only it didn't involve cooking.

She wasn't as hopeless in the kitchen as her mother claimed—she had, in fact, never burned water—but what were the chances the Prescotts would be satisfied with scrambled eggs and BLTs?

The thick gray drizzle enveloped her the rest of the way to Lake Forest. Roadside landmarks disappeared in the mist, but every couple of miles a green and white highway sign leapt from the fog like a Halloween goblin. Once she reached the tony suburb, finding Strathmoor became an even greater challenge. Along the lake, mansions hid behind ivy-covered walls and massive iron gates. The roads were poorly marked—probably to keep the riffraff out. If you didn't know where you were going, you probably didn't belong in Lake Forest in the first place. By the time she'd driven down the wrong lane three times, Zoë was cursing her GPS in language that would have given her grandma hives.

On the fourth try, she spotted a gate with an elaborate "P" worked into the black wrought iron. She checked the address number on the stone wall and released a pent-up breath.

Finally.

She pulled into the driveway in front of the gate and rolled down her window. But when she reached for the button on the intercom, her finger fell several inches short. *Rats.* Lack of height was one of the few disadvantages of her precious car.

She cut the engine then swiveled in her seat and unfolded her legs. If there was a graceful way to exit the Mini in a skirt, she had yet to discover it. That was a minor annoyance since she rarely wore skirts, but she'd dressed up today, wanting to make a good impression on her new client.

As she stepped out, a high-pitched buzz caught her attention. She glanced down the street and spied a pair of black-clad motorcyclists, side by side, approaching rapidly. It couldn't be coincidence. They had to be the same idiots who'd tried to play chicken with her earlier, but why would they follow her here?

As they neared, they slowed their bikes and gunned the engines. The dark shields of their helmets obscured their faces, lending an air of menace to their solid black figures, like a pair of ninjas preparing to strike. Zoë shot a quick glance over her shoulder at her bag still on the passenger seat of the car. Her weapon was inside. Could she reach it in time, if necessary?

Before she could act, the cyclists cruised by, moving just fast enough to stay upright. As they passed, one raised two fingers to his helmet in a parody of a salute. Then they revved their motors and roared off down the street.

Adrenaline zipped through Zoë's veins. Air filled her lungs in short, sharp pants.

What the hell?

She glanced around, allowing the solidity of iron and stone to bring her back to the present situation. She was here to do a job, which was starting off a lot less routine than she'd anticipated. She stepped up to the two-way speaker next to the gate, took a deep breath, and pushed the button. "Zoë Hargrove to see Mr. Prescott."

A male voice crackled in response. "Miss Hargrove, please come in."

When the gates parted silently, Zoë climbed back in her car and drove through. A subtle shiver slithered through her body. The grounds of Strathmoor had probably been lovely once, but now dark, tangled woods surrounded the broad swath of weedy lawn. The woods would be an excellent hiding place for a pair of deadly ninjas.

For the love of Pete, Hargrove, pull yourself together. This is a job, not some C-grade graphic novel.

She slowed the car, grabbed the bottle of water for a quick swig, and surveyed the house at the end of the drive. The sprawling stone mansion was an early twentieth century version of an English country manor, complete with parapets and numerous fancifully-shaped chimneys. It was the perfect place for a rum-running gangster and his machine gun-toting cohorts. Zoë pictured a string of long black Packards delivering bleached blonde flappers in fringed dresses for a night of hot jazz and cool hooch. At the moment, however, only a non-descript brown Ford sedan sat parked at the base of the stone steps.

Not wanting to box in the other car, she eased forward and followed the driveway along the side of the house. Behind the house, she found a wide, cobblestone courtyard in front of a turreted, two-story structure that looked more like a mini-castle than a place to park cars. Only the array of garage doors revealed its true purpose. She flipped up the visor mirror to smooth her short, dark brown bob and refresh her lipstick. No point in looking as ruffled as she felt. Then she retrieved her rolling suitcase, locked the car, and headed around the house to the front door.

Mr. Prescott had been as vague about the duration of the assignment as he had about the other details. "Until everything's sorted out," he'd said. Whatever that meant. When she glanced up at the imposing stone façade before climbing the steps, a sharp pang poked her chest. What had she been thinking when she'd accepted this assignment? She probably should have called Madelyn first, even in the Bahamas. No one would believe Zoë was a chef. Not only could she barely cook, but she hadn't even had time to find a proper white coat to help look the part.

Then her old drill instructor's harsh bark rang in her ears. *Suck it up, Hargrove! You got yourself into this. Make it work.* She shoved her doubts aside, squared her shoulders, and pressed the antique brass doorbell.

A moment later, the wooden plank door swung open to reveal a tall, thin, middle-aged man wearing brown corduroy trousers and a tweed jacket. Wispy curls of indeterminate color topped a high forehead above bemused brown eyes. "Welcome to Strathmoor, Ms. Hargove. Come in, come in."

When he shook her hand, the strength of his grip surprised her. His appearance suggested a man more at home with mental than physical labor.

"I'm Lyman Prescott."

Her eyes adjusted to the lower light as she stepped through the doorway into a dark-paneled, baronial foyer with black and white checkerboard floor tiles. A pair of gilt bronze wall sconces in the form of Greek maidens holding torches lit the heavily carved oak staircase. They looked as though they'd been converted from gas to electricity at some point during the life of the house. The aura of a bygone age was so strong Zoë half-expected Frankie "No Nose" himself to appear at any moment.

She glanced further into the foyer and realized she'd interrupted a meeting of some kind. Behind Lyman Prescott stood two men and a petite, very pregnant blonde with her right arm in a cast. The thin man on the left could only be a cop. His small notebook, pencil, and matter-of-fact expression gave him away. Besides, no one but a cop would wear that rumpled brown suit, sad green tie, and industrial-grade orthopedic shoes.

Zoë glanced from him to the other man and took a quick half-step back. She was tall, especially in the burgundy stilettos she'd chosen that morning to compliment her charcoal suit, but this man was several inches taller and heavily built, like a professional athlete just past his prime. He wore a black suit with a white shirt and black tie, and a black-brimmed cap dangled from the fingers of one hand. Black hair curled above a strong, square forehead and prominent nose that listed to the right, as if it had been broken a time or two. But it was the intense expression in his dark eyes that made her stomach clench. She was used to masculine appreciation, but this was different. This man wasn't undressing her with his eyes; he meant to flay her open to discover her secrets. And the lines between his brows suggested he didn't like what he saw.

Lyman followed her gaze with a small, confused frown then waved his right hand in the general direction of the blonde. "Oh...yes...ah...allow me to introduce my wife. Marian, dear, this is Ms. Hargrove, the personal chef I told you about."

Zoë turned and smiled. "Please call me Zoë."

"Of course, of course." Lyman's voice had an edge of strain. "We don't stand on ceremony here, do we, my dear?"

"We certainly don't. You'll have to bear with us. We're not used to having household staff. I'm Marian. I'd shake your hand, but..." She tipped her cast with a rueful twist of her lips.

Marian Prescott was a lovely woman, especially when she smiled, and the tiny crinkles fanning out from her cornflower blue eyes suggested she smiled often. Golden hair tumbled casually from a big clip high on the back of her head. She appeared to be at least fifteen years younger than her husband, but the warm affection in her gaze suggested she was no trophy wife. Between her advanced pregnancy and broken arm, Marian's need for assistance in the kitchen was obvious, but that didn't explain her husband's decision to hire a bodyguard.

"I'm pleased to meet you. I'll try to be as much help as possible." Zoë glanced at the cast. "I'm so sorry about your arm. That can't be easy, especially now."

Marian shook her head and patted her tummy with her left hand. "Between my arm and my belly, I'm pathetically helpless for the next month. Thank heaven the doctor says the cast can come off before the baby's born."

Zoë turned back to Lyman. Phoenix, Ltd.'s personal protection business placed the highest priority on client confidentiality, so she didn't want to ask questions in front of the other men, but she needed more information. The presence of the police detective troubled her. And who was the big guy in the suit? He looked like a nightclub bouncer who was looking for an excuse to toss her out on her rear.

Lyman glanced at the two men. "This is Sergeant Lewis of the Lake Forest Police, and this is our chauffeur Dominic Rosetti."

Both men nodded in acknowledgement, but neither smiled. Maybe the sergeant was here to arrest the chauffeur for stealing the silver.

Lyman cleared his throat. "The sergeant is investigating a series of...er...incidents we've been having lately, but I believe he has finished with his questions for the moment. Haven't you, Sergeant?"

Sergeant Lewis flipped his notebook closed and tucked it into his pocket. "I think I've got what I need for now. I'll be in touch. Be sure to call me if you have any further problems." He handed Lyman a card.

"I'll do that. Thank you." Lyman ushered the man out and closed the door. He seemed relieved and offered a tentative smile. "Now, Zoë, I'm sure you would like to see your quarters and get settled."

"That would be great, but first, I wonder if I might have a word." She glanced at Marian's questioning face and ignored the glowering chauffeur. "To go over the details of the job one more time. I want to be sure I've got everything straight before I start."

"Oh, of course. Of course. We can talk in my study."

"Do you need me? If not, I'm going back to my book." Marian heaved a small sigh. "Reading is about the only thing I can do these days, and even then it's a challenge to turn the pages with this thing." She shot an accusatory glare at her cast.

Lyman squeezed her shoulders and dropped a kiss on top of her head. "Zoë and I just have a few business details to iron out. Put your feet up and enjoy yourself, dear." When Marian waddled toward the living room, grumbling, he turned to Zoë and gestured to a hallway off the foyer. "Right this way."

She followed Lyman into a sumptuous library with floor-to-ceiling shelves filled with leather-bound volumes. They were impressive, but that had doubtless been the original owner's intent. She wondered if anyone ever read them. A variety of well-worn science and engineering texts filled a lower shelf. Those were probably Lyman's.

He closed the door and motioned for her to sit while he remained standing. "I suppose you want to know why you're here, besides to cook, of course."

Besides that, yes.

She tried to suppress the niggling worry as she removed a small notebook and pen from her bag and crossed her legs. "I need to know everything you can tell me about the situation. You said you wanted a bodyguard for your wife."

"Yes. I contacted your firm specifically because the website said all your agents are female and able to work undercover as members of the client's staff. The references you gave me were all very pleased with your services."

Zoë smiled and nodded. "The agency has a sterling reputation."

He steepled his fingers and tapped his lower lip. "There's one aspect of this job that may be a little different. First and foremost, Marian must not suspect the true reason you're here."

She frowned. This was an unexpected wrinkle. "Our undercover personas are generally for the benefit of the public and any potential threats because people tend to ignore the help, especially when they're women. As a rule, we don't hide our identities from the clients themselves."

"That may be, but you'll need to hide it here. I can't imagine how Marian would fuss if she knew I'd hired a bodyguard for her. She's already upset about not being able to do much for herself. A bodyguard who could also cook seemed like the perfect solution. I just want her to be safe." He sank into a battered brown leather wing chair and ran both hands through the curly wisps atop his head. "She is everything to me."

Zoë nodded, pen poised, waiting for him to continue. When he hesitated, she leaned forward and gave him an encouraging smile. "I understand." She didn't, but hopefully, she would soon. "Why don't we start at the beginning?"

He clasped his hands in his lap. "The beginning. Yes. That would be three months ago." He raised his gaze to meet hers. "It all started with Victor Watanabe."

She wrote the name in her book. "What started, exactly?"

"The incidents—the calls, the accident, the break-in. That's why the police were here. Someone broke into this room last night through that window." He gestured toward one of the tall, leaded glass casement windows that overlooked the front lawn. The antique metal latch was bent and twisted.

"What was stolen?"

"That's the oddest thing—nothing, as far as I could tell. And if the burglars went through the rest of the house, they left no trace."

She frowned. "Do you have a security system?"

His pale face flushed, and he glanced away. "Yes, but sometimes I get distracted and forget to set it. Besides, there's not much of real value left in the house. I'm afraid the family fortunes have dwindled since my grandfather's day."

"You'd be surprised what thieves might find of interest, but regardless, you don't want strangers in your home."

"I certainly don't. I've tried to downplay the whole thing for Marian's sake, but the idea of someone sneaking around in the middle of the night is intolerable."

"Why don't I take over responsibility for setting the alarm at night? That way you won't have to worry about it."

He dipped his head. "Thank you. That would be a great relief."

"So, let's get back to the break-in. You believe the perpetrator was this Victor Watanabe?"

Lyman rose to pace in front of the carved limestone fireplace. "I don't know who else it could be. He claims to be a representative of a Japanese company, Ichiro Electronics, but industrial spy is more likely. He showed up here about three months ago with an offer to buy GRAMPA."

Her hand stilled, and she stared at him. "I don't understand. A Japanese company wants to *buy* your grandfather?" An image of Frankie's moldering corpse flashed through her mind.

Lyman dismissed her question with a wave. "No, no, no. They want to buy GRAMPA, my robot. His official name is the Great Robotic Automatic Meal Preparation Assistant or GRAMPA for short."

Zoë breathed a small sigh of relief that Frankie "No Nose" could continue his eternal nap in peace. "I take it you don't want to sell GRAMPA."

Lyman bristled. "Absolutely not. He is the culmination of my life's work. I've had a number of inventions in the past but never managed to time them right. This time is different. GRAMPA's different. He's unique. And with a few more adjustments, he'll be ready for the marketplace. I've told Victor Watanabe I'll never sell, but he refuses to take no for an answer. He keeps showing up every week or two with a new offer."

"And you believe he's harassing you to try to persuade you to sell your invention."

His soft brown brows drew together in a perplexed frown. "There's no other explanation for what's been happening. About three months ago, someone started calling the house at odd hours and hanging up as soon as I answered."

Zoë could think of another plausible explanation for the calls but kept it to herself. While Marian didn't seem the type, she would hardly be the first pretty young wife with an older husband to have a lover on the side.

Lyman resumed his pacing. "Then a couple of weeks ago I had an accident, and the car was wrecked. That's when Marian insisted on hiring Dominic to drive me." He stopped and faced Zoë with a look of determination. "She thinks I wasn't paying attention, but I swear a crazy motorcyclist tried to run me off the road."

A chill snaked up her spine. She doubted Lyman Prescott had ever been an observant driver — she could easily picture him lost in thought instead of concentrating on traffic — but his mention of the biker set warning bells clanging in her brain. "Are the police investigating the accident?"

He waved a hand in the air, as if brushing aside an invisible insect. "They say they are, but they don't hold out much hope of finding anything. The motorcyclist sped off, and I was too flustered to provide a detailed description."

She caught her lip between her teeth. There couldn't be a connection between the bikers she'd encountered that morning and Lyman's accident, could there? How could anyone outside of Phoenix, Ltd. have found out about her assignment and intercepted her on the road? And even if they could, why would they?

She made a note to call Sergeant Lewis. She hadn't gotten the license numbers, but she knew the makes and models of the bikes she'd seen. Maybe he could find a link.

Lyman's brows pinched. "I'm not concerned about my own safety, but you must protect Marian."

"So far, the incidents you've described appear to have been directed at you. Has anyone bothered Marian or made threats against her?"

"Not yet, but what if someone tries to break into the house during the day? I'm usually in my workshop in the cellar, and I might not hear. Or they might try to kidnap her to force me to give them the plans to GRAMPA. She hasn't been able to drive since she broke her arm, but now that you're here, I know she'll welcome the opportunity to get out." He paused. "I assume you carry a firearm."

She nodded. "I have one in my purse, which I'll take whenever we leave the house."

Lyman pressed his lips together and shook his head. "That's not good enough. You might not be able to reach it in time."

Zoë considered her Glock 26 and her wardrobe. The small gun was ideal for normal bodyguard assignments, when she wore a jacket and wasn't trying to conceal her identity from her client. It would be much more difficult to hide under casual indoor clothing. "Marian and I will be in close quarters every day. She's sure to notice if I wear a holster."

He threw his hands in the air. "Wear a big sweater, or strap it to your ankle like they do in the movies. I don't care. You'll have to find a way. Nothing can happen to her or the baby."

His anxiety was spiraling out of control. She had to reassure him she could handle this assignment if he let her do it her way.

"Mr. Prescott, your wife will be safest if we limit her exposure to firearms as much as possible. No matter how careful one is, accidents can happen."

"But what—"

"Before joining Phoenix, Ltd., I served in the Army Military Police for eight years. I received extensive training in hand-to-hand combat, including methods of subduing adversaries without a weapon. Short of an armed invasion, I'm confident I can eliminate any threat that presents itself inside this house. When we're away from the estate, as I said, I'll be armed. Nothing will happen to Marian or the baby, I promise you." She rose and tucked the notebook into her bag.

After a second, the tightness around his eyes and mouth eased, and he reached for her hand. "I'm so glad you're here. I know I made the right decision hiring you."

Warmth kindled in her chest at the gratitude in his eyes. Lyman Prescott was her first solo client, and she was determined not to let him down. He might be eccentric, but he clearly adored his wife. "Thank you. There are a few things I need to attend to as soon as possible." She pictured the tangled woods she'd seen on the way in and wondered about the condition of the wall surrounding the property. "I'll need to inspect the house and grounds, as well as your security system."

He pursed his lips. "If you can wait until this afternoon, Marian usually takes a nap around one o'clock. She might get suspicious if she sees the new chef poking around the shrubbery."

Zoë nodded. "I think I can wait a few hours."

"Excellent. Then if you'll come with me, I can show you to your room so you can get settled before lunch."

Lunch.

She swallowed hard. They would undoubtedly expect her to begin her new duties immediately. What appetite she had deserted her as she pictured her last attempt at gourmet cooking—a soggy concoction of overcooked pasta and undercooked shrimp. Maybe she could sell her new clients on the delights of peanut butter and jelly.

As they stepped into the hallway, Lyman added, "Oh, and by the way, I probably should have mentioned that one of the reasons I gave Marian for hiring you was to help test GRAMPA. I hope you don't mind a little electronic help in the kitchen."

She stifled a snort.

Sure. Why not? The robot was probably a better cook than she was.

Chapter Two

Nick Rosetti waited in the foyer, black chauffeur's cap in hand, until Lyman Prescott returned with the new cook. He hadn't seen a cab pull up, so she'd probably driven her own car. Good. If that were the case, Lyman wouldn't expect him to drive her around, and he could continue to focus on his primary objective.

Lyman stopped in front of Zoë's compact rolling suitcase and puckered his brow. "Is this your only luggage?"

She laughed—a warm, light sound. "I'm afraid not. I left the larger bags in my car. I'll get them."

When she turned toward the door, he halted her. "Dominic can carry them for you."

"That's not ne—"

"I'll take care of it." Nick stepped toward her with his hand outthrust. "Just give me your keys."

Her curved lips thinned to a tight line. "That won't be necessary."

Lyman touched her arm lightly. "Please, Ms. Hargrove..."

The tension in her shoulders eased, and she smiled at him. "It's Zoë, remember?"

"Yes, Zoë. Please let Dominic carry your luggage." Lyman hesitated, and an unreadable look flashed between them. "I wouldn't want you to injure yourself before you even start work."

She released a breath and nodded. "I wouldn't want that either." She turned to Nick and lifted her chin. "I'll go with you. I have the key right here." She shouldered her purse and marched toward the door.

Nick crossed the foyer in three long strides and caught up with her as she reached the door. His hand closed around the brass knob before she could reach it. When he opened the door, she brushed past him, both hands clutching the straps of her shoulder bag as if she expected him to try to snatch it and run.

Maybe he was being too touchy. He'd been on edge ever since Lyman announced he'd hired a personal chef. Nick had only been at Strathmoor a week and was still in reconnaissance mode. Given Marian's condition, hiring a chef made sense, but the addition of a newcomer to the household was a complication he didn't need.

But now that she was here, he had to admit the new chef was a stunner—tall and lithe, with the long, lean muscles of a dancer beneath her form-fitting gray suit. And those legs. She had to know what spiky heels did to her legs, not to mention a man's libido. Normally, he went for long-haired blondes, but Zoë Hargrove's chin-length dark hair formed the perfect frame for a pair of big, heavily-lashed, green eyes.

All in all, a very nice package. Just not the package of a chef.

Real chefs stood on their feet all day. They wore sensible shoes. They didn't wear wine-colored stilettos and have legs like a Vegas showgirl.

He wanted to believe she was exactly who Lyman said she was—a personal chef and nothing more—but his investigator's nose wouldn't let him. The woman was a mystery, and mysteries made him itch. Even beautiful ones.

Their footsteps crunched on the pebble sidewalk as they crossed in front of the house and headed down the driveway toward the garage without a word. When Zoë stopped beside a red Mini Cooper, Nick held out his hand again, and she rummaged in her purse.

She produced a key and pressed the remote button to unlock the doors. "I can carry my own luggage."

"I'm sure you can, but Mr. Prescott asked me to do it, and I like to keep my employer happy."

He opened the back hatch and sized up her bags, one red and one black. Then he reached in, grabbed a handle in each hand, and tugged. The red one slid out easily, but the black one jerked back against his shoulder like it was bolted to the floor of the car. He applied more muscle, and the case grudgingly thumped and bumped its way out of the car and onto the driveway.

He scowled at the suitcase, then at its owner. "What have you got in here, a collection of dumbbells?"

Her lips curved as if she were enjoying a private secret. "Mostly shoes—a book or two, but mostly shoes."

"Nobody needs that many pairs of shoes. What do you wear, steel-toed work boots?"

"If it's too heavy for you, I'd be happy to carry it myself."

Heat rose up his neck. "I can carry the damned suitcase." To prove it, he jerked the bag up with a single heave. "It's only awkward because you drive this clown car. I don't know why a full-grown adult would buy a kiddie car like this."

Her smile widened, but her eyes narrowed. "I love my car. It's cute and fun, and I don't have any trouble getting in and out—probably because I'm still young and flexible."

Now she was making cracks about his age? He still had a few good years left before forty. Life might have beaten him up a little, but she couldn't be more than six or seven years younger than he was. He bit back the words forming in his brain before they spilled from his mouth, hefted the bags, and headed back toward the house. The only sound was the crunching of her heels on the gravel behind him.

When he reached the foyer, Lyman and Marian were waiting. Nick set the bags down, and Zoë cruised past him.

Marian gave her a friendly smile. "If you follow me, I'll show you to your room."

"My dear, you should let me do that," Lyman protested. "You shouldn't be climbing all the way to the third floor."

She rose to her tiptoes and planted a quick peck on her husband's cheek. "Nonsense. I need the exercise. Since I can't see my feet, I won't promise to watch my step, but I do promise not to tip over."

"We'll be careful." Zoë glanced back over her shoulder. "And I'm sure the luggage won't be a problem for Dominic."

Nick gave her a tight-lipped smile. "Not at all."

He picked up the bags again and watched Zoë's shapely backside as she and Marian climbed the grand main staircase, headed to the servants' quarters on the third floor. He didn't mind carrying her luggage—not too much, anyway—but it would have suited his purposes better if they'd put her next to him in the suite of rooms over the garage. However, since he had no say in the matter, he would have to adjust. If he wanted to maintain his cover, accommodation was the name of the game.

Lyman walked up behind him. "Nice looking girl, isn't she?"

Nick nodded. "I only hope her cooking's as good."

Lyman's fingers began tapping the banister in staccato rhythm like a telegraph operator in an old movie. "I'm sure it will be. The agency assured me Ms. Hargrove is quite competent in the kitchen."

Nick shot him a sharp look. The man was as jittery as a junkie in need of a fix. What was it about the new chef that suddenly made him so nervous? One more question to add to the growing list.

He followed the women to the warren of rooms on the third floor that had been the old servants' quarters and set Zoë's bags in the small room with yellow flowered wallpaper that Marian had selected for her. "Will there be anything else?"

"Not right now." Marian smiled. "I'll show Zoë where everything is and be down in a minute. Thank you."

"Yes, thank you, Dominic." Zoë's smile showed a few too many teeth, almost as if she were daring him to respond.

He didn't.

Instead, Nick tipped his chin in a short nod and headed back downstairs. He'd never been much of a smooth talker and couldn't afford to mix it up with the new chef right now, no matter how sexy her legs were. It was more important to come up with a plausible reason to stick close to Lyman for the rest of the morning. When he'd accepted the job as the Prescotts' chauffeur, he hadn't considered how much downtime it would entail and how much more difficult that would make his primary task. It might have been easier if Marian had wanted him to play the part of the butler, but at least Nick knew how to drive. He didn't have a clue how to butle — if that was even a thing.

A few minutes later, the old stairs creaked as Marian descended, carefully gripping the banister with her left hand. "Zoë will be down for a tour of the kitchen as soon as she unpacks."

Lyman pushed past Nick and bounded up the steps in a loose-limbed gallop.

When he reached for his wife's elbow, she shooed him away. "Will you quit fussing? I'm fine."

He persisted. "You'll wear yourself out."

"I'm perfectly healthy, and the exercise is good for me. I can't sit around like a brood hen for the next few weeks."

Her husband frowned and shook his head. "I should have fixed the elevator ages ago. Don't know why I didn't."

Marian smiled and patted his arm. "You were busy with GRAMPA, dear."

Lyman turned to Nick. "Dominic, you don't, by any chance, know how to repair an elevator, do you?"

Nick had never seen any sign of an elevator at Strathmoor and didn't know if he could fix one. He wasn't a mechanic, but he was good with his hands, and a motor was a motor. Besides, it would give him the excuse he was looking for to stay in the house. "I'd be happy to try if you show me where it is."

Lyman nodded. "I would appreciate that. I should have repaired it myself, but as Marian pointed out, I've been busy." He tilted his head and regarded Nick with a hopeful look. "I still don't believe I need a driver, but you might turn out to be useful after all. The elevator is over here."

He led Nick to a door in the wall behind the staircase. "It runs between my workshop in the cellar and the second floor hallway. If you can get it working again, it would be a great help to Marian."

Nick opened the door to what he'd assumed was a closet and found the folding metal doors of an antique elevator, probably installed when the house was built. The interior was fitted with carved and polished panels that matched the woodwork in the foyer. It was a work of art, but function was another matter. "I'll give it a try. When was the last time this thing ran?"

Lyman pursed his lips. "About twenty years ago, I think. Or it may have been longer. I can't remember for certain."

"I'll get the tool box from the garage and see what I can do."

He retrieved the tools and after a twenty minute search, located a cobweb-encrusted wooden step ladder in the basement and lugged it to the main floor. He grabbed a flashlight from the toolbox, climbed the ladder, and poked his head through the hatch in the car's ceiling.

No wonder the motor didn't work. It was filthy. Blackened oil and dust coated the entire thing. He'd have to disassemble it and clean each part before he could begin to diagnose the problem. This was going to be a long, messy project. He climbed down and eased the polished wooden hatch back into place.

The control panel was next. After a few turns of the screwdriver, he peered into the wall at a tangle of outdated wiring. Replacing the wiring would be the first order of business. He didn't want to burn the house down before he got the elevator running.

Lyman popped his head into the car. "So, do you think you can fix it?"

"I'll give it my best shot." Nick replaced the screwdriver in the toolbox.

Lyman nodded. "Excellent." He stepped back and called out, "Marian, dear, Dominic is going to fix the elevator for you."

Nick couldn't make out her muffled reply, and Lyman's voice receded as he continued his conversation.

Footsteps sounded on the other side of the wall. It must be Zoë, coming down to start lunch. He latched the tool box and stepped out of the elevator into the foyer to find her standing at the bottom of the stairs. He felt a brief pang of disappointment that she'd exchanged her snug little gray suit for a raspberry-colored sweater and slim black slacks and her stilettos for a pair of matching flats.

Her smile taunted him when she held out her hand. "Let's try this again. Hello, Dominic, wasn't it?"

"Nick."

"And I'm Zoë."

The strength of her grasp surprised him, and he scanned her with a quick, assessing glance. Her sweater and slacks weren't skin tight, but they hugged her body closely enough to caress the firm curve of muscle here and there. She was clearly in top shape—a shape you didn't get from standing around peeling potatoes. And the way she moved—fluid and purposeful—spoke of training. The question was what kind of training? Maybe she ran or played tennis in her free time, but he sensed it was more than that.

Her smile faded, and she released his hand. "Fine. Nick. Can you direct me to the kitchen?"

He met the challenge in her clear, green gaze with a challenge of his own. "Sure. Follow me."

****

Zoë chewed her lip as she contemplated Nick Rosetti's long legs and broad, black gabardine-clothed back. A couple of hours on the job, and she'd already entered into a battle of wills with the chauffeur. She should probably try to do something about that. Unnecessary friction in the household could be dangerous. If she wasn't careful, she'd blow her cover and her assignment before she even started.

Her grandmother's frequent admonition about drawing more flies with honey than vinegar rang in her head. She could try being nicer to Nick, but it ran against her grain. He might be attractive in a burly, surly, he-man sort of way, but his whole demeanor spelled arrogance and aggression. Having grown up with five older brothers, she'd learned early that if she didn't stand up for herself, she'd end up mucking out the stalls alone.

Zoë pondered her options as she followed him to a roomy kitchen with solid white cabinets, red linoleum countertops banded in chrome, and a checkerboard floor that matched the foyer. The room looked as though it hadn't been touched since the forties. In the center of the room, Marian stood face-to-face with a robot that was nearly as tall as she was. The robot was silent and still—no lights flashing or gears humming—but her wary expression suggested she expected it to attack her at any moment.

Zoë stepped forward. "I take it this is GRAMPA."

The other woman wrinkled her nose. "Yes, but I wish Lyman would leave him in the workshop. I hate running into him here. He creeps me out."

Zoë had to agree. The robot was clunky and homemade looking, like something out of an old sci-fi movie. It was hard to believe a modern Japanese company would be interested in buying it. Maybe there was something in the internal electronics or software that was worth buying—or stealing.

She leaned down to examine a panel of red buttons on GRAMPA's chest. "How does he work?"

"I'm not sure."

"He works by voice command. You talk to him, like your phone, only he doesn't talk back." Lyman entered the kitchen with a battered notebook in his hand and flipped through the pages. "As the name suggests, he's a meal preparation assistant, like a personal sous chef. At this point, he's programmed to measure and chop ingredients. I plan to add additional features as soon as I've perfected the basic functions."

Zoë recalled her most recent attempt to mince garlic. Sticky bits had ended up everywhere. "I bet there'll be a huge demand. GRAMPA could take most of the grunt work out of cooking."

Lyman beamed. "Exactly! The home cook can have all his or her ingredients prepared in the correct amounts just like chefs on television."

"He got the idea while I was watching a cooking show one afternoon." Marian's pretty lips turned downward in disgust. "I can barely make toast, and those TV cooks make everything look so easy."

Her husband slid an arm around her shoulders. "I thought it would be more efficient if everything she needed was sitting on the counter in a row of neat little glass bowls."

Zoë had to agree with Marian. She'd never had much success trying to duplicate a recipe from a cooking show. She invariably forgot some ingredient or added something at the wrong time. Lyman might be on to something with GRAMPA. "I know I'd appreciate that."

"Good." His head bobbed enthusiastically. "Shall we try him out now?"

"Sure. Why not?"

"Excellent." He pulled a compact remote electronic controller from his jacket pocket, flipped a switch, and manipulated the tiny joy stick. The robot came to life, rolled across the room, and stopped in front of the counter. "Okay, we're ready to go."

Zoë held back a couple of steps. She half-expected the contraption to come at her with blades flailing. "Did you have a particular recipe in mind?"

"I thought we'd start with something simple, like vegetable soup, to test his chopping skills."

"That sounds good."

She shifted her gaze to the robot. *Better you than me, Bub.*

Marian bent over to open the door of a large lower cabinet. "I think there's a big pot in here somewhere."

Zoë jumped when Nick appeared beside her. She'd forgotten he was still in the room. Why was he hanging around the kitchen? Didn't he have something automotive to do, like change the oil or wash the car?

He laid a hand on Marian's arm. "I'll get it. Why don't you sit down?" She headed to a white-spindled chair at the farmhouse-style kitchen table while he retrieved a tall pot from the cabinet.

Lyman peered into GRAMPA's innards through an open panel in the back. "The vegetables are in the refrigerator."

Assuming his statement was directed at her, Zoë pulled open the door of the old-fashioned white Frigidaire and found a large yellow onion, a couple of potatoes sprouting eyes, a half bag of carrots, and a bunch of celery with browning leaves. She grimaced. The robot would have to be a miracle worker to beat her in the cuisine department with these ingredients.

"I'm sorry there's not much in the fridge," Marian said. "I don't really cook, but I think there's a bag of corn in the freezer and maybe some canned tomatoes in the pantry."

Zoë found the corn amid stacks of frozen dinners and two cans of tomatoes in the walk-in pantry. She set them on the counter, where Lyman had lined up a series of glass bowls.

His eyes gleamed. "GRAMPA, one cup of onion, chopped."

A panel on the robot's chest slid open, revealing a ten inch square stainless steel chamber. Then a second panel opened below the first. Zoë stared in fascination when the robot raised one mechanical arm, picked up the onion with a claw-like hand, and set it in the top opening. Next, it selected a bowl, placed it in the bottom chamber, and both doors slid shut.

"That's amazing," she said. "How did it know what to pick up?"

"Do you see these sensors?" Lyman pointed to a pair of discs where the robot's eyes would have been, if it had had eyes. "GRAMPA is programmed to recognize a large range of ingredients and utensils, so when I instructed him which ingredient to choose and the amount needed, the sensors scanned the counter, and he retrieved the correct items."

"Wow. Every home cook in America is going to want one of these."

He beamed. "I hope so."

She leaned closer to inspect the control panel. "So what happens next?"

"We wait."

Loud metallic noises emanated from machine's insides like a bad case of robot indigestion.

"When it's finished, the door will open." Lyman raised his voice to be heard above the whirring and chopping. "The skin will come out here." He pointed to the panel on the robot's lower back.

When the noise stopped and the lower door in the robot's chest slid open, Lyman reached for the bowl. Eager anticipation sagged into a disappointed frown. "The separation sequence needs more work." He handed the bowl to Zoë. "Maybe you can do something with this."

She frowned at the bits of papery brown skin mingled with pale yellow chunks of onion.

Like what? Toss it in the garbage?

"Let's try the carrots. It's a different process."

He requested four carrots, diced. Zoë watched in amazement as the robot used its rubber-padded pincers to pick up the correct number of carrots and another bowl. After a minute or so of whirring and clanging, the door opened again.

The carrots had been pulverized to a soft mash.

Lyman held the bowl up and squinted at it. "Hmm. That might have been my fault. Not sure I got the setting right." He handed her the second bowl. "I'm going back to my workshop to make some adjustments to the software. Call me when lunch is ready."

She stared at his back as he headed down the basement stairs. Even Julia Child couldn't turn this mess into something edible.

"I can't wait to see what you're going to do with that." Nick raised one brow and shot a pointed glance at the carrot puree.

She balanced the bowl in her hand like a softball and narrowed her eyes.

His lips twitched, but he remained silent.

Marian reached for the bowl. "I think we can dump this." She wrinkled her nose at the orange glop. "It might be useful once the baby arrives, but I like food with a little more texture."

Zoë checked her watch. It was eleven-thirty. Time to take charge of this circus before they all starved. "How about pizza?"

Marian's face brightened. "That sounds wonderful. I haven't had pizza in ages — maybe not since Lyman and I were married three years ago. He's not much for going out."

Zoë couldn't imagine her new employer in a noisy, dimly lit pizza joint, but her heart went out to his young wife. Three years without pizza? That was a major sacrifice to ask of any woman in the name of love.

Then Marian's smile faded. "I'm pretty sure we don't have what you need to make pizza."

"Maybe not, but Giordano's does. I'll give them a call. What do you want on yours?"

Marian hesitated for a second. "Peppers, mushrooms, and black olives. I'll share with Lyman. He'll eat anything."

Zoë nodded. That was reassuring. If he wasn't much of a foodie, maybe he wouldn't notice her lack of culinary skills.

Nick's deep voice interrupted her thoughts. "I'll take pepperoni and Italian sausage."

Why was he still here? Maybe it was her imagination, but he always seemed to be watching her. Cooking was enough of a challenge without a critical audience.

She dismissed the provocation in his dark gaze with a half-shrug. She had a job to do, and she refused to let Dominic Rosetti's presence affect her. Now where was her phone? Oh, yes, upstairs in her purse. She glanced around the kitchen and spotted a white, vintage-style princess phone on the wall next to the fridge.

"I think there's a phone book in this drawer." Marian produced a fat volume and handed it to Zoë.

She couldn't remember the last time she'd seen an actual phone book, but took it and flipped the pages until she found the number she needed. After she placed the order, she turned to Marian. "Lunch should be here before too long. Why don't you put your feet up and rest?"

Marian sighed. "It seems like all I do these days is rest, but I'm afraid my ankles agree with you." She headed toward the door. "I'll be in the living room, reading. There's money for the delivery man in the top left drawer of Lyman's desk."

After she left, Nick leaned his hips against the counter, crossed his arms in front of his chest, and cocked his head, as if expecting an answer to some unasked question.

Zoë pressed her lips together. "You can go back to doing whatever it is you do. I can handle things from here."

He didn't move. "What kind of personal chef orders take-out pizza?"

She crossed her arms to mirror his. "One with an empty refrigerator and pantry."

He eased away from the counter, opened the fridge, and perused the shelves. "There must be something in here a creative cook could use to put together a meal."

She clenched her teeth at the emphasis he put on the word *creative*. Was he naturally a donkey's behind, or was he purposefully trying to antagonize her?

"You want creative?" She marched to the pantry, grabbed a nearly empty box of corn flakes, and thrust it into his hand. "See what you can do with these."

Only a monumental application of self-control kept her from making a suggestion out loud. Instead, she turned her back and began searching for plates and glassware.

When the doorbell rang a half hour later, she headed for Lyman's office to get change for the delivery driver, but Nick was ahead of her. He paid the delivery man and carried the armful of cardboard boxes and Styrofoam containers to the kitchen.

He set the pile on the counter with a questioning glance. "How many people did you plan to feed?"

She plucked the receipt from his fingers and lifted the lid of each container, checking the contents against her order. "There are two pizzas for lunch, chicken parmesan for dinner, plenty of salad, and a box of brownies."

His lips parted in a genuine smile—the first she'd seen. It softened his rugged features in a disturbingly attractive way. "That sounds great. I don't know what the Prescotts used to eat before Marian broke her arm, but since I arrived, we've relied on the contents of that freezer."

"A lot of Skinny Suppers, then, I take it."

Pretty much like the freezer in my apartment.

"Yeah. Not enough to keep a hamster going." He opened the lid on the brownies and peered inside with a look of pure food lust.

She slapped his hand away. "Get out of those. They're for dessert." She shot a glance at his sturdy, muscular body. "Besides, you don't look like you're wasting away."

He shrugged, but unexpected heat flared in his gaze. "A man's got to keep his strength up. You never know when you're going to need it."

Zoë turned her attention back to the food, but her stomach tightened, quashing her appetite.

What's up with this guy?

Coming from any other man, his words would have been a come-on. Nick made them sound like a threat. She was usually good with people, but he was impossible to read. And he seemed awfully nosy for a chauffeur. Weren't good servants supposed to be invisible except when their services were required?

After she completed her security assessment of the estate, she would see what a Google search turned up on him. If the results didn't satisfy her, she'd call in Risa, Phoenix, Ltd.'s queen of research. One way or another, she would solve the puzzle of Dominic Rosetti.

Chapter Three

As Lyman had predicted, Marian went upstairs after lunch to rest. Nick returned to tinkering with the elevator, and Lyman showed Zoë the control panels for the security system before heading down to his workshop in the basement.

With everyone else safely occupied, she began her inspection on the main floor. Strathmoor's security system was adequate, if not state of the art. All the windows and doors were equipped with magnetic sensors that would set off an alarm if opened when the system was armed. Motion sensors were also placed in strategic locations. The system could be armed or disarmed from panels by the front and back doors and in the Prescott's bedroom.

The second and third story windows, however, were unprotected. The system designer must have decided the risk of entry was slight because the windows were so high, but since there had already been a break-in, that weakness would need to be addressed as soon as possible.

After finishing her review of the interior, Zoë grabbed her short, quilted jacket and headed outside. The morning rain had stopped, leaving a carpet of sodden red and brown leaves on what passed for a lawn.

Every breath sent a small cloud of mist into the lingering fog. Poking around the outside of the house, the first thing she noted was the lack of exterior lighting. Two large carriage lamps flanked the front door, but that was about it. The long driveway from the gate to the house had only one lamppost. An intruder could easily approach the house undetected. At the very least, motion-sensing floodlights should be added to the corners of the building, along with some general landscape lighting.

She began her inspection of the perimeter of the property at the front gates. The ironwork was old but appeared sound, much more solid than the wall attached to it. She tramped through tangles of dead weeds, stopping occasionally to examine crumbling sections of the wall and pick small burrs off her pants. There were no cameras anywhere. The place was about as secure as her parents' farmyard in Middle-of-Nowhere, Iowa. She would have to speak to Lyman about installing a few cameras and hiring masons to repair the stonework as soon as possible.

A forest of massive hemlocks obscured the northern border of the grounds. They had probably been attractive when Frankie "No Nose" had employed a staff of gardeners to prune and maintain them. Now, their long, sweeping limbs had grown together into a nearly impenetrable dark green mass.

Zoë picked her way through the mist-shrouded giants, scrambling over fallen limbs, until she found the wall again. Hidden in the damp, perpetual shade of the hemlocks, this section was in even worse repair than the front. Here and there, capstones had given up and tumbled to the ground, leaving the top of the wall as jagged and uneven as an ogre's teeth.

She spotted a hefty limb that had fallen against the top of the wall. It would have to be removed to prevent easy access from the neighboring property, but if she could climb it, she might be able to get a view down the entire length of the wall. She grabbed one of the small side branches and pulled herself up onto the log. It didn't wobble under her weight, so she reached for another branch and took a tentative step. So far, so good.

But when she shifted her weight, her foot slipped, almost sending her to the ground. Her arms flailed before she caught another branch and managed to right herself. If she'd had any idea she might need to climb a tree, she would have changed out of her smooth-soled flats before she left the house. For the first time in years she missed her old combat boots. Her first act as a civilian had been to ditch the ugly, heavy things, but half way up the damp, slippery tree limb she would have welcomed their gripping power.

She took a deep breath, adjusted her footing until it seemed solid, and tried another step. No slipping. Good. Grasping the small branches with each hand, she inched her way up the limb until she could almost see over the top of the wall. If she could stretch a little, one more step should do it.

She reached for the next branch to pull herself up and —

"What the hell are you doing up there?"

Zoë inhaled sharply and snapped her head around to identify the intruder. As she turned, her left foot slipped, and her fingers lost their grip. The branches slid through her hands, scraping her flesh and leaving behind bits of bark and dead, dry needles. She kicked her feet wildly and grabbed at the branches, trying to avoid the inevitable, but gravity won out. With a shriek, she dropped from the limb and crashed down on the source of her predicament.

Nick Rosetti.

As her weight took them both to the ground, the air *oofed* from his lungs. His arms tightened around her for an instant before he released her with a curse.

She scrambled to her feet and scowled at him. "What are you doing here? You made me fall."

Nick grunted, pushed to his feet, and scowled back. "You wouldn't have fallen if you hadn't climbed up there in the first place. What were you trying to do?"

She couldn't tell him the truth and wouldn't even if she could. She straightened her jacket and brushed a few stray needles away, gritting her teeth when her injured palms touched the fabric. "I was exploring the grounds."

She might as well have told him she was picking daisies. He pressed his lips together and narrowed his eyes. "From a fallen tree? In this weather? Give me a break." His big hand closed around her upper arm. "What were you really doing up there?"

She jerked out of his grasp. "I told you, I was exploring—not that it's any of your business. I wanted some fresh air, and Mr. Prescott suggested I might enjoy a tour of the estate."

Nick gave a huff of disbelief. "Yeah, right. Because it's so beautiful, especially in the rain."

She lifted her chin and shot a challenging glare straight into his dark eyes. "It isn't raining."

"It's not exactly tree-climbing weather, either." He peered up toward the top of the wall. "What were you trying to see?"

Zoë frowned. He was as tenacious with his suspicions as a bulldog with a bone. She ran a quick glance over his body, sizing him up. Tough, but not too tough for someone accustomed to pulling drunken soldiers out of bar fights. Nick might have several inches and sixty pounds on her, but she was fast. She could take him down if she had to, but that would be even harder to explain than sightseeing in the fog. Better to extricate herself quickly and get back to the house.

"I don't see how my activities should be of any concern to you." She tugged her jacket smooth and headed toward the house.

"Wait up." He hustled forward and matched his stride to hers. "I'll walk you back."

She kept her gaze straight ahead. "I'm not likely to get lost from here."

"Maybe not, but—"

"Aah!" Pain shot through Zoë's ankle. Her leg gave way, and she crumpled to the soggy ground.

Damned root. If only she'd been paying more attention to her footing and less to the disturbing man beside her.

Nick reached down and pulled her up to stand on one foot.

As soon as she gained her balance, she released his hand and sucked in a quick breath through her teeth. Her palms still stung, and now she'd turned her ankle. This was shaping up to be a difficult day all around, and a big part of the problem was standing in front of her.

His face wore a look of mild disgust. "Are you always such a klutz?"

"I am not a klutz," she gritted out.

"Then it must be those shoes. Only a fool would hike through the woods, much less climb trees, in little pink ballerina shoes."

She bristled at the insult to one of her favorite pairs of flats. In retrospect, they might not have been the

40

wisest choice, but her footwear was none of his business. Zoë had grown up wearing worn out, hand-me-down boots from one of her brothers and had gone straight into the Army out of high school. Now that she was a civilian and could choose her own wardrobe, pretty shoes had become a near-obsession. They reminded her she was a woman, and she loved them. Period. End of story.

"They're not ballerina shoes. And they're not pink — they're raspberry. Regardless, my shoes are not the problem. My only problem right now is you." But one tentative step brought another stab of pain.

With a huff of disgust, Nick slid his right arm around her waist and half-lifted her off her feet. "Put your left arm over my shoulder and lean on me."

She opened her mouth to protest but realized the pain in her ankle had disappeared as soon as he'd shifted the weight off her foot. As a test, she tentatively lowered it to the ground. *Yow!* She had no choice but to accept his help. Without it, she would never make it back to the house unless she crawled.

She mustered as much dignity as possible. "Thank you."

"You're welcome."

She refused to turn her head, but she could swear she heard a smile in his voice.

They slowly made their way out of the woods and across the lawn with Zoë half-limping and half-hopping.

"You know, this would be a lot faster and less awkward if I carried you."

The image of herself in Nick's arms brought a traitorous pang of something she chose not to examine too closely, immediately followed by a sudden fear. Lyman couldn't see her like this. If he thought she was injured and unable to do her job, he'd send her packing before nightfall, and her first attempt to prove herself to Madelyn would end before it began.

As soon as they topped the front steps, she slipped her left hand from Nick's grasp and released his shoulder. His right hand still supported her ribs, but some of her weight transferred back to the injured ankle. She tested it gingerly. It still hurt, but the pain was bearable. "I can make it from here on my own."

He opened the door then faced her with a skeptical frown. "At least let me help you to your room. It's two flights up."

She hobbled toward the stairs, refusing to give in to the sharp jabs that came with each step. "That's what banisters are for. I'll be fine."

She probably looked like a one-legged stork trying to climb the stairs, but by the third step, all she cared about was reaching the relative comfort of the bed in her tiny attic room.

By the time she reached the third floor, she was breathing like she'd run a 5K. She collapsed on the bed and slipped off her shoe. Her ankle was swollen and starting to bruise, but she could wiggle her toes and nothing seemed to be broken. If she could find something to wrap it, she'd be fine in a couple of days. The problem was how to do so without either of the Prescotts finding out.

Three loud raps sounded on the door, and panic squeezed her chest. Was it Lyman or Marian? What if one of them had seen her? She grabbed her shoe and tried to stuff her foot back in.

"Who is it?" she called.

The door opened, and Nick stuck his head in. "It's me."

Zoë let her shoe drop to the floor with a soft thump. "What do you want?"

He strode into the room without waiting for an invitation. "I brought you these." He held up a zippered plastic bag of ice, a hand towel, and a rolled Ace bandage.

Embarrassment formed a lump in her throat. He'd known exactly what she needed and spared her the risk of being seen and possibly losing her job. Her mother would pop a gasket if she didn't make at least a minimal effort to be polite.

"Um...thank you. That was very thoughtful."

He flashed her a sharp look then shrugged. "I didn't like the idea of the cook being stuck up here for days. In case you haven't noticed, I like to eat, and everyone else around here is hopeless in the kitchen."

"You could always cook for yourself."

"I'm hopeless, too." A dimple appeared beside his thoroughly masculine mouth.

There he goes again with the mixed signals. When he'd discovered her up the tree, she'd been sure he was going to call Lyman or the cops. And now he was showing her his dimple.

Zoë sat up straighter and stiffened her spine. "As you so graciously pointed out earlier, all I've fed you so far is take-out pizza."

"Yeah, but I have high hopes."

"Well, I guess you'll have to wait and see. At any rate, thank you for the first aid supplies." She held out a hand. "I can take it from here."

"Not just yet."

For a big man, his movements were deceptively quick. She'd barely opened her mouth to object when he was beside her on the bed with her left leg across his lap.

43

"Let me see that ankle."

She tugged against his hold then winced when the pain returned.

He adjusted his grip to ease the pressure but didn't release her. "Stop wiggling. I've treated plenty of sprained ankles before."

"So have I."

"I've played hockey since I could stand."

"I have a brown belt in taekwondo."

His dimple reappeared. "I guess we're both pretty tough then, aren't we?"

How could she hold out against dimples? She had to try. "You'd better believe it."

"So, tough guy, are you going to let me wrap your ankle?"

She rolled her eyes. "If you insist."

He wrapped the ice bag in the towel then used the Ace bandage to fasten it to her injured ankle with the speed and skill of an experienced trainer. When he had finished, he lifted her leg off his lap with surprising gentleness, set it on the bed, and stood. "Hand me that pillow, will you?"

She twisted, grabbed the second pillow from the head of the bed, and tossed it to him. He raised her foot and settled it on the pillow. "Better?"

She had to admit the pain was nearly gone. "Yes."

He straightened and pulled a small bottle of ibuprofen from his pocket. "I'll get you a glass of water. Take a couple of these and keep your foot elevated the rest of the day. You'll feel much better by dinner time, and no one will be the wiser."

What?

She blinked. "You aren't going to mention my accident to the Prescotts?"

"Why should I? You were just *exploring*. Perfectly innocent, right?"

Apparently, playtime was over.

She gave him a tight smile. "Perfectly."

After bringing her a cup of water from the bathroom and watching her swallow the painkillers, he left.

After his footsteps thumped down the stairs, Zoë fished her electronic tablet out of her bag. If Nick Rosetti was an ordinary chauffeur, she was Kate Middleton's cuter sister. She typed his full name into the search engine and watched as the results popped up. Listing after listing of Dominic Rosettis, but were any of them the right one?

She quickly discounted social media links to an aging Italian opera singer and a rotund restaurant owner in Seattle. He probably wasn't a chiropractor from Athens, Georgia, either. She gave up after twenty minutes and countless unlikely references. The only entry that caught her attention was an article in the *Detroit Free Press* from a year ago about a police detective who had been involved in a shootout in which a bystander had been killed. Unfortunately, the article hadn't included a photo, so she had no way of knowing if he was the same man who seemed hell-bent on complicating every aspect of this job.

She glanced at the time on her tablet. Four-thirty. Risa would still be manning the reception desk at the Phoenix, Ltd. office on Michigan Avenue in downtown Chicago, providing her unique blend of administrative backup, research, and tech support to the staff in the field. Zoë wished she'd had the foresight to snap a photo of Nick at some point when he wasn't looking, but she had every confidence Risa would be able to ferret out the truth even without a picture. She picked up her phone and placed the call.

****

Nick lay propped on the bed in his room over the garage with his laptop resting on his thighs. He needed to get back to the house to work on the elevator, but with Lyman safely tucked away in his workshop, he could spare a few minutes to see what he could find out about the mysterious Ms. Hargrove.

He'd been concerned the moment she appeared at Strathmoor, but this afternoon, when she'd inspected every door and window, his instincts had switched into high gear. He didn't know if she was casing the place for a robbery, looking for information to sell to Victor Watanabe, or involved in some other illicit scheme. Whatever her intent, she clearly wasn't here to cook. She'd responded to his attempted peace offering with caution, and since he no longer had the legal authority to haul her in for interrogation, he'd have to rely on more indirect methods.

He gave a passing glance to the cute Google Doodle of a puppy jumping in a pile of leaves and typed in her name. Only a few possibilities popped up, and after looking at their pictures, he quickly dismissed them. Even allowing for a change of hairstyle or color, none resembled the owner of the long, shapely leg he'd wrapped his hands around a few minutes ago. Who was she? If she actually worked for a personal chef service, as Lyman claimed, the company ought to have a website listing its personnel. Besides, what young woman in this day and age had no Internet footprint—no Facebook, Twitter, or Instagram account?

Of course, he didn't have those things either, but his invisibility was a matter of choice. Was hers?

46

He closed his laptop and swung his feet off the bed. Time to check on Lyman and get back to work on the elevator. Maybe he could drag something useful out of the elusive, tree-climbing imposter at dinner.

Nick was still in the elevator behind the stairs when slow, uneven footsteps sounded overhead. Zoë must be coming down to fix dinner. He refused to call heating take-out and putting it on plates cooking. By the time he stepped into the foyer and wiped his grimy hands on a rag, she had nearly reached the bottom of the stairs.

"I see you changed your shoes." She had switched to a sensible pair of black leather sneakers.

She sucked in a short breath and grabbed the banister with both hands to keep her balance. When she turned her head, green eyes narrowed in accusation. "You almost made me fall. What's the matter with you, sneaking up on a person like that?"

"I was just making an observation."

"Well, don't."

He suppressed a grin. "Sorry. Maybe your ankle making you extra grumpy."

She took two careful steps down. "My ankle is fine. I used the ace bandage to wrap it after the ice melted."

He raised one brow. "If you say so. Just don't expect any more toting and fetching from me."

"Believe me, I won't."

He stood his ground as she crossed the foyer and disappeared through the kitchen door. She appeared to be walking with her usual confident gait, but that didn't mean much. She would probably refuse to show any sign of pain in his presence out of sheer stubbornness. He retrieved his toolbox and headed back to the garage to clean up for dinner.

When he returned to the house, the tantalizing aromas of garlic, tomato sauce, and melting mozzarella and parmesan cheeses met him at the door. His mouth watered, and his stomach growled. He hadn't eaten a decent meal since Sunday dinner at his mom's house two weeks ago with his sister and brother-in-law. While Nick stuffed his face with baked manicotti, Kenny had mentioned a potential job babysitting an eccentric inventor whose wife was afraid someone might be trying to kill him. Nick had spoken to Marian the next day, and three days later here he was, ostensibly working as the Prescott's chauffeur. Since then, Lyman had insisted he join them for meals, but the pickings had been pretty slim.

He strolled into the kitchen and found Zoë dumping Giordano's salad into a large wooden bowl. She'd set the kitchen table with white dishes and red place mats and lit a couple of candles. The big room felt cozy and almost romantic. There was even an uncorked bottle of red wine, three goblets, and a tumbler of ice water for Marian.

As he approached, she glanced over her shoulder. "Would you let the Prescotts know dinner is ready? Marian is in the library, and I think Lyman is still down in his workshop."

"Sure." He gave an appreciative sniff. "The food smells great. Too bad you didn't cook it."

Her nostrils flared for a second before she turned her attention back to the salad bowl and scattered a small bag of croutons over the contents. "What does it matter who cooked it?"

He sauntered closer and leaned one hip against the counter. "Well, you are being paid to cook. So far, all I've seen you do is pick up the phone."

48

"Fortunately, you don't sign my paycheck." She grabbed the bowl and a pair of matching flat wooden spoons and carried them to the table.

"True. Lyman seems to think you're a highly-qualified chef."

"Who says I'm not?"

He eased away from the edge of the counter and met her gaze head-on. "Are you?"

She stared back, then her lips curved in a hard, tight smile. "You'll just have to find out—if you're here long enough."

"Why wouldn't I be?"

"You don't seem to have much to do. As far as I can tell, the Prescotts rarely leave the house."

"I find ways to make myself useful."

She spooned the chicken parmesan onto a big oval platter and set it on the table. "Well, make yourself useful now and call the Prescotts. The food is getting cold."

Five minutes later, they were all seated around the table, helping themselves family-style.

"This looks delicious." Lyman spooned a healthy portion onto Marian's plate then nodded at Zoë. "I applaud your resourcefulness."

She shot Nick a look that all but shouted, "So there!" He was surprised she didn't stick her tongue out, too.

Instead, she smiled and poked her fork into her salad. "I thought Marian and I might go to the grocery store tomorrow morning. That way she can show me what you both like and help plan the menus."

Marian's eyes sparked. "I'd love to. Since I can't drive with this," she raised her right arm a couple of inches, "and Lyman's been too busy to take me, I haven't left the house in two weeks."

"Excellent idea." Lyman nodded as he sliced a bite-sized piece of chicken. "And while you're there, will you get more vegetables? I've made some adjustments to GRAMPA's settings and want to give him another try."

"Absolutely. Is there anything else you'd like to add to the list?"

He chewed for a minute then swallowed. "Can you make gingersnaps? Grandfather's cook used to make them when I was young. I loved her gingersnaps."

Zoë smiled. "I love gingersnaps, too. Anything else?"

Nick seized the opportunity to toss out a test question. "How about some osso buco? It's great this time of year." Any trained chef should know how to make his mother's autumn specialty.

Zoë froze, and her eyes rounded.

Gotcha.

"I'm afraid Italian food isn't my specialty." She dropped her gaze to her lap and made a show of rearranging her napkin.

If the situation were different, he might feel guilty about putting her on the spot, but he didn't. "What is your specialty?"

She took a long, slow sip of wine. He could almost see the cogs turning and wondered what she'd come up with.

"German food. My specialty is German food."

"Oh, schnitzel and spaetzle?" He was willing to bet she didn't know sauerbraten from strudel.

Her eyes burned with a dark green flame. "Of course."

"My grandma used to make bratwurst with the best German potato salad," Marian said before popping a cherry tomato into her mouth.

Zoë kept her gaze locked on Nick's. "Mine, too."

"That's kind of lowbrow cuisine for a professional chef."

She tipped her head and slowly flashed her long lashes. "I cook what my clients like to eat."

"A very sensible approach," Lyman interjected.

"This is a little tricky to eat left-handed, but it's delicious." Marian raised a forkful of chicken covered with oozing cheese. "I wouldn't mind having it again."

Nick chuckled. "Looks like you'll have to brush up on your Italian."

Before Zoë could respond, the phone on the wall jangled. Nobody made a move to answer it. Another ring. Nothing. Nick glanced at the Prescotts, who continued eating, then at Zoë. She shrugged. The kitchen phone was too old to have a built-in answering machine, but maybe there was a newer model somewhere else in the house that would pick up. Another ring, then another. After six rings he was ready to jerk it out of the wall or answer it himself.

Lyman blotted his mouth on his napkin. "Zoë, why don't you get that?"

The two exchanged a long look before she pushed her chair back from the table and nodded. "Good idea."

She crossed the room and picked up the old-fashioned, corded receiver. "Prescott residence."

A brief silence ensued before Zoë frowned. "Who the hell are *you*?"

Chapter Four

"Who was on the phone," Lyman asked.

Zoë stared at the receiver in her hand. "I don't know. He hung up." She set the receiver back in its cradle. Adrenaline still coursed through her veins. She didn't know what she'd expected when she picked up the phone, but that wasn't it.

"I wonder if it was the same caller who's been bothering us for the past three months." Lyman propped his elbow on the table and rubbed a forefinger across his upper lip. "Although that person never spoke. I don't even know if the caller was male or female."

Zoë returned to her chair at the table. "This was definitely a man."

"Have a drink then tell us what he said." Nick pushed her goblet toward her.

She took a slow swallow of the rustic Chianti she'd found in the back of the pantry and waited for the resulting glow. Ah…there it was. She set the glass down and scanned the three questioning faces at the table. "As soon as I spoke, he shouted, 'who the hell are you?' I was so startled I almost dropped the phone."

"Your come-back was perfect." Marian's eyes widened. "I would never have been able to stay so calm."

Calm? Zoë shook her head. "It just popped out. I was too surprised to think."

Nick leaned forward and placed a hand on her arm. "What can you tell us about his voice?" As he spoke, his fingers tightened.

Zoë frowned and tugged her arm from his grasp. "Not much. He sounded angry."

"Did he sound young? Old?"

She thought for a second. "Kind of in the middle, I guess."

"What about an accent?"

Nick's staccato questioning was getting on her still-jumpy nerves. "What is this, some kind of interrogation?"

He sat back and ran a hand through his thick, black hair. "You heard Lyman—this may be the same caller who's been harassing them for some time, the caller he reported to the police. Now someone has heard his voice. Sergeant Lewis will want to know about it, and the best time to recall details is right after an incident occurs. Play the call back in your mind. Did the man have any noticeable accent?"

A tiny burst of satisfaction soothed her nerves. She might not have the answers he wanted, but she now had at least a partial answer to a big question of her own. His words gave him away. Nick Rosetti was now, or had been, some kind of cop.

"So...?" He dipped his chin and raised his brows.

"I'd call it a classic Chicago accent—hard and flat."

"Would you recognize his voice if you heard it again?"

"Maybe, but I doubt it."

Lyman interrupted Nick's stream of questions. "I don't think we need to do anything more this minute."

He picked up the wine bottle and topped off their glasses. "I'm sure we'll be safe for the next hour. I'll call Sergeant Lewis as soon as we finish eating, and Zoë can fill him in. In the meantime, let's eat our dinner before it gets cold."

The tight lines around Nick's mouth eased a fraction, and he nodded.

Marian tapped the rim of her water glass with her spoon. "Tonight I decree there will be no more worrying. We have brownies for dessert, and tomorrow — gingersnaps!"

Lyman patted her hand with a doting smile on his face. "Hear, hear, my dear."

After they had both spoken briefly to Sergeant Lewis, Zoë cleaned up the kitchen, loaded the dishwasher, and went in search of Lyman. She found him in his study, poring over a book of what looked like some kind of engineering tables.

He glanced up when she entered the room. "Come in, come in. I'm working on an issue with GRAMPA's hydraulics."

"May I?" She nodded toward the door.

He raised his brows. "Oh…of course."

She closed the door with a soft click and approached the desk with her small notebook in hand. "I wanted to give you an update on my security assessment this afternoon and make a few recommendations for upgrades."

He nodded and waved toward a side chair. "Please have a seat."

She scooted the chair closer to the desk, crossed her legs, and flipped back the cover of her notebook. "First, the security system in place appears to be adequate."

He bobbed his head. "Good. Good."

"But it needs to be extended to the windows on the upper floors."

"We can do that." He hesitated then pulled open the center desk drawer. "And here is the code so you can set the alarm at night." He handed her a slip of paper.

An unlocked center desk drawer – the first place a thief would look.

If it were anyone but Lyman, she would be amazed at the lack of forethought. For him it seemed to be par for the course. "Don't you have a safe or some other secure place to keep the code?"

His expression brightened. "Oh, I keep the drawer locked." Then his face sagged. "That is, sometimes...when I remember."

"And where do you keep the key?"

He reached in his pocket and pulled out a wad of keys. "It's on this ring...I think..." His brow furrowed. "Or maybe..."

"We need to find a safe place for your valuables. I'm sure Marian has some jewelry you'd like to protect, and you must have important papers."

A gleam sparked in his eyes. "Absolutely. Grandfather's big safe is still in the basement. It would be the perfect place to keep my notes and working drawings for GRAMPA secure from prying eyes."

Frankie "No Nose's" safe would be decades old. What were the chances the lock still worked? "I don't suppose you have the combination."

Lyman opened the drawer again and began rifling through the mass of disorganized papers. "Aha!" He waved a brittle, yellowing piece of lined notebook paper. "I knew it was here somewhere. Grandfather used to let me keep my coin collection in his safe when I was young."

Zoë smiled and reached for the paper. "May I? I think it would be best if I held on to this and the key for tonight. Tomorrow we'll see if the combination still works. In the meantime, I have a few other suggestions to improve security around the estate."

She laid out her recommendations for increasing exterior lighting and repairing the wall, and Lyman agreed to make the calls first thing in the morning.

She pushed back her chair and stood. "Excellent. I'll make one last sweep of the house around eleven before I arm the security system. Will that be too early for you and Marian?"

He responded with an impish chuckle. "Oh, no. I used to work late some evenings, but these days Marian gets sleepy by nine, and I like to go up with her to keep her company. I rub her feet. It helps her relax."

He rubs her feet without being asked. Absent minded professor business aside, the man's a saint.

At the door, she paused with her hand on the knob and turned. "I'll leave you to your work and see you for breakfast at eight. Please remind Marian about our trip to the store in the morning."

"I will, but I know she's looking forward to it. She's been feeling pretty cooped up the past couple of weeks."

She left him to his work, closing the door with a soft click, and turned to find herself face-to-chest with Nick Rosetti. Her heart jumped to her throat and, without thinking, she shoved hard against his rock-solid chest with both hands.

Nick stumbled back a step and rubbed his chest. "You pack a quite a wallop."

"Oh, stop it. I didn't hurt anything but your pride." She kept her voice low but made no effort to suppress her annoyance. "That's the second time today you've snuck up and nearly scared me to death. If you startle me again, you're going to get a lot more than a bruised ego."

His expression was all innocence. "I was coming to ask Lyman a question."

She stepped past him. "I don't believe you. I think you were listening at the door, or maybe even peeking through the keyhole."

He snorted. "Nobody peeks through keyholes except in old British mystery movies. Besides, was there anything going on in there that would interest me?"

Nice try, Sherlock. "Not a thing."

He glanced at her feet. "You ankle seems a lot better. Lucky for you I know my way around an ice pack."

She lifted her left foot and rotated the injured joint. She hated to admit it, but he was right. "It is better."

Humor glinted in his eyes, and his damned dimple reappeared. "Do you want some help upstairs?" He made a show of glancing around the foyer. "No witnesses."

Zoë closed her eyes and counted to three. "No, thank you. I'm going to the kitchen to work on my grocery list for tomorrow. You might as well go out to the garage and do whatever it is you do."

"I think I'll watch television in the living room with Marian for a while."

"When I walked past, she was watching *The Bachelor.*"

"Oh, good. One of my favorites."

One eyelid flashed so quickly she almost missed it before he strolled off toward the living room. Her jaw sagged as she stared at his retreating back.

What the...? Did I imagine it, or did that jackass just wink at me?

She shook her head and returned to the kitchen.

Since the fridge and pantry had so little to offer, she started her list with basic staples. After that, things got complicated. Besides the gingersnaps Lyman had requested and the bratwurst Marian wanted, Zoë had no idea what to prepare. She knew how to boil water for dried pasta and dump a jar of marinara in a pot but suspected that would only invite more snide comments from Nick. She tapped her pen against the notepad for a couple of minutes then had a brainstorm. Pulling out her phone, she started searching, and twenty minutes later she had two pages of ingredients — including everything she needed to make schnitzel and spaetzle.

Take that, Nick Rosetti!

She stayed awake half the night, chewing on the problem of the Prescott's so-called chauffeur. An email from Risa had been waiting for her when she returned to her room. True to form, the Phoenix, Ltd. super sleuth had dug up enough information to confirm that *her* Nick Rosetti was indeed the same man who, until last year, had been a detective with the Detroit PD. He had left the force after a shootout with a gangbanger in which an innocent civilian had been killed. The exact circumstances of the incident had been under investigation at the time the article was written, and Risa hadn't found any follow up.

She had, however, found a recent address in Arlington Heights, as well as evidence that he'd applied for and received an Illinois Private Investigator's license, but that was all. Nothing to suggest he'd gone to work for an existing agency or set up his own.

So he had wormed his way into the Prescott household, presumably to investigate or spy on the inhabitants. According to Lyman, Marian was the one who had hired Nick as a chauffeur, and it was hard to believe she had any motive other than to keep her husband safe. So who might have an ulterior motive for wanting to plant someone on the inside? Victor Watanabe and Ichiro Electronics? Or maybe some other outside party with an interest in GRAMPA?

The following morning, Zoë continued to ponder the possibilities while she showered and dressed. She was pleased to discover that whatever else he might be, Nick was a good field medic. Her ankle barely squawked when she tested her full weight on it. She wouldn't need the extra support of her sneakers, but high-heeled boots were probably out of the question. Instead, she slipped on a pair of adorable red ballet flats to go with her black leggings and red-and-white-striped sweater.

Her soft steps reverberated through the silent house as she descended the stairs. The Prescotts must still be in bed. She paused on the landing and glanced out the window, across the paved courtyard, at the garage. The shades were drawn on the second story windows. She'd better disarm the security system before Nick came looking for breakfast and set off the alarm.

A tiny voice in the back of her head warned, *he might be dangerous*, but she dismissed it. His behavior and attitude might be inappropriately assertive for a chauffeur, but they were not surprising for a police officer. And she didn't sense he posed any threat to Marian. He was always polite and solicitous in her presence. She would keep a close watch on him, but Zoë couldn't imagine Nick harming Marian in any way, and Marian's safety was her main concern.

She flipped on the overhead light in the kitchen and opened the refrigerator door, hoping she'd overlooked something edible. She found a partial quart of orange juice that didn't smell too sour and a half gallon of milk that had expired the day before. After a good long sniff, she decided the milk was probably okay for this morning. She located the remnants of a loaf of whole wheat bread behind a half-empty jar of kosher dills then stopped when her fingertips brushed against something long and flat.

Could it be? She stroked the smooth Styrofoam surface. It had to be. She shoved the remaining odds and ends aside and broke into a gleeful little dance when she extracted an untouched carton of eggs. She was saved! If there was one thing growing up on a farm had taught her, it was how to cook eggs.

"Do you always get this excited about eggs?"

She spun, and the carton slipped from her fingers. Her chest tightened as the yellow foam container hit the floor and popped open. Eggs bounced out and hit the black and white tiles, some breaking instantly and others wobbling a few feet away to die. One bold escapee made it all the way under the kitchen table.

Deep male laughter broke through her horror.

He was laughing. The idiot was laughing!

She marched to the sink, grabbed a roll of paper towels, and threw it straight at Nick's face with the velocity of a minor league pitcher.

"Hey!" he protested, raising his arms to fend off the missile.

"You will clean up that mess," she said between clenched teeth. "Then you will drive to the convenience store and buy another dozen eggs. You will be back here by seven-thirty."

His cheeks flushed a dull red. "Now wait a—"

She held up a hand to stop his words. "No excuses. No complaints." She glanced at the old-fashioned clock above the sink. "You have half an hour. Get going."

He jerked a couple of paper towels from the roll. "You're awfully bossy for a cook."

"Hah! I'm a pussycat. Have you ever seen Gordon Ramsey?"

Nick muttered something unintelligible but squatted and began wiping up the broken eggs. Five minutes later the floor was clean.

When he left the kitchen without a word, Zoë called out after him, "And pick up a fresh loaf of bread while you're at it."

Chalking one up for her side, she got out the bowls and pans she needed, set the table for breakfast, and started the coffee.

Twenty minutes later Nick marched into the kitchen and set the grocery bag on the counter as gently if it contained nitroglycerine. "I hope whatever you plan to do with these is worth the trip. The roads iced up overnight, and I was lucky not to end up in a ditch."

She reached into the bag and pulled out a carton of eggs and a loaf of bread. "It'll be better than the dry cereal you would have gotten if you hadn't made the trip. Besides, a little ice shouldn't be much of a challenge for a professional driver."

Before he could respond, Marian wandered into the room wearing fluffy slippers and a pink robe that struggled to cover her belly. "Mmm, that coffee smells delicious. The doctor says I can only have one cup a day, so I have to make it count."

Lyman followed her, dressed in gray trousers and a dark blue sweater with leather elbow patches. "I'll have some, too."

Zoë herded them toward the table, ignoring Nick. "Why don't you take a seat and I'll bring you each a cup. Would you like scrambled eggs or French toast?"

Nick plopped down in the same spot he'd occupied the evening before.

Marian closed her eyes and smiled. "That sounds like heaven. I don't think I can choose." Her smile faded as she opened her eyes. "But I'm sure there's not enough —"

"We have plenty," Zoë assured her. "Nick *kindly* went out early and bought fresh eggs and bread." She glanced at him and bit back a smile. There was nothing kind about his expression.

Lyman gave Nick a nod of approval. "That was very thoughtful of you, Dominic."

"No problem." His reply might have been directed to Lyman, but his gaze never left Zoë.

She tried to decide if he was being surly or pouting, but his mood didn't matter. Either way, she refused to indulge his childish behavior. Breaking eye contact, she turned to the Prescotts. "Why don't I make a big platter of eggs and another of French toast? Then everyone can have whatever they want."

"Excellent idea," Lyman said.

While the others sipped their coffee and chatted at the table, Zoë whipped eggs and milk with a fork then soaked bread slices and melted butter in a big skillet. She might not know how to make Oscar's Buckwheat, or whatever it was Nick had referred to last night, but even her mother would admit she made darned good scrambled eggs and French toast.

As she flipped the toast, she had a sudden thought that sent her into five minutes of blind panic. She had completely forgotten syrup. There was none in the pantry, and she didn't remember seeing any in the refrigerator. And who wanted plain French toast? *Blech.*

What else might work? Fresh fruit? None. Powdered sugar? Of course not. Cinnamon? Too much to hope for. There must be something. Improvise.

When she pulled open the refrigerator door again and scanned the meager contents, her gaze settled on a half-empty jar of raspberry jam. She said a little prayer as she cranked off the stuck-on lid and peered inside, but her hopes sank when she saw the crusty sugar crystals on top. Still, it was her best option.

She set the jar in a small pot of water on the stove and turned up the heat. Now would be a good time to have three arms, she thought as she stirred the jam and tended the eggs and toast. The jam slowly began to melt, and the sugar crystals dissolved until it formed a nice, thick syrup. She gave the spoon a quick lick. Not bad. It wasn't maple, but it would do.

She set the platters on the table, topped up everyone's coffee, and collapsed into her chair. Tiny beads of moisture dampened her hairline, and her ankle had begun to ache again. Cooking was harder work than she'd expected. How had her mother managed to serve three meals a day to a family of eight and make it look easy? Zoë wished she'd paid closer attention instead of running off after her brothers every chance she got.

None of her previous assignments with Phoenix, Ltd. had required such a demanding cover. She had mainly assisted her boss or other agents and provided back-up. The longest role she'd had to play was a couple of hours as a Wal-Mart stock girl. That's one reason she'd been so excited about this job. It offered the first opportunity to run her own operation and make decisions in the field. It also offered the first opportunity to screw up big time. For years, she'd ignored her mother's warnings about the dangers of being impulsive—spontaneity was too much fun. But now she was beginning to wonder if she should have taken a little longer to think this one through before jumping in with both feet.

Marian swirled the last bit of bread in the last drop of syrup on her plate. "I can't remember French toast tasting this good."

"And I believe I'll have another spoonful of those eggs." Lyman reached for the platter.

Their enjoyment of her simple offerings boosted Zoë's outlook. With a little luck she might pull this assignment off yet.

Nick didn't offer any compliments, but he didn't complain, and not a single crumb remained on either platter by the time she cleared the table.

While Zoë tidied the kitchen, Marian went upstairs to get ready for their shopping expedition. She was so excited one would have thought they were going to a Hollywood premiere instead of the grocery store. Zoë had a twinge of misgiving as they approached her Mini Cooper. She loved the compact car, but she wasn't eight months pregnant.

"Would you rather take another car?" she asked as Marian eased her bulk into the passenger seat.

Marian jerked the seat belt across her belly and clicked it into place. "Oh, no. I've always wanted to ride in one of these. "

When they reached the iron gates at the end of the driveway, Marian pulled a garage door-style opener from her purse and pushed the button. The gates swung open. After the car drove through, she pushed it again, and they closed on command.

"I love doing that." She returned the opener to her purse. "Growing up, I never dreamed I'd live in a place with a big gate like a palace."

Zoë checked for traffic then turned left onto the deserted road. "It is a beautiful house. Are you originally from this area?"

"I was born in Chicago and lived in the city until I married Lyman."

"How did you meet?"

"I've been a bank branch manager for the past few years, and Lyman was one of my customers." Marian frowned at her cast. "I hadn't planned to start my maternity leave for a couple more weeks, but I can't get any of my work clothes on over this thing, and my computer skills have been reduced to a laughable, one-handed hunt-and-peck"

"If you don't mind my asking, how did you break your arm?"

Marian shook her head with a rueful smile. "I'm embarrassed to admit it, but I slipped in a puddle of melted ice cream at my own baby shower."

Zoë shot her a quick glance. "Ice cream?"

She nodded. "Um, hmm. My co-workers threw me a party in the break room after hours, and Charlene in Accounting brought an ice cream cake. We were playing some silly game where the others tried to guess my circumference—if you can believe it—and a piece of the cake somehow ended up on the floor. I guess I wasn't paying attention, but I stepped on it, and down I went, like an elephant on roller skates."

"At least you can laugh now. It must have been frightening at the time."

"It was certainly startling. At least the baby wasn't hurt."

"I'm not surprised Lyman is so protective of you. Your accident must have scared him to death."

"I'm sure it did, but he's always been that way." Marian turned to Zoë. "I know we must seem like an odd couple—everyone says that—but Lyman's the sweetest man I've ever met."

Zoë smiled. "It's obvious he adores you."

Marian settled back against the seat. "He treats me like a princess—sometimes a little too much like one. He's always worried something is going to happen to me."

"Some men can be overprotective."

"I think he worries about Jimmy."

Zoë shot her a quick glance. "Jimmy?"

"My ex-husband."

Oh.

"We got married right after I graduated from high school and he finished the police academy."

Zoë stopped at a light then turned right onto a broad commercial street. "So he's a police officer?"

"Not anymore." Marian stared out the window at the damp gray skies and scarf-wrapped pedestrians going about their business. "Lyman is convinced he's a threat, but I've known Jimmy since we were kids. He would never do anything to hurt me."

"I'm sure your husband's just concerned about you."

"I know, but sometimes I wish he'd relax. I'm not a child, and I can make decisions for myself."

Marian clearly needed a friend to confide in, and under different circumstances, Zoë would have been happy to oblige. She enjoyed the woman's enthusiasm and normally upbeat outlook. As it was, she had no business interfering in her client's marriage.

She spotted the upscale supermarket she'd found online and signaled a turn into the parking lot. "Here we are. Are you ready to see how much damage we can do?"

Marian gave her an impish smile. "More than ready."

An hour later, Zoë wondered how seventeen bags of groceries were going to fit into the Mini. As soon as they'd entered the store, Marian had started pointing out items that caught her eye. Zoë piled them in the cart, adding the items from her list. She swallowed hard when the cashier rang up the total, but at least they had enough staples for the next couple of weeks, as well as a few fun splurges for Marian.

Two cheerful bag boys pushed the loaded carts to the car, and Zoë watched in awe as they lowered the back seats and tucked every last bag into the back of the Mini as if they did it every day. Of course, they probably did. When she tried to tip them, they refused and hustled back inside.

As Zoë started the car, Marian reached behind the seat and pulled a box of imported dried figs from one of the bags. "You must be a bad influence on me. I never bought things like this when I shopped on my own." She tore open the paper wrapping. "And since I broke my arm and Lyman wrecked his car, we've been using a delivery service."

"I'm sure Nick would have been glad to drive you." *That is supposed to be his job, after all.*

Marian hesitated before popping a fig into her mouth. "Mmm. This is delicious."

Zoë looked both ways then eased out of the parking lot, half expecting her car to bottom out from the extra weight. "Have you finished shopping for the baby?"

"Between my job and Lyman spending every waking minute working on his robot, there hasn't been much time. I ended up ordering almost everything online." Marian half-turned. "Would you like to see the nursery when we get home?"

"I'd love to. Do you know if you're having a boy or a girl?"

Marian shook her head. "We want it to be a surprise."

"What about the ultrasound?"

"We asked the technician to hide the telltale parts."

Zoë glanced in the rearview mirror and tapped the steering wheel with one forefinger. Marian's pleasure over their trip to the grocery store had sparked an idea. "If you still need any baby items, we could plan an outing to a fancy baby shop downtown and go out to lunch."

"That would be awesome, but I don't know what Lyman would say. He likes me to stick close to the house."

Zoë squared her shoulders. "You leave Lyman to me." He might worry about his wife's safety if she went out alone, but he couldn't complain if she were accompanied by an armed bodyguard.

Marian was still happily planning their trip to the baby shop when they pulled up to the gate at Strathmoor. She retrieved the opener from her purse, pushed the button, and the gates slowly swung open.

As she drove through, Zoë noticed a big black Lexus with dark-tinted windows parked in front of the house. Lyman had promised to call the security company this morning, but it was unlikely the vehicle was theirs.

"Do you recognize that car?" she asked.

Marian's lips tightened. "I'm afraid so."

Chapter Five

"That's Victor Watanabe's car." Marian's frown deepened. "I had hoped he wouldn't come back. Lyman will be upset."

Zoë wanted to check the man out, but that could wait. She pulled around to the courtyard and parked near the back door. She was out of the car, with her hand on the passenger side door handle, by the time Marian had unbuckled her seat belt and gathered her purse.

Zoë reached in to help her out. "When we get inside, why don't you lie down and rest a little? Nick can help me with the groceries."

Marian tightened her grip on Zoë's hand and heaved herself out of the low-slung car. "I hate to admit it, but that's not a bad idea. The doctor wants me to put my feet up several times a day to help with the swelling. We can look at the nursery this afternoon."

As they walked through the foyer, Zoë noticed the door to Lyman's office was closed. Raised voices emanated from within. She waited while Marian made her way up the stairs then went in search of Nick.

She found him kneeling in the side hallway, around the corner from the door to Lyman's office. As soon as she approached, he scrambled to his feet.

"What are you doing?" she demanded.

He held a screwdriver in one hand and a pair of needle-nosed pliers in the other. "Fixing that outlet." He pointed the pliers at an electrical outlet in the wide wooden baseboard.

"It looks fine to me."

He raised one thick, dark brow. "And you're an electrical expert?"

"I know enough to know you have to take the switch plate off to do any work."

He slipped the tools into his shirt pocket. "I just finished."

Zoë took a step closer and lowered her voice. "Are you sure you weren't lurking out here to eavesdrop?"

Nick let out a snort of laughter. "Lurking? Really?"

"What else would you call it?"

"I'd call it doing my job."

"As I understand it, your job is to drive the car."

"I fill in as a handyman, too."

The latch on Lyman's office door clicked, and the heavy brass knob turned. Zoë and Nick turned in unison.

A stocky Asian man in a black suit, carrying a black leather briefcase in one hand, stepped out. His cheeks were flushed, and the muscles in his jaw flexed. "Our latest offer is very generous. You will regret your decision."

Lyman followed and herded him toward the front door. "I don't believe I will."

Zoë glanced at Nick and read silent agreement in his eyes. Together they fell into step behind Lyman.

After Lyman opened the door, Watanabe paused at the threshold. "May I tell my superiors you will at least consider it?"

A tiny tremor shook Lyman's hand as it gripped the knob, and his knuckles turned white. "Tell your bosses I don't want to see or hear from you again. If I do, I will file a harassment lawsuit. I have already been in touch with the police."

Victor Watanabe's face mottled purple and red. He gave a sharp nod, turned, and marched toward his car.

Lyman shut the door with a solid thud then leaned against it. He glanced from Nick to Zoë then gave a shaky laugh. "I know it's early, but I believe I could use a nip of Grandfather's special blend about now."

Alarmed by his pallor, Zoë reached for his arm. "Come sit down, and I'll get you a glass. Is that what you keep in the decanter in your office?"

He nodded. "I hate confrontations of any kind, but that man won't take no for an answer. I just want him to go away and leave us alone."

Nick reached for the door knob with a look of stolid determination. "Don't worry about him. I'll make sure he gets the message." He opened the door and stepped outside, pulling it shut behind him with a loud click.

Zoë wasn't sure what he planned to do. He probably wouldn't punch out a Japanese businessman in the driveway, but who could say? In the two days she'd known him, Nick Rosetti had been anything but predictable. At least his physical presence was more intimidating than his employer's. She led Lyman into the living room then brought him an inch of whiskey in a cut-crystal tumbler. He swallowed it in one swift gulp then gasped and coughed.

He blinked a couple of times and coughed again before handing the glass back. "I'm afraid I've never been much of a drinker. Grandfather would be gravely disappointed."

The front door opened and closed moments before Nick walked into the living room.

"Watanabe won't be bothering you anymore."

"Thank you, Dominic. I hope you're right." Lyman turned to Zoë. "I hope you and Marian had a better morning than I did. Because of that blasted man, I didn't get much work done on GRAMPA."

"We had a very fruitful outing. I'll let her tell you about it." Her hand flew to her mouth. "The groceries! Omigosh, I forgot the groceries!"

She grabbed Nick's sleeve and dragged him toward the kitchen. "You...come help me right now."

He stumbled as she pulled him through the back door at full speed. "You left the food sitting out in the driveway all this time?"

"It wasn't that long. Besides, it's cold outside. Everything will be fine." She jerked open the back hatch of the Mini and prayed she was right.

"It might be cold outside, but you clearly had the heat cranked up in the car." He peered into a bag as he hefted two more from the back with the other hand. "There better not be any ice cream in here."

There was.

She bit back the word on the tip of her tongue. Marian had been so excited about the key lime pie sorbet. If it was melted, Zoë would have to make a quick ice cream run after lunch. "Just help me get everything inside."

Nick helped put the food away with remarkable efficiency and only a few cracks about the more unusual items, most of which could be blamed on Marian's pregnancy cravings. Before putting the sorbet in the freezer, Zoë gave it a squeeze. The carton flexed, but only a little. There was still hope. She would check it again in a few hours.

Because she'd been gone most of the morning, lunch consisted of sandwiches and deli coleslaw, but at least the bread was fresh and the meat and cheese sliced thin. The others had nearly finished their leftover brownies when Zoë's phone rang. She glanced at the caller ID: Madelyn Li—the owner of Phoenix, Ltd. and her boss. Her stomach did a flip flop. Madelyn must be back from her honeymoon, and Risa would have filled her in on the Prescott job.

"Excuse me. I need to take this." She hurried out of the kitchen.

"Feel free to use my study," Lyman called after her.

As soon as she closed the office door, she tamped down her nerves and answered the call. "Hargrove here."

As expected, her boss's voice replied. "Zoë, it's Madelyn."

"Hi, Boss. How was Nassau?"

Madelyn sighed. "Hot, and how many times have I told you not to call me Boss?"

Zoë's laugh cracked a little. "More than I can count."

"Risa tells me we have a new client, and you took the initiative to accept the job on your own."

Zoë couldn't tell from Madelyn's tone whether she approved or not. "That's right."

"How are things going? Have you run into any significant problems?"

"So far, so good."

"I'm glad to hear it. Please tell Mr. Prescott I'll call him later this afternoon for his perspective and to thank him for his business."

Zoë's stomach tightened. The job seemed to be going well, but would Lyman give her a good report? "Will do." She heard the sound of shuffling papers on the other end.

"I don't see a duration or end date for the job in the file."

"It's open-ended at this point."

"Okay. In a week or so, I'll send Casey to fill in for you so you can have a couple of days off."

Casey Callahan was Zoë's favorite fellow operative at Phoenix, Ltd. She was warm and friendly, and the Prescotts would love her. Maybe too much. Casey was also a fabulous cook. What if Lyman asked to make the switch permanent?

"Um...I'm not sure that will work. It might raise Mrs. Prescott's suspicions... I'll get back to you on that next week."

"I'll discuss it with the client. I'm certain he doesn't expect you to work twenty-four/seven indefinitely." Madelyn's tone signaled her switch to boss mode.

"Whatever you say, Boss."

"And stop calling me Boss."

Zoë rang off and returned to the kitchen with only a minor dent in her confidence.

"Is everything okay?" Marian asked when she walked in.

Zoë smiled and began collecting the dirty plates from the table. "It was the head of the agency I work for. She was just checking in to find out how things are going." It was always better not to lie, if possible.

"And what's the name of this agency?" Nick had a self-satisfied look, as if he'd tricked her and knew it.

Her brain froze.

If she gave him the correct name, he'd figure out her cover in a couple of minutes on a computer. Madelyn insisted the identities of her agents be kept confidential, but the company had a robust, professional website that explained its business in detail.

She sent a questioning glance to Lyman, who gave his head a tiny shake. *Think fast.* "Um...We Cook for You." *Sheesh.* That was so lame there couldn't possibly be a company in Chicago with that name.

Nick seemed satisfied for the moment—at least he didn't grill her any further. He excused himself to continue his work on the elevator, and the others headed off to their afternoon pursuits—Lyman to tinker with GRAMPA and Marian to read. Zoë spent the time reviewing her recipes for dinner and organizing everything she would need. This meal was critical. She'd run out of excuses.

She had decided to make old-fashioned chicken and dumplings for a couple of reasons. One—she'd watched her grandmother make it for Sunday dinner more times than she could count, and two—she'd found a recipe on the Internet that didn't look too hard. Two hours later she was covered in flour from head to foot, and the dumplings didn't look much like Grandma's. But the kitchen smelled delicious, and all the ingredients were finally in the same pot, simmering on the stove, so she counted it as a win.

"Do you always make such a mess when you cook?"

The sound of Nick's voice startled her like a cold hand on the back of her neck. She spun and dropped the big metal spoon, which clattered to the floor, creating a slippery puddle of pale yellow broth.

She glared at him. "Always." *And are you always such a jackass?*

He grabbed a paper towel and squatted by the puddle. "I'll clean this up for you."

"Yes, you will."

He tossed the dirty spoon into the sink and blotted up the mess. "There. Good as new." Pushing to his feet, he turned toward the pot on the stove and sniffed the air. "That actually smells good."

"You don't have to sound so surprised."

"Yeah, I really do." A slow grin spread across his face.

Zoë gritted her teeth. After growing up with five older brothers, she recognized a male who thought he had the upper hand. "If you don't want to eat my cooking, you can always go out. There's a fast food burger place on the highway about fifteen minutes from here."

His grin widened. "But free food is one of the perks of the job."

She turned her back with a wave toward the fridge and pulled open the silverware drawer to set the table. "The Skinny Suppers are still in the freezer. Help yourself."

Nick stepped behind her—so close his breath stirred the top of her hair. She had a sudden vision of his arms sliding around her but gave herself a mental kick.

Don't be silly. Why would he do a thing like that?

"Don't be so touchy. I'm looking forward to tasting your…um…whatever that is."

"It's chicken and dumplings." She grabbed a handful of cutlery, slammed the drawer shut, and then thrust the utensils into his hands. "Make yourself useful and set the table."

****

Nick took the silverware and did as he was told but rewarded himself by sneaking an occasional peek at Zoë. He couldn't remember when he'd had as much fun teasing a woman. It might have been the time he'd switched his sister's toothpaste with a tube of his father's hemorrhoid cream when he was thirteen. Angela had shrieked like a howler monkey and chased him through the house with a metal-bristled hairbrush. Zoë was keeping a tight rein on her anger, but he could almost see smoke rising from her ears as she organized the rest of the meal.

The more time he spent around her, the less convinced he became that she posed a danger to the Prescotts — her reactions were too genuine. Besides, she was too much of a klutz. But he still wondered what she was doing here. Was it possible she'd managed to convince the owner of a bona fide personal chef agency she actually knew how to cook?

When everything was ready, she sent him to call Marian and Lyman to dinner. He found them in the living room, watching the news. Before he could speak, a change in the anchor's tone caught his attention.

"...and in developing news, a brazen bank robbery occurred this afternoon at the Evanston branch of the First National Bank of Chicago. Two masked gunmen ordered the customers to the floor before almost making off with thirty-five thousand dollars. As the men fled, a guard fired one shot, and they dropped the bag containing the money. One robber lost his mask, and witnesses were able to give a detailed description to police. If you have any information about this man, please contact the Evanston Police or the FBI at this number."

A police artist's sketch of the perpetrator appeared on the screen.

"Oh, my God." Marian whispered the words against fingers pressed to her lips.

Nick's chest tightened. Her skin was pale and waxen, as if every ounce of blood had drained away.

Lyman reached for her hand with a worried frown then glanced at Nick. "That's her bank — the place we met." He slid an arm around his wife's shoulders and cradled her against his chest, speaking softly against her hair. "It's all right. The report didn't mention any injuries to employees or customers. I'm sure the vice president would have called if any of your staff had been hurt."

She pulled back a short distance. "I'm sure you're right. I just had a little dizzy spell. I'm fine now."

Nick had seen dizzy spells and was pretty sure that wasn't one, but he couldn't contradict her in front of her husband.

Lyman hopped up. "I'm calling the doctor."

"No, no. Don't do that. I'm sure I just need to eat."

Eat. Oh, yeah. "That's what I came to tell you. Dinner is ready."

When they walked into the kitchen, Zoë pointed to the table. "I hope you don't mind eating in here. The dining room seemed kind of formal."

Lyman pulled out Marian's chair and seated her then took his place at one end of the table. "I've always preferred eating in the kitchen. The dining room is beautiful, but it was designed to seat twenty-four. We would either have to cluster at one end or shout at each other."

Marian gave her husband a shaky smile. "I think the kitchen is cozy."

Nick was relieved to see the color returning to her face.

Each place was set with an individual tossed salad and a big bowl and spoon. Zoë placed a white china tureen with a matching ladle on the middle of the table then slid into the empty chair next to Nick. "I wasn't sure if you like white or dark meat, so please help yourselves."

After Lyman served Marian and himself, Nick filled his bowl with a couple of dumplings and a nice leg and thigh.

Zoë eyed his bowl then swirled the ladle in the tureen. She brought up a plump breast and offered it to him. "Are you sure you don't need this, too? I wouldn't want you to go hungry."

"I'm fine. Besides, I've always been a leg man." He allowed himself one pointed glance at her very fine legs then grinned.

Her face flushed pink, and she focused on filling her bowl, her frustration permeating the air in an invisible cloud. Nick choked back a laugh. He was sure he'd be getting an earful if Lyman and Marian weren't sitting there. He cut off a piece of dumpling with his spoon, scooped it up along with some broth, and slid it into his mouth.

Gack.

He swallowed quickly before his taste buds had a chance to rebel. What had Zoë done to the broth? Or, more accurately, what hadn't she done? The dish looked fine and smelled appetizing, but it tasted like someone had briefly dunked a cooked chicken in a pot of hot dishwater, minus the detergent. He glanced around the table. Lyman had set his spoon down and was regarding his food as if it were a perplexing math problem.

Marian's wrinkled nose spoke for her. Zoë had just brought her spoon to her lips.

When the first sip hit her tongue, she grimaced. Then her eyes widened. "The salt!"

That sealed it as far as Nick was concerned. No experienced chef would ever forget such a basic ingredient.

"The broth does seem a bit…er…lightly seasoned," Lyman said. "Perhaps—"

Zoë jumped up from the table. "I'll get it." She ran to the stove, grabbed the salt and pepper shakers from the counter, and scurried back. "I forgot to put these on the table. I…um…don't believe in over-salting. It's unhealthy, especially for pregnant women. Bad for the blood pressure."

Nick raised one brow. "What if I prefer a little flavor in my food?"

"Then you'll die young. Here." She slammed the shakers down in front of him.

"I'll take those when you're finished," Lyman said.

"Me, too." Marian held out her hand.

Lyman patted it. "Just a dash, my dear. Your doctor said you'd have less trouble with your ankles if you restricted your salt."

Marian heaved an injured sigh. "I can't wait for the baby to come. I'm really getting tired of being pregnant."

Her husband gave her an indulgent smile. "It won't be much longer."

After everyone doctored their food, the meal proceeded without incident. With a liberal application of salt and pepper, the chicken and broth weren't half bad, and the dumplings turned out to be surprisingly light. For dessert, Zoë served cookies and the salvaged key lime sorbet.

Marian took one bite and closed her eyes with a blissful smile. "Mmm. This is almost worth the low-salt thing. In fact, I think I could live on sorbet for the next few weeks."

After dinner, Zoë remained in the kitchen, and the Prescotts retired to the living room to watch television. Nick worked on reassembling the parts of the elevator motor he'd cleaned. Tomorrow morning he should be able to give it a test run. When Lyman and Marian went to bed, he said goodnight and went out the back door toward the garage, but instead of going directly to his quarters, he headed around the side of the house to begin his nightly patrol.

Heavy clouds obscured the moon, making it difficult see, even after his eyes adjusted to the lack of light. He rounded the corner and glanced up at the windows in the Prescott's bedroom. Soft light glowed through the slit in the heavy drapes. Unless he opened the curtains, Lyman wouldn't see a light outside.

Nick withdrew a small, powerful flashlight from his coat pocket. Swinging the beam across the lawn and stopping briefly here and there to examine the denser shrubs and trees, he made his way around the house and grounds. As expected, he saw nothing unusual or out of place, so he switched off the flashlight and walked back across the courtyard to the garage.

He'd feel better if the estate had a few motion sensor lights but hadn't been able think of a plausible way to broach the subject with Lyman. After all, security wasn't supposed to be the chauffeur's domain. Once he'd completed his rounds, he retired to his apartment and settled down in front of the small television with a bag of pretzels and a beer.

The next morning, after breakfast, he drove Lyman to the hardware store in the Bentley to pick up some parts for GRAMPA. Driving the huge vintage car and wearing a black chauffeur's cap, it was impossible not to feel like an extra from *The Great Gatsby*. At least Lyman didn't expect him to wear jodhpurs and knee-length boots.

When they arrived home, a van marked North Suburban Security was parked in front of the house.

Lyman peered out the window as they drove past on the way to the garage. "Oh, good. They're early. I decided it was time to upgrade the security system."

Since Nick didn't believe in telepathy, he wondered where the idea had come from. Lyman Prescott was one of the least practical men he'd ever met.

He found excuses to surreptitiously monitor the installers' work, but it wasn't easy. Every time he turned around, Zoë Hargrove seemed to be in the room or passing by outside. By their third encounter, his internal radar was blaring. Her presence couldn't be coincidence, and he was pretty sure it wasn't because she found him irresistible. The time had come to flush her out.

That evening, true to her word, she served schnitzel with spaetzle. Marian and Lyman carried on as if Wolfgang Puck himself was in the kitchen, and Zoë basked in their praise, shooting Nick triumphant little glances between bites. He had to admit it wasn't bad, but given his choice, he'd rather have his mother's stuffed manicotti any day.

After dinner, Marian went into the living room with her husband in tow for her usual evening fare of sitcoms and crime dramas. Nick remained at the kitchen table, pretending to read Lyman's discarded newspaper while he waited for an opening. Zoë, however, continued to clean up the leftovers and load the dishwasher as if he were invisible. After ten minutes, he tossed the paper aside and sauntered over to stand beside her at the sink. She had a heavy cast iron skillet in her hands and was up to her elbows in suds.

Her brow furrowed as she scrubbed hard at a bit of stubborn residue. "What do you want?"

"Just to see if you need any help."

She blew out a puff of air that ruffled her bangs. "I don't *need* any help, but you're welcome to dry if you want. Grab a towel."

He snagged a towel off the handle of the oven and picked up a pot from the dish drainer. "Dinner was pretty good tonight."

"Overwhelming praise, indeed." Her words were clipped and tight.

That didn't go over too well. If he was going to get her where he wanted her, he'd have to do better. "You look tired."

"Gee, thanks. Just what every girl wants to hear."

Nick shook his head. He'd never been glib around women, but even he usually did better than that. If his mother were here, she'd whack him in the back of the head with a wooden spoon. "What I meant to say was you've had a busy day. I wondered if you'd like to put your feet up and watch a movie with me tonight after Lyman and Marian turn in. My sister gave me the new Jason Statham action flick for my birthday."

She hesitated. "The Prescotts' bedroom is right above the living room. The sound might disturb them."

"My apartment has a small sitting room with a TV and DVD player."

"I don't know. You're right—I am tired."

She was waffling. Time to dangle the ultimate carrot. "There's also a microwave...and I have popcorn."

Her eyes sparked, and the corners of her mouth tipped up. "Popcorn?"

He nodded. "With real butter."

Her smile broadened. "Count me in. I'll be over around nine-thirty."

"I'll be waiting."

Chapter Six

A band of anxiety tightened around Zoë's stomach as Nick's broad back disappeared through the kitchen door. She had just agreed to a—what, a date?—with a man she barely knew and almost certainly didn't like, despite his dimple. Alone together in his apartment. What on Earth had possessed her?

It wasn't that she didn't trust him— not exactly— and she was confident she could take care of herself. But something about Nick Rosetti had set her on edge from the moment she'd laid eyes on him. Maybe it was the hint of menace in the solid strength beneath his black suit or the bold suspicion in his dark eyes. Who knew? Yet here she was, about to spend the evening with the man. Why? What kind of woman allowed herself to be seduced by the mere mention of buttered popcorn?

After she finished her kitchen chores, she went to her room to freshen up. Nick was right about one thing—it had been a long day. She splashed water on her face then regarded herself in the mirror. He was right about another thing too—she did look tired. Her ankle ached, and it showed. A little blush and a fresh swipe of mascara were the best she could do. He could like it or lump it.

As she left the house, she set the alarm and locked the back door. A blaring light caught her by surprise when she stepped onto the back porch—one of the new security lights. She was pleased Lyman had wasted no time acting on her advice. She was far from an expert, and her boss probably would have made numerous high-tech, state-of-the-art recommendations, but at least the estate was safer tonight than it had been yesterday.

Her confidence slipped a notch as she crossed the courtyard. She'd picked apart her response to Nick's invitation but hadn't stopped to question why he'd made it. Was this his way of offering an olive branch, or did he have some ulterior motive? She was about to find out.

She climbed the exterior staircase to the second floor of the garage, squared her shoulders, and gave the door a sharp rap.

He opened the door with a smile. The ends of his dark hair were still damp and trying to curl. "Come on in."

She stepped into a small living room with a low, steeply-pitched ceiling. The sofa and TV sat across from each other, tucked under the eaves. She shot a questioning glance at Nick, who stood under the highest point in the center of the room.

He replied with a half-grin and a shrug. "You get used to it. I've only hit my head three times this week. You should see the bedroom. I had to pull the bed out several feet from the wall so I could sit up without knocking myself out."

She bit back a smile at the mental picture. "I'll take your word for it."

"Here's the movie I thought we could watch." He tossed her a small, flat DVD case.

It was an undemanding film with a glamorous European setting and lots of martial arts action—one of her favorite genres and the perfect way to relax after a long day.

She handed it back. "This looks great. I love these movies. The villains are villainous, and the heroes are invincible."

"Yeah, too bad it's not like that in real life." Nick popped the case open and set the disc in the player. "Have a seat." He gestured toward the old brown corduroy sofa. "I'll throw the popcorn in. Do you want a beer?"

He was so casual—almost too casual. She'd be better off with all her wits intact. "Not tonight, thanks. Do you have anything else?"

He squatted in front of the dorm-sized refrigerator and opened the door. "Root beer and cola."

"Diet?"

"No. I'm sorry."

"Don't be. I hate diet soda. That stuff will kill you. I'd love a root beer. I haven't had one since I was a kid."

He rose, popped the cap off the bottle, and handed it to her. "You're in for a treat. This is made locally by a boutique brew pub in Lincoln Park."

She tipped the bottle and took a swig. The dark, spicy flavor filled her mouth as the bubbles tickled her nose. "Mmm. You're right. It's delicious."

In a few minutes the hot, buttery scent of popcorn filled the small space. Nick joined her on the sofa, settling the bowl between them. Then he propped his feet on the battered wooden coffee table and pushed a button on the remote.

Zoë tossed a handful of popcorn into her mouth and settled back as the film opened with a fast, expensive black sports car careening around the hairpin turns of a corniche on the Riviera. Within minutes the hero was showing off his considerable martial arts skills by thrashing a slew of lesser-skilled bad guys.

Nick took a long swallow from his beer bottle. "I like a good action flick, but I always wonder why none of those goons ever pulls a gun."

She drew back and regarded him with mock distain. "I bet you love movies that are nothing but heavy weapons fire and explosions."

He grinned. "Some of my favorites."

"But there's so much more skill involved in martial arts. Look at his moves." She pointed to the screen with her bottle as the hero flew through the air and took out a pair of opponents with simultaneous kicks to the jaw. "It's almost like ballet — violent ballet, maybe — but it's an art form."

Nick tilted his head and ran his gaze over her body. "You look like a ballet dancer. Did you dance as a kid?"

She tried to brush aside the nervous flutter in her stomach with a laugh. "Not unless you consider a pitchfork a dance partner."

His questioning gaze prodded her to elaborate.

She munched a kernel of popcorn and pondered how much to tell him. Her entire life didn't have to remain secret, but one question could easily lead to another, and lies always came back to bite you. She decided to give him enough to satisfy his immediate curiosity, but no more. "I grew up on a farm in Iowa."

His brows rose. "I never would have taken you for a farm girl." His gaze zeroed in on her shoes.

"I wore different boots then."

"You must have."

They watched a few more minutes of the movie, including a wild car chase and the introduction of a slinky Asian heroine with fast hands and faster feet.

Nick finished his beer, set the bottle on the coffee table, and stretched his arm across the back of the sofa. "So if you didn't dance as a kid, you must have started — what was it you said, taekwondo?"

She'd learned taekwondo in the service, but he didn't need to know that. She saw no reason to raise unnecessary red flags, and eight years as an MP was an unlikely background for a personal chef. She shook her head. "No, that came later, but I was always a scrappy kid — I had no choice, growing up with five older brothers."

"You have five older brothers? "

"Yep. Adam, Benjamin, Charlie, Dan, and Eddie. Do you see a pattern there? My mom really wanted a girl, so she kept trying. She named me Zoë to let the world know she was done." She sighed and took another pull from her root beer. "Sometimes I think she wishes she'd stopped at five."

As soon as the words left her mouth, she wanted to take them back. So much for revealing as little as possible. But there was something about the casual atmosphere — the shabby little sofa, the root beer, the popcorn, and the movie — that had lulled her into lowering her guard, if only for a moment.

Then it occurred to her that Nick had arranged everything about the evening with a purpose. He'd slipped his questions into the conversation so naturally. If she hadn't caught herself, she might have spilled her entire life's story by the end of the movie. But then he used to be a police detective. For all she knew, he was still a detective. One thing was certain — he was a skilled interrogator. If she wanted to maintain her cover, she'd have to watch every word she uttered in his presence.

"I'm sure your mom is proud of you."

She tuned back in at Nick's subtle probe. This time he was trying to draw a response from her without asking an overt question. She refused to take the bait.

"Look at that kick." She pointed to one of the villains on the television screen. "His form is so sloppy. I don't know what the stunt coordinator was thinking."

Her attempt at deflection worked.

Nick turned his attention back to the film. "He looks okay to me."

Zoë snatched the remote from the coffee table and backed the picture up to the beginning of the fight scene. "Look at the angle of his leg." She hopped off the couch, crossed the room, and touched the television screen with her finger. "Here, see. His center of gravity is all wrong. He's off balance. His kick wouldn't have enough force to knock a feather off Jason Statham's shoulder, much less drop him to the ground."

The dimple appeared in Nick's cheek. "You really take your action flicks seriously, don't you?"

She straightened her spine. "I appreciate accuracy. Come here, and I'll show you."

"I don't think—"

Her lips parted in a mocking smile. "Chicken."

Something sparked in his eyes, and he hauled himself up from the sofa. "Okay, you win. But I don't think this is a good idea. I probably outweigh you by sixty pounds."

She grinned. "At least."

This should be fun. If she'd learned one thing dealing with brothers, it was that men were simple creatures. When faced with a challenge, especially from a woman, they let their egos — not to mention other parts — overrule their brains. And after all the grief Nick had given her over the past few days, she was looking forward to dumping him on his backside.

"Now come after me," she said, beckoning with her hands.

"How?"

Zoë shifted her weight from foot to foot. "Any way you want."

"This room's too small."

"Excuses, excuses."

He shrugged. "Okay, but if you break the TV, you're buying a new one."

"Deal."

As she expected, he lunged toward her with both arms outstretched, and she knocked them aside with one swift kick.

"You're fast." He dipped his head in acknowledgement.

A surge of confidence made her bolder. "Try it again. Come on."

This time when he stepped forward, one hand shot out, latched onto her wrist, and jerked her toward him before she had time to react. When she hit the solid wall of muscle, a deep chuckle rumbled through his chest. She clenched her teeth. The arrogant ass was laughing at her. She'd show him!

She raised her foot to bring her heel down on his arch, but he must have anticipated her move. He shifted his weight, brought one foot behind her ankle, and knocked her off balance, sending them both to the floor. Hard.

He'd somehow managed to slip both arms behind her back to cushion the fall, but his weight still forced the air from her lungs in a *whoosh* when he landed on top of her. She lay still for a moment, stunned. She couldn't move. His big body pinned her to the floor, trapping her arms between them, and his face loomed inches above hers. As she struggled for air, her breath came in short, sharp pants.

He pushed up a couple of inches, easing the pressure on her chest. "Are you okay?"

Good question. She drew a full breath and stared into the depths of his coffee-colored eyes, where concern mingled with something more dangerous. As she started to nod, his head descended toward hers.

He's going to kiss me.

An unexpected thrill zipped through her.

What the – ? We barely know each other. Do I even want to kiss him?

Before she could make up her mind, Nick's warm mouth touched hers. His kiss began with a teasing nip of her lower lip.

Not bad. Maybe even a little fun.

She decided to reserve judgement.

But the second his lips became more insistent, the old panic rose in her throat, determined to drag her back to the time and place she'd fought so hard to escape. Suddenly, she was eighteen again — terrified and woozy from her first beer — crushed beneath the weight of a boy she'd known all her life and never feared...until that moment. His hot breath filled her lungs, suffocating her, and his hands were everywhere, squeezing and pawing.

Raw instinct took over. Her brain zeroed in on one clear thought — she had to free herself. She had to escape. Now.

She forced her hands up between their bodies and shoved against Nick's shoulders with every ounce of strength she possessed. As soon as her arms were free, she jammed the point of her left elbow into the inside of his right, knocking him off balance, and rolled out from under his body.

Once she was out of reach, her breathing slowed, and her head began to clear. She was safe. She was not eighteen. It was not graduation night. She was not lying in the stubbly grass behind the Halvorsen's barn. And Jeremy was nowhere in sight.

Damn. That memory hadn't slipped through her defenses in years. Had it really been so long since she'd kissed a man that she'd forgotten to keep her guard up?

She sat up and forced herself to face Nick. He must think she was crazy, or worse.

He had pushed up and rocked back onto his heels and was rubbing his right elbow. "Why the hell did you do that?"

Part of her wanted to apologize or explain, but she quashed it immediately. No way was she opening that door to him. Her scars were none of his business. She rammed the ugly memories back into the dark recesses of her subconscious where they belonged, determined to lock them up and throw away the key.

Her heart still pounded as the adrenaline rush subsided. "You were crushing me. You weigh as much as my grandpa's brindle bull."

"I doubt that." He rose and extended a hand, but she ignored it and clambered to her feet on her own. As soon as she shifted her weight to her injured ankle, a sharp jab of pain brought a rush of tears to her eyes. She blinked them away, hoping he hadn't noticed.

He eyed her closely. "Where did that move come from? It didn't look like any martial art I've ever seen."

"It's not. I've learned to improvise over the years."

"Like when you're flat on your back under your opponent." One corner of his mouth tipped up with classic, testosterone-fueled smugness. "They probably don't teach that in the dojo."

Her stomach tightened at his graphic description, but the echo of her earlier fear faded quickly, leaving only a residue of prickly irritation. "You didn't need to flatten me, you know." She bent to brush her pants with both hands. "I wasn't going to hurt you."

"No, you weren't."

"I was just demonstrating the correct technique."

"For what? Knocking me on my butt?"

"No, although I admit if things had gone right, that would have been the end result."

He crossed his arms and set his jaw. "And I was supposed to stand there like a chump and let you show off?"

"That would have been the gentlemanly thing to do."

He snorted. "I bet. You like to have your cake and eat it too, don't you?"

A budding headache throbbed in Zoë's temple. The evening hadn't been a complete disaster, but it had come close. While her brief devolution into a quivering mass of terror had not been strictly Nick's fault, the outcome was the same. On top of that, she hadn't learned anything useful about him, yet he'd succeeded in prying far more from her than she'd intended.

"I'm tired. I think it's time to call it a night." She took a step toward the door but stumbled when her injured ankle threatened to drop her to the floor.

His smug expression evaporated into one of concern, and he reached for her elbow to steady her. "Does your ankle hurt again?"

She clenched her teeth and forced herself to take a step without limping. "Just a little. I'll be fine." She took another step toward the door. "I'll see you tomorrow."

Before she could move, one heavily-muscled arm wrapped around her back, while another caught her behind the knees and lifted her into the air as if she were a child. He shifted her weight until her body rested against his chest.

She twisted in his arms. "Put me down! What do you think you're doing?"

His brows pinched together in a formidable frown as he kept his gaze straight ahead. "I'm taking you to your room. It's my fault you're injured. I never should have gone along with your little game tonight."

He pushed through the door and began to descend the stairs. Zoë instinctively clutched his neck.

"It wasn't a game," she protested.

"Sure it was. And while I enjoy a wrestling match with a beautiful woman as much as the next guy, I shouldn't have forgotten your ankle."

She didn't respond. Her brain was stuck on *beautiful*.

She wasn't sure how to interpret his off-handed comment. Males had been telling her she was pretty all her life. Eventually, she'd come to understand they usually wanted something in return. But Nick had tossed the words off too matter-of-factly to qualify as a compliment. Besides, if he'd wanted to press his advantage, he'd had ample opportunity a few minutes earlier when he'd had her flat on her back underneath him, as he'd so delicately put it.

He shifted her slightly. "Can you get the door?" His voice held a hint of strain. "I've got my arms full."

She realized they'd reached the back porch of the main house. "You can put me down any time. In fact, now would be good. I need to disarm the alarm."

He shifted her again and raised one brow. "Lyman gave you the code to the security system?"

"Yes." *And please don't ask me why.*

She couldn't think of a plausible reason why her new employer would give the security code to the new cook. And since Nick was already suspicious about her presence in the household, any excuse she gave would only compound his misgivings. "Please put me down so I can get inside without setting off the alarm and scaring everyone to death."

He lowered her gently to her feet, and she punched in the alarm code.

When he followed her through the door, she halted and turned. "You can go home to bed. You've done your duty."

He closed the door behind himself. "I want to make sure you get upstairs safely."

Zoë waved her hand toward the security keypad in exasperation. "As you saw, I set the alarm when I left. There's no bogeyman hiding in the house."

"I won't have the elevator fixed for another day or two. You can barely walk, and your room is two long flights up."

She heaved a sigh. Unfortunately, she couldn't force him to leave. He'd proven that tonight. "There's no arguing with you, is there?"

"Nope."

"Then do what you want. You will anyway."

She turned and hobbled through the dark kitchen toward the foyer. His shoes slapped the tile a few feet behind. When she reached the bottom of the stairs, she turned. "Go home. I'm fine. Really."

He nodded. "If you can make it to the landing on your own, I'll bring you a bag of ice."

She cleared the first step with her sound right foot then tentatively placed her left on the second step. As soon as she transferred her weight, pain shot through her ankle and up her shin. She gasped and grabbed the banister. Two seconds later, she was back in Nick's arms.

"Put me down," she hissed in protest. "It took me by surprise, is all."

"Shut up." Teeth clenched, he left it at that.

She told herself she didn't want to make a scene and risk waking the Prescotts, so she might as well settle back and enjoy the ride. It almost worked.

As he carried her up the grand staircase, visions of Tara flashed through her mind. Although he didn't take the stairs two at a time like Rhett Butler, all she needed was a lush, red velvet dressing gown to transform into Scarlett O'Hara. Oh...and the anticipation of a night beyond her wildest dreams.

That was so not happening.

By the time they reached the third floor, He was breathing heavily. He carried her into her room and tossed her on the bed.

She winced when she hit the mattress. "If you're out of shape, you don't have to take it out on me. No one told you to carry me up here."

He ignored her jibe and turned. "I'll get the ice."

By the time he returned, she had changed into yoga pants and a loose T-shirt.

He handed her the zippered plastic bag of ice cubes. "I'll let you handle that, since you're such an expert with injuries." Stopping in the doorway, he turned. "Oh, and

I'll need the security code to arm the system on my way out."

She bit the inside of her lip. Had his TLC been nothing more than an excuse to get the code out of her? But what choice did she have? He would never allow her to hobble downstairs with him and then make her own way back up.

She gave him the code. He winked and disappeared into the hall.

****

Zoë spent the next couple of days babying her ankle and avoiding Nick. She still saw him at meals, but she stayed away from the foyer where he was working on the elevator as much as possible. The sight of him brought back memories of the feel of his lips on hers and being carried in his arms, memories it would be safer to forget.

Instead, she ended up spending most of her time with Lyman. Despite the man's eccentricities and permanent air of distraction, she was surprised by how much she enjoyed working with him in the kitchen, experimenting with GRAMPA. He'd made great progress with the software, and the robot could now measure and chop vegetables like a pro. By working the results into her menus, Zoë had also upped her own culinary game. Her skills were nowhere near professional, but at least she no longer worried about cutting off her finger or setting the kitchen on fire.

On the afternoon of the third day after her evening with Nick, she was in the kitchen baking a batch of Lyman's favorite gingersnaps when the phone on the wall jangled. With Lyman in his basement workshop and Marian napping upstairs, she wiped her floury hands on a towel and picked up the receiver.

"Hello," Marian's voice answered. She must have picked it up in the bedroom.

"I've got to see you. Now."

Zoë didn't recognize the man's voice, but his accent and tone seemed vaguely familiar.

"What do you want?" Apprehension tinged her words.

"I'll tell you when I see you. It's important."

Maybe Marian had a brother. Family speech patterns were often similar, and that might account for the sense of familiarity.

She hesitated then sighed. "All right. I'll meet you at the summer house at the back of the property in half an hour. Do you think you can find it?"

"I'll be there."

After Marian hung up, Zoë gently set the receiver back in its cradle. What should she do? She could hardly admit she'd overheard the conversation and forbid Marian to keep the appointment. All she could do was follow at a discreet distance, get as close as possible without being seen, and be prepared to act the instant she sensed a potential threat.

She glanced at the clock and then at her cookie recipe. The cookies were on the trays, and the oven was hot. If she popped them in now, they would be ready before Marian left to meet her caller. She slid the trays into the oven and waited with one eye on the clock and the other on the doorway to the foyer. She had just moved the last cookie to the cooling rack when a creak from the stairs followed by soft footsteps on the tile floor caught her attention.

After slipping on a black jacket to cover her pink sweater and grabbing her Glock from her purse, she tucked herself just inside the kitchen doorway and poked her head out in time to watch Marian disappear through the front door. Zoë waited for her quarry to get far enough from the house not to hear the door open and close then followed, keeping well back and using trees and shrubs for cover. When she entered the hemlock woods, she had to pick up her pace to keep Marian in sight.

The fanciful wooden summer house sat in a small clearing among the towering trees. With its delicately carved, white-painted gingerbread woodwork, it conveyed the impression of a fairy dwelling in the forest—a perfect counterpoint to the solidity of the stone main house—and must have been a cool retreat from the heat of Chicago summers in the days before air conditioning.

When Marian entered the clearing, a man stepped from behind the building and walked out to meet her. He was dressed from head to foot in full black motorcycle leathers and still wore his helmet. Zoë judged him to be about five foot nine or ten with a wiry build. She crept as close as she dared, stopping behind a tree with a trunk nearly as wide as her body. From this vantage point she could observe the couple clearly, although she was too far away to hear their conversation.

Marian said something then the man removed his helmet. He had wavy dark red hair and sharp, pointed features, reminding Zoë of a fox. If he was Marian's brother, there wasn't a hint of family resemblance. Additionally, the narrow red stripes at his knees and elbows jolted Zoë's memory. She'd seen a suit like that before, and recently. One of the ninja cyclists had worn leathers with that pattern. She pulled her phone from her jacket pocket, zoomed in, and snapped a shot. She would send it to Risa later on the off-chance she could identify the man.

While the two talked, Zoë tried to get some sense of the tone of their conversation from their body language. The man didn't appear to be angry, but he took an aggressive stance, moving steadily closer to Marian as he spoke. She backed away, maintaining the distance between them, and her posture and gestures appeared conciliatory.

Suddenly, the tenor of the conversation seemed to change. The man's features tightened, and he grabbed Marian's injured arm. Zoë raised her gun and prepared to break from her cover, but before she could move, Marian jerked away and strode as quickly as her pregnant belly would allow — straight toward Zoë.

Chapter Seven

Nick twitched aside the curtain on the kitchen window as Marian broke out of the woods and marched across the lawn toward the front of the house. He'd been wrapping up the final adjustments to the elevator motor when she'd slipped out the front door fifteen minutes earlier wearing a white down-filled parka draped over her shoulders and no hat or gloves. He'd assumed she just wanted to pop outside for a minute and hadn't been concerned until Zoë sneaked out behind her.

Only the reminder of his obligation to guard Lyman had kept him from following. Instead, he'd set his tools aside and moved to the kitchen, where he could keep an eye on the women and watch for signs of trouble.

By the time he returned to the foyer and glanced out the diamond-paned window, Marian had nearly reached the front entrance. Zoë must have caught up with her somewhere along the way because the two of them were walking up the steps together. As they approached the front door, Nick swung it open.

Deep red color stained Marian's cheeks, and moisture glinted in her eyes. He would have chalked her appearance up to the cold wind except for the small furrows between her brows and look of worry behind the tears. She'd only been gone a few minutes. Had Zoë said or done something to upset her?

"Good afternoon, ladies. Did you have a nice walk?"

Marian slipped off her coat and dropped it in his waiting hands. "I think I'll go lie down for a while."

Nick frowned. "I've almost got the elevator running, but in the meantime let me help you up the stairs." She looked worn out, and it might give him an opportunity to find out what had happened outside.

But Marian brushed him off with a shadow of a smile. "That's sweet of you, but I'll be fine on my own."

Zoë unzipped her black jacket. "I'll bring you a cup of tea and some cookies in a few minutes."

"That sounds great. Thanks."

Nick waited, ready to help if Marian showed the slightest sign of faltering. When she reached the second floor with no trouble, he headed for the kitchen. If she wouldn't talk to him, maybe he could get the information he wanted out of Zoë. He found her removing a steaming mug from the microwave.

"Tell me what happened out there."

She spun and dropped the cup. Boiling water splashed the front of her pants, and shards of broken pottery shot across the tile floor.

Her empty hand shook as she pinned him with a furious green gaze. "Why do you keep doing that?"

He squared his stance and crossed his arms. "Something happened outside to upset Marian. What was it?"

Zoë glanced at the mess on the floor. "I don't know what you're talking about. Nothing happened. She wanted some fresh air."

She was lying. Marian hadn't been seeking fresh air. And if she had, why would Zoë have followed so stealthily instead of walking with her? "She looked unhappy when she came in, upset about something."

A wary look flashed in her eyes then vanished. "She's just tired. You try carrying around a twenty pound basketball all the time, and see how you feel."

He raised his brows and dropped his gaze to her smooth, flat stomach. "Are you speaking from experience?"

"No, but I have this thing called empathy—obviously a foreign concept to you."

She marched over to the broom closet, opened the door, and pulled out a mop. When she thrust it into his hand, his fingers tightened automatically.

"Make yourself useful and clean up this mess while I make Marian another cup of tea."

He hesitated for a moment then pushed the broken pieces of pottery into a pile. "I saw you, you know."

She stilled with a teabag dangling from her fingers. "What?"

He continued mopping without looking up. "I saw you sneak out after her."

"Don't be ridiculous. I wasn't sneaking."

Was it his imagination, or had the pitch of her voice risen a tone or two?

She placed three gingersnaps on a small plate and picked up the new mug of tea. "I'm taking these to Marian, and I expect to see this floor clean when I come back." With a cool glance she turned and left the room.

Her straight back and brisk stride told him she was hiding something. She had been from the moment she arrived. He only hoped he had enough time to figure out what it was.

That night at dinner, Marian remained quiet and subdued—not her usual bubbly self. Her blue eyes drooped with fatigue, and the faint worry lines persisted between her brows.

Lyman didn't seem to notice. He dominated the conversation with excited updates on his latest progress with GRAMPA. "...and the puree function worked perfectly on the butternut squash. Didn't it, Zoë?"

She smiled and raised her spoon, brimming with creamy orange soup. "Better than any food processor."

Lyman poked his knife into the butter then slathered it on his roll. "Dominic, how are you coming with the repairs to the elevator?"

"I think I've got it fixed. We can test it after dinner, if you like."

"Excellent!" He turned to Marian. "Won't it be wonderful not to have to climb those stairs every day?"

She gave her husband a wan smile. "Wonderful."

When Zoë collected the soup bowls, she frowned at Marian's half-empty bowl. "I wish I'd known you didn't like butternut squash. I would have been happy to fix you something else."

"No, no, it was delicious. I'm just not very hungry tonight."

Zoë pursed her lips. "Maybe the next course will be more appealing—roast pork with rosemary and apples."

Nick's ears perked up. The soup had been tasty, but the main course sounded even better. Maybe he'd been wrong in his initial assessment. Zoë might not have been much of a cook when she arrived, but her skills seemed to be improving with each meal. However, that still didn't explain why she'd been following Marian that afternoon.

"That does sound good. I'll do my best," Marian said.

The pork turned out to be a little dry, but the gravy helped. After the first few bites, Nick poured a second generous dollop across his serving and dug in.

Zoë sliced off a bite then paused. "Marian, if you're not too tired, I was thinking tomorrow might be perfect for our excursion into the city. We're supposed to have a bright, sunny day for a change."

The fatigue left Marian's eyes, and her face brightened with a genuine smile. "I'd love to!"

Lyman's brow furrowed. "What's this, my dear?" Although he addressed the question to his wife, he pinned his gaze on Zoë.

She glanced at Marian then replied quickly. "I thought Marian might enjoy a shopping trip to Chicago to buy a few things for the baby at Le Bébé Élégant and have lunch at a cute bistro I know."

Lyman leaned forward and lowered his chin. "Are you sure this is a good idea?"

She gave a single, definitive nod. "Absolutely."

"It will be so much fun." Marian's voice brimmed with enthusiasm.

He reached for her hand and gave it a squeeze. "Then, of course, you must go." He turned back to Zoë. "Were you planning to take that little roller skate you drive?"

She hesitated as if it were a trick question. "Um...yes."

He settled back in his chair. "I'd feel better if Dominic drove you in the Bentley. It's bigger and heavier. It will be safer on the highway and has more room for your purchases."

Nick paused with his fork halfway to this mouth. His real duties required him to stay at Strathmoor, but as the ostensible chauffeur, he could hardly refuse a direct request to drive the client's wife.

Zoë narrowed her eyes at him, but when he shrugged, she turned back to Lyman with a nod. "Of course."

Nick searched his brain for an alternative. He was pretty sure he'd rather stick an icepick in his eye than spend a morning traipsing after Marian and Zoë, cooing over baby paraphernalia. "Maybe I could drop them off in front of the store then pick them up when they're ready to come home."

Lyman took a long swallow of water. "I don't know. It's a long drive into the city and back, just to turn around and do it again."

"It would be good for the engine—a chance to blow out the cobwebs. I bet that car hasn't seen the top side of thirty miles an hour in years. Besides, parking downtown is a nightmare. The ramps weren't engineered for cars with a turning radius as wide as the Bentley's. I wouldn't want to scrape a fender, or worse."

Lyman shook his head. "No, no, we wouldn't want that. All right, go ahead—as long as you have Marian home in time to rest before dinner."

"I can call him a half hour before we're ready to leave," Zoë volunteered. "So we don't waste time waiting around."

Lyman appeared satisfied. "Good idea." He picked up his fork and stabbed a bite of pork and apple. "Now let's finish this delicious meal. I'm anxious to try out the elevator. Not only will it be good for Marian, but it will also be very useful for moving GRAMPA between floors. You'd be amazed how heavy he is."

To Nick's relief, the elevator rumbled into motion as soon as Lyman pushed the button. It creaked and lurched a little, but nothing a good oiling wouldn't solve. He gave the Prescotts a ride down to the basement then up to the second floor and back, and Lyman pronounced himself delighted.

When they stopped at the main floor, Nick opened the brass grate to let them out. "I'll grease the pulleys and cables tonight. By tomorrow she should be good as new."

Marian met his gaze with gratitude in her big, blue eyes. "Thank you so much, Nick. It will make getting around a lot easier for me, both before and after the baby arrives."

Her smile made every messy, frustrating minute of his work on the antique motor worthwhile. He hadn't done much that left him with a sense of satisfaction and accomplishment in the past year—not since his life went to hell and he left Detroit.

****

The next morning Nick helped Marian and Zoë into the back seat of the grand 'forty-six Bentley for the trip to downtown Chicago. While they settled and chattered about Marian's shopping list, he popped an antacid and wished he'd brought ear plugs. It was bad enough leaving Lyman home alone, even for a couple of hours, but since he had no choice, all he could do was lock the doors, set the alarm system, and cross his fingers. An even bigger worry was the trip itself.

In its day, the Bentley had been the height of luxury, but it drove like a tank and lacked all modern safety features. The thought of driving two women—one eight months pregnant—at highway speed down I-94 in traffic gave him heartburn. The car was in the best possible condition, and he was a highly experienced driver, but they probably would have been safer in the Mini.

He breathed a huge sigh of relief when he pulled to the curb in front of the store and helped Marian out onto the sidewalk.

She released his hand with a grin. "Thanks, Nick. I know you didn't want to drive us, but I felt like a movie star in the back of that car."

"My pleasure. And don't worry—I'll get back to the house as quick as I can."

She nodded. "I appreciate that."

Zoë glanced up from her phone and handed it to him. "Put your number in there, and I'll call you when we're nearly finished—probably sometime around two."

He did as she asked before handing it back. "I'll be waiting on pins and needles."

Her eyes said, *Are you always such a jerk?* But her lips settled for, "Good."

Nick chuckled, got back in the car, and made it to Lake Forest in record time.

He left the car in the driveway, since he'd be taking it out again soon, and climbed the steps to the back door. After fishing the key out of his pocket, he reached up to disarm the security system.

The light was green.

His heart thudded in his chest. He'd watched Zoë set the alarm before they left. He'd even congratulated himself for weaseling the code out of her. What if—

He took a deep breath and assessed the situation. There were no strange vehicles visible anywhere outside. Maybe the system had malfunctioned. He stuck the key in the lock and turned the knob. It was unlocked.

His pulse picked up speed.

Grabbing his Ruger LCR from the holster clipped to his belt, he burst through the door into the kitchen. A quick scan showed the room to be empty with everything exactly as they'd left it. His first priority was to locate Lyman, so he ran to the study.

Empty.

Next stop—the workshop.

He eased the cellar door open, trying not to give himself away. With his weapon drawn, he tiptoed down the stairs until he could see Lyman standing at his workbench, wearing magnifying goggles and soldering a tiny circuit board. A glance around the room proved he was alone. Nick holstered his gun and adjusted his jacket to hide it. He clumped down the last three steps to announce his presence.

Lyman turned and flipped up the goggles. "Ah, Dominic, did the Bentley give you any trouble?"

"None at all, and the ladies seemed pretty excited when I dropped them off."

"Marian was looking forward to a girls' day out. She'll be so glad when that cast comes off and the baby's born." He sighed. "I know I should probably take her out more, but I've been so wrapped up in my work."

Nick didn't know how to respond, so he moved to the other topic he wanted to discuss. "I noticed the back door was unlocked when I came in."

Lyman turned back to his project and adjusted his goggles. "I needed some wire from the garage. I didn't seem to have the right gauge down here. I must have forgotten to lock the door after I returned."

"That's fine." It wasn't, but what could he say? "I'll lock it and set the alarm when I leave to pick up the ladies."

Lyman didn't reply. He had re-immersed himself in his micro-electronic world.

Nick shook his head and went back upstairs. He didn't pretend to understand the scientific mind, and that was fine.

At noon, he took Lyman a ham sandwich with potato salad then ate alone in the kitchen. He was more than ready when Zoë called at two-thirty to say she and Marian would be ready to come home in a half hour. With Lyman toiling silently in the basement and the women out of the house, Nick had felt like the lone occupant of a cavernous mausoleum.

Thirty minutes later, he picked Marian and Zoë up where he'd dropped them off, but this time they were accompanied by a mountain of packages.

He glanced from the pile to the storefront. "Where's the Going-Out-Of-Business sign?"

Marian laughed. "There's still plenty left inside."

"Are you sure?"

She grinned at Zoë. "I didn't even buy everything I wanted, did I?"

Zoë smiled and picked up the smallest box. "We can always come back."

Nick opened the back door and helped Marian into the car then loaded her purchases into the trunk. After helping with the packages, Zoë climbed in beside her. The drive home began with lots of conversation about all the adorable this-that-and-the-others at Le Bébé Élégant and the wonderful food at Lucy's Kitchen, but the back seat fell silent by the time they reached Evanston. When Nick glanced in the rear view mirror, his gaze met Zoë's. She smiled and tipped her head. When he adjusted the mirror, he saw Marian had fallen asleep. She only awoke when they pulled into the driveway and stopped to open the gate. Nick parked in back as close to the porch as possible to make unloading more efficient.

Zoë popped out as soon as he turned off the engine. "I'll get the door." She bounded up the steps, rummaged in her bag until she found her key, then raised her gaze to the alarm panel.

Nick was helping Marian out of the car when he heard his name. He straightened to find Zoë glaring at him from the back porch.

"You forgot to re-arm the system when you left to pick us up."

"I didn't forget." He slipped his hands through the handles of several shopping bags then lifted a stack of three boxes.

"Well, it's not on now, and the door's unlocked."

He straightened and peered over the top box. Despite Lyman's assurances, he must have forgotten the lock and alarm again. Unless he chose to engage, the man had the attention span of a gnat. "Lyman must have gone out to the garage again for more wire. Don't worry about it."

He followed Marian up the steps and into the kitchen. "Where do you want this stuff?"

"You can take it up to the nursery, but first I want to show Lyman what we bought." She turned to Zoë. "I hope he won't freak out when he sees all these packages."

"Not a chance." She unzipped her jacket and stuffed her gloves into the pockets. "He's at least as excited about the baby as you are."

Marian's lips curved in a sweet smile. "That's true."

Nick set his load on the kitchen table. "I'll get the rest."

"I'm going to find Lyman. He's probably his workshop. He's *always* in his workshop." Marian opened the basement door and stuck her head in. "Lyman, are you down there?"

"Yes, dear, but don't come down right now."

Nick stopped half-way across the kitchen. Lyman's voice sounded strange—edgy and higher-pitched than usual.

Marian turned to Nick and Zoë with a huff and an eye roll. "I hate having to yell at him down these darned stairs." She took two steps down the stairs then shouted again. "Then you come up. I want to show you want we bought."

"Stay right there." Lyman's words were rushed and his voice strained. "I...I can't come up right now. I'm...uh...in the middle of something."

Nick had heard the sound of fear enough times to recognize it. He pushed past Zoë and started down the stairs. When he stopped behind Marian, she turned worried eyes in his direction.

"Stay here," he whispered. "I'll go."

She nodded.

He slipped past her and inched his way down, step by step, praying the old wood wouldn't creak and give him away. A few feet from the bottom he crouched and scanned the room. Lyman hovered next to GRAMPA in front of his work bench. Ten feet away a figure dressed all in black and wearing a ski mask waved a pistol at him.

"Give me the plans," the man demanded in an odd, growly voice.

"I don't know what you mean." Lyman's voice shook.

"I want the drawings—the blueprints, or whatever you call them—to that thing over there." He waved the pistol at GRAMPA. "Now."

The man advanced until his weapon was only a few inches from Lyman's chest. Nick reached behind his waist, drew his gun from the holster, and aimed for the center of the intruder's back.

"Drop your weapon," he ordered.

As the gunman turned his head, Lyman shouted, "Brûlée!"

GRAMPA scanned the top of the workbench, picked up a compact kitchen torch with one pincer and a lighter with the other. At the clicking sound of flints striking, the attacker turned and all three men stared as the robot lit the torch.

Lyman pointed at the man in black. "Brûlée!"

GRAMPA rolled toward the man with the flaming torch pointed directly at his face.

The intruder stared as if he couldn't believe what he was seeing. "What the—?"

Nick had reached the bottom of the stairs and shouted, "Drop your weapon. Now!"

"Lyman!"

Startled by the cry almost in his ear, Nick spun to find Marian peering over Zoë's shoulder directly behind him. "Get back upstairs. Call the police."

At the mention of the word *police*, the gunman frantically scanned the room for an avenue of escape. The women still blocked the stairs, staring in horror at the scene below. With Nick advancing from one side, pistol drawn, and GRAMPA approaching relentlessly from the other with a flaming torch, he appeared to be out of options.

Suddenly, he bolted for the elevator, waving his gun. "Get back! Get back!"

Dragging the metal gate across the opening, he slammed his fist against the button. As the outer door closed, Nick rushed forward.

Bang!

The reverberation of the gunshot in the stone-walled basement dazed him for a moment. He shook his head to stop the spinning, but his ears still roared, and everything around him seemed to move in slow motion. The man in the elevator had disappeared. Across the room, Lyman staggered to his feet.

"Are you hurt?" Nick's voice sounded hollow and muffled to his own ears.

Lyman brushed a hand across his forehead, leaving a small smear of blood then glanced at his hand. "Only a cut, probably from a chip of stone from the ricochet. But Marian—"

When Nick turned, he saw the women huddled at the bottom of the steps. Zoë had thrown her body across Marian, and still had her arms wrapped around her.

He rushed over and squatted beside them. "Are you two okay?"

Zoë nodded.

He pushed to his feet. "Stay here. Don't come up until I give the all clear."

She nodded again and slowly released Marian. By that time Lyman had joined them, tears gathering in the corners of his eyes. He reached for his wife, and they clung together. Nick exchanged a glance with Zoë then crept up the stairs.

The intruder was likely long gone, but it didn't pay to take chances. He moved through the house quietly and methodically, clearing each room in turn. As soon as he was satisfied the house was empty, he phoned the police then called for the others to join him in the kitchen.

Lyman looked like he'd stepped off the railroad tracks just before a train roared through. His wispy curls sprung from his head at a dozen angles, his eyes were round with shock, and his shirt hung partially untucked.

Nick settled both Prescotts at the kitchen table. "The police will be here soon." He glanced at Zoë. "Why don't you make some tea?"

"Of course." She crossed to the sink to fill the kettle.

Nick pulled up a chair across from Lyman and regarded his dazed expression. He wanted to ask a few questions before the police arrived and took charge, but he wasn't sure the man was ready to answer them.

"Lyman."

Lyman stared at Nick for a moment as if trying to focus. "Yes?"

Nick tried to frame his questions without sounding judgmental or accusatory. "Do you have any idea how that man got in the house?"

Lyman shook his head. "No. I've been busy in the workshop all day."

Zoë brought the hot tea, two cups at a time, and joined them at the table.

"I've been working on adding voice commands to GRAMPA," Lyman continued. "Since the purée went so well, I wanted to try brûlée." He turned to his wife. "I wanted to surprise you with crème brûlée tonight. I know how much you like it."

Marian pulled him close and planted a soft kiss on his lips. "And you did a wonderful job. GRAMPA brûléed perfectly."

Nick cleared his throat. "We noticed the door was unlocked and the alarm disabled when we got home."

Lyman raised his head. "I'm afraid that was my fault. I needed more wire. I guess I forgot to lock up when I came back inside."

He looked so morose and repentant, Nick felt sorry for him. "I'd be happy to carry any supplies to your workshop. Tomorrow you can show me what you need."

"Thank you." Lyman ran a hand through his hair. "Sometimes I have trouble planning ahead. I'll get an idea that takes me in another direction and..." His voice trailed off as he stared through the back window.

Slowly, he straightened and turned to Nick with a clear, sharp gaze. "Now there's something I'd like to ask you, Dominic. Why do you carry a gun?"

Nick's thoughts raced as he scrambled for an answer.

Zoë leaned forward and rested her elbows on the table. "Yes, *Dominic*, tell us. Why *do* you carry a gun?"

Chapter Eight

Zoë couldn't wait to hear his response to her question.

"I'm fully licensed, and the gun is registered." Nick turned his attention to Lyman. "I had it with me because I was driving the ladies downtown. Chicago can be a dangerous city."

Zoë gave a huff of disbelief. The evidence against him just kept piling up. Lyman hadn't known about Nick's gun and certainly hadn't asked him to carry it. No professional chauffeur would carry a weapon on duty except at the express direction of his employer. Besides, the Magnificent Mile of Michigan Avenue boasted more cops per block than the entire police forces of some small towns.

Nick shot her a glare then turned back to Lyman. "I knew you would want them to be well-protected, and it always pays to be prepared."

She rolled her eyes. *So now the man's a fricking boy scout.*

Lyman nodded. "I do feel better, knowing you were armed. Considerably better, in fact — especially in light of what happened here."

Zoë choked back an objection. She'd been armed, too. Was Lyman no longer confident she could protect his wife?

The faint chime of the doorbell interrupted any further conversation.

Nick jumped up. "Sit tight. I'll get it."

Zoë ignored his direction and rose to follow. She stopped in the kitchen doorway while he opened the door to two uniformed officers. Was it her imagination, or was there something odd about the way he greeted them? Their handshakes seemed a bit too long under the circumstances, and one even clapped him on the back. When he led them toward the kitchen, she slipped back to join the Prescotts at the table.

Nick approached and introduced the two cops. "Mr. and Mrs. Prescott, this is Kenny...er...Officer Zolnicki and Officer Swanson of the Lake Forest Police Department."

After a few initial questions, Officer Kenny went downstairs with Nick and Lyman, while Officer Swanson stayed in the kitchen to question Marian and Zoë. When he requested specifics about the gunman's voice and appearance, Zoë gave as detailed a description as she could, but Marian merely uttered single-word answers. Her pallor spoke of exhaustion and shock.

Concerned for her client's condition, Zoë interrupted the officer's note-taking. "This has been very disturbing for Mrs. Prescott. Do you have many more questions?"

He closed his notebook and tucked it back in his pocket. "I think that's enough for now. A detective will stop by tomorrow to wrap things up."

Because Lyman was still in the basement with Nick and Officer Kenny, Zoë accompanied Marian upstairs and helped her change into casual knit pants and a bell-sleeved sweater that fit over her cast. When she came back, the officers had gone, and Nick and Lyman stood in the kitchen as if neither had any idea what to do next.

She gently took Lyman's arm and led him into the foyer. "Why don't you go upstairs with Marian? I know she'd feel better, and I think you would, too."

His eyes held a blank, shell-shocked expression. "Yes. I must go to Marian." He took a couple of steps toward the stairs.

"I'll bring you both something to eat in a little while. How about tomato soup and grilled cheese sandwiches? That's what my mother always gave us when we needed comforting."

He hesitated and turned with a nod. "That sounds nice."

She returned to the kitchen to find Nick leaning over with his head stuck in the refrigerator. "Looking for something?"

At the sound of her voice he jerked up, banging his head on the top shelf. He drew back with a scowl and rubbed the back of his head. "Do that again and I might have to shoot you — accidentally, of course."

She gave him a tight-lipped smile. "Not much fun being surprised like that, is it?"

He ignored her question and glanced back in the fridge. "I'm starving. There's nothing like a shoot-out to give a man an appetite."

"I wouldn't call one shot a shoot-out."

"Close enough."

He found a plastic container of carrot sticks and popped the lid to peer inside. He must have been satisfied because he closed the fridge door and bit the end off a carrot with a loud crunch. Munching away, he followed her to the sink where she washed her hands before starting the Prescott's supper.

He leaned one hip against the counter in his usual casual stance and chose another slice of carrot. "You didn't seem too upset by what happened downstairs."

Zoë snagged a dry kitchen towel from the front of the stove. "What did you expect me to do—start screaming?"

"Most girls would."

She turned and crossed her arms to keep from smacking him. "I am neither *most* nor a *girl*." Staring directly into his eyes, she dared him to contradict her. Her adrenaline hadn't crashed yet from the earlier confrontation, and she wouldn't mind a fight if Nick kept pushing her.

After a moment, his body relaxed. "No, I guess you're not. What I meant to say was you really kept your cool down there."

She lifted one brow and dropped her arms to her sides. "Good save."

"Good enough to buy me a sandwich and a bowl of soup?"

She almost laughed at his look of hopeful expectation. "Sure, but I have to warn you, the soup's coming out of a can. I don't have it in me to do much more tonight."

His cocky expression returned. "I think you can be forgiven, under the circumstances."

She gave his shoulder a light punch. "Gee, thanks. Now make yourself useful and see if you can find a couple of trays."

While he rummaged through cupboards, she dumped two cans of tomato soup in a pot and started making sandwiches. Nick's apparently chummy relationship with Officer Kenny had piqued her curiosity. There might be a perfectly reasonable explanation, but it felt like one more wrinkle in his story.

She gave the soup a casual stir. "You seemed pretty friendly with the officers earlier. Have you met them before?"

He had his head in a cabinet and didn't look up. "You could say that. Hugh Swanson and I play on the same hockey team, and Kenny Zolnicki is married to my sister Angela."

Ah.

So, Officer Kenny was Nick's brother-in-law. His ties to the local police were even closer than she'd imagined. He spent his recreational time with at least one and was related to another. She'd always heard cops were a brotherhood. Apparently, those bonds remained tight even if one left the force or changed cities.

"So you play hockey."

"Uh, huh."

"That explains a lot." Like the battered condition of his nose.

He pulled his head out of the cabinet and straightened. "Oh?"

She suppressed a smile and nodded. "Too many pucks to the head."

Since the elevator was off-limits until the police evidence techs finished with it, Nick helped her carry the Prescotts' trays upstairs. Afterward they ate together, largely in silence, at the kitchen table. By eight o'clock Zoë was fighting a serious case of the nods. Lyman and Marian spent the remainder of the evening in their room, and Nick seemed to run out of steam as well. He retired to the garage without any further wise-guy comments, leaving her to turn out the lights, set the alarm, and drag herself up to her room.

After she washed her face and brushed her teeth, she pulled on her pj's and slipped into bed with her tablet. She'd received an email from Risa that morning with the results of her search for the identity of the man Marian had met in the garden. With all the excitement, she hadn't had a chance to read it yet. As soon as she'd powered up, she opened the message.

Bingo!

As usual, Risa had hit pay dirt. Zoë read the summary of her findings in the body of the email then opened the first attachment. It was a scanned copy of a seven-year-old newspaper article, including photos of two apparent mug shots. The headline read, "Rogue Cops Sentenced to Ten Years in Drug Scandal." She held the tablet closer, trying to make out the faces in the grainy photos. One was definitely the man she'd seen earlier with Marian. The article identified him as Jimmy Mahoney, a former Chicago P.D. narcotics officer who had been busted selling dope in an Internal Affairs sting operation.

The second attachment was a short article from June indicating both former cops had been released on probation after serving six years.

Zoë set the tablet on her lap. Hadn't Marian said her ex-husband was named Jimmy and that Lyman considered him a threat?

She would ask Risa to check public records for a marriage license in the names of Jimmy Mahoney and a woman named Marian, but she was confident her suspicion would prove correct.

Maybe Lyman was wrong about Victor Watanabe and Ichiro Electronics, and the threats had nothing to do with GRAMPA. Maybe Jimmy Mahoney was behind them all.

Could he have been the armed man in the basement? She tried to picture the wiry, red-haired man she'd seen yesterday. From her vantage point behind Nick's back she hadn't been able to get a good look at the intruder. Everything had happened so fast she couldn't be sure, but the gunman had appeared to have been about the same height and build as the man in the garden. There hadn't been any unfamiliar cars near the house, but she'd seen Jimmy Mahoney with a motorcycle the day before. He could have stashed it in the woods and escaped the way he got in.

Zoë made a mental note to inspect the grounds for tracks in the morning to see if she could find another entrance point to the property. The police would undoubtedly do their own investigation, but she wasn't willing to share her suspicions until she had more evidence.

And then there was the added twist that the intruder hadn't demanded money, only the plans to GRAMPA. What would Mahoney want with a vegetable-chopping robot? Was his motive simple jealousy, and he wanted to ruin Lyman? Or was there something more?

The whole puzzle made her head hurt. She set the tablet aside with a yawn, turned off the light, and slid down under the covers. Maybe tomorrow would bring a flash of brilliance. If not, it might be time to consult the boss. Madelyn had an uncanny way of examining the facts of a case and ferreting out the players' motives.

****

After a visit from Sergeant Lewis and a crime scene technician the following morning, the next two days passed quietly. Marian seemed subdued and spent more time than usual in her room. Lyman worked on GRAMPA's liquid measuring skills in his workshop, and Nick had taken to patrolling the grounds like a sentry. Since the elevator had been released by the police and was back in service, he had no further excuse to be in the house all day. He still wore his black suit, so a stranger might think he was a servant merely taking a smoke break or a casual stroll, but Zoë knew better.

To her, he seemed more like a prison guard. She couldn't decide if his presence was reassuring or disturbing, but she found herself looking for him every time she passed a window. She should have been nervous—knowing he was armed—but strangely, she wasn't. Whatever Nick was doing at Strathmoor, he'd proven he meant the Prescotts no harm.

Unfortunately, his new pastime meant Zoë was stuck in the house. He was bound to see her if she searched the grounds for motorcycle tracks or a point of exit Jimmy might have used. She didn't want to explain herself to Nick, and besides, he would probably laugh at her suspicions and theories.

Friday morning, over blueberry waffles, Marian reminded Lyman of her doctor's appointment at eleven o'clock. "I can hardly believe it—only four weeks until the baby's due." Her eyes sparkled.

He squeezed her hand. "The months have flown by, haven't they?"

"Until I did this." She lifted her cast with a glum expression. "I have a feeling these last weeks are going to feel like years." She sighed and rested her left hand on the napkin-covered mound of her belly. "I'm antsy and tired at the same time, and it's hard to sleep with this in the way. Sometimes I wish I could take it off and set it aside for a few hours."

"It won't be much longer, my dear." Lyman hesitated before his brows pinched together in a little frown. "I know I should come to your appointment with you, but I'm at a critical juncture in my work. I don't suppose you could reschedule for later in the afternoon."

Marian's eyes widened. "You've got to be kidding. Dr. Moseby is booked solid for weeks. You stay home and work. I'm sure Zoë can drive me. Besides, there's nothing for you to do at the doctor's office but sit and wait. This appointment will only take a few minutes. You can come next time."

"I'd rather Dominic drove you. Zoë can go along, too." His gaze met Zoë's, and a silent message passed between them. He wanted an armed bodyguard with Marian at all times, and two would be even better. After the incident in the workshop, she couldn't really blame him.

She nodded. "I'd be glad to. Maybe Nick can find a nearby coffee shop. I doubt he would enjoy twiddling his thumbs in an obstetrician's waiting room."

Nick looked offended. "Hey, I enjoy a dog-eared copy of *Parents* magazine as much as the next guy."

Marian laughed. "Then you're in for a treat."

"How long does it take to get to your doctor's office?" he asked.

"About twenty minutes."

"I'll bring the car around at ten-thirty."

Zoë rose and gathered the empty breakfast dishes. After depositing them in the sink, she straightened and glanced out the window. A wintry mix of sleet and snow was rapidly turning the lawn white. The roads would be a nightmare, and the Bentley didn't have a limited-slip differential or anti-lock brakes. It probably even pre-dated the invention of snow tires.

She pressed her lips together and considered the alternatives. If this were a normal assignment, she would call Risa to bring one of the Phoenix, Ltd. cars, but there was no way she could explain that to Marian.

She turned to the group at the table. "The weather is horrible. I think we'd better take the Mini. It's small, but at least it has all-wheel drive. "

Lyman shook his head with a worried frown. "It would be better to cancel the appointment."

Nick joined Zoë at the sink and craned his neck to peer out the window. "It doesn't look that bad. We'll take my truck. It can handle a little ice and snow, no problem."

She hadn't seen any cars around the estate besides Frankie "No Nose's" Bentley, so Nick must keep his vehicle in the garage.

At ten twenty-nine, Zoë waited by the front door for Marian. The elevator rattled and hummed before the door slid open.

Marian pushed back the brass gate and exited with a grin. "I know I should probably take the stairs for exercise, but this thing is so much fun. I love it! Who would have ever guessed that one day Marian O'Shaunessey would live in a house with an elevator?"

Nick waited at the bottom of the steps next to a late model dark blue SUV with oversized tires. When Zoë stepped out from under the overhang of the porch, tiny pellets of sleet stung her cheeks and had already coated the stone steps with a lumpy layer of ice. She grabbed the wrought iron railing with one hand, and Marian did the same, but before either could take a step Nick bounded up the stairs and slid one arm around each woman.

"I've got you. Hold on tight." He maneuvered them both down the steps and into the car.

He drove with caution, but Zoë was grateful there weren't many vehicles on the road. The defroster and wipers kept the front windshield clear, but ice was forming on the side windows where the sleet melted when it hit the glass and re-froze before it could run off.

About three miles from Strathmoor, they reached a long stretch of roadway bordering a marsh. It would have been peaceful and picturesque on a nice day, but today steam rose from the unfrozen water, and ducks huddled together among tall clumps of lifeless cattails. As they passed over a corrugated metal drainage culvert, a noise caught Zoë's attention, and she swiveled to look out the back window. A pair of black motorcycles with riders crouched low was coming up fast from behind.

"Nick—"

He met her glance in the rear view mirror. "I see them."

"I think I've seen them a couple of times before." The taut thread in her voice tightened further.

"What is it?" Marian frowned and tried to turn but was hampered by the bulk of her belly.

"Just a couple of guys on motorcycles driving too fast for the conditions," Nick replied. "There's nothing to worry about."

The whine grew louder as the cyclists bore down on the car.

"What's the matter with them?" Marian's confusion had given way to panic. "They're right next to us!"

"Hang on." Nick gripped the wheel and pushed the gas pedal. The SUV began to accelerate away from the motorcycles.

Marian's knuckles whitened on the arm rest, and Zoë reached for her purse. She had no idea what the men were after, but if Nick couldn't outdrive them, she wanted her weapon close. The whine increased until only a pane of glass and a couple of feet separated her from the nearest rider. Her palms began to sweat, and her pulse pounded in her throat. She slipped her hand into her purse and wrapped her fingers around the grip of her Glock.

Suddenly, one cycle pulled ahead of the other until it was even with the front bumper. Nick jerked the wheel, tapping the first rider. He crashed to the pavement and skidded to the side of the road, while his bike bounced end-over-end another twenty feet before coming to a stop. Instead of stopping to check his downed companion, the second biker sped past the wreckage and disappeared down the road.

The SUV's momentum had carried it across the center line, but when Nick tried to correct, the vehicle lost traction on the icy road despite its heavy tires and four-wheel drive. Zoë instinctively thrust her arm in front of Marian, who screamed as they spun out of control and plowed into a tree. The airbag exploded in Nick's face, and the impact threw both women hard against their seatbelts.

A deep, aching pain arced across Zoë's chest from the seatbelt digging into her breasts. She dragged her eyes open. Dust particles from the airbag floated in the air, and someone moaned. She coughed. In the front seat, Nick stirred, muttered an epithet, and reached for the clasp of his seatbelt.

"Is everyone okay?" His raspy voice grated on her ears.

"I think so. What about you?"

He rubbed his chest and winced. "I'm going have one helluva a bruise from the airbag, but I think that's all. I'm just glad the windshield held."

Beside her, Marian stirred and moaned.

The baby!

Marian's eyes were closed, and her head leaned back against the headrest. Her hands clutched the sides of her belly as if she were preparing to take a free throw shot. Because the shoulder strap of her seat belt crossed her chest between her breasts, and the lap belt lay snug across her thighs, she shouldn't have been injured, but her sounds of pain sent fear rocketing through Zoë. She quickly released her seat belt, then Marian's, and covered Marian's hand with her own.

"Marian, look at me. Are you hurt?"

"The baby." She moaned, and her hand tightened. "I think it's coming." Fear and pain mixed in her blue eyes. "It's too early."

Zoë placed her hand directly on Marian's belly. It was rock hard. Her chest tightened. "Nick—"

"On it." He raised his phone, gave the nine-one-one dispatcher clear, succinct details about their situation and location then ended the call. "The ambulance is on its way."

Zoë turned and met his worried gaze. "I think Marian should lie down while we wait."

Nick nodded. "Good idea. I've got a blanket in the back."

He shoved his door open, walked around to open the rear hatch, and retrieved a folded green blanket. Zoë scooted out the opposite side of the car then helped

Marian stretch out. She unzipped her jacket and tucked it under the other woman's head then helped Nick spread the blanket.

He patted Marian's ankle. "It won't be much longer. I think I hear sirens already."

Zoë tilted her head and listened closely. A chorus of faint wails sounded in the distance.

Thank heaven.

She glanced back at Nick as he straightened.

Oh, God, no!

The downed cyclist now loomed behind Nick with a tire iron raised in one gloved fist.

She grabbed her Glock from the floor of car where she'd dropped it and aimed with both hands. "Nick, duck!"

In one fluid movement, he dodged to the side, spun, and drove a fist into the biker's leather-clad gut. As the man released his weapon and bent forward, clutching his middle, Nick grabbed one shoulder in each hand and rammed his knee into the assailant's groin. He dropped like a rock. Nick pulled the man's hands together behind his back and knelt with one knee pressing him against the pavement.

"Get me a couple of zip ties. They're in the back." His breath came fast, sending quick white puffs into the frosty air.

When Zoë returned her gun to her purse, she glanced at the pair of handcuffs nestled at the bottom. Deciding there would be fewer awkward questions if she got Nick what he asked for, she hurried to the back of the SUV, opened the hatch, and began sifting through the loose odds and ends.

"They're in a bag in the cardboard box."

She found the bag, pulled out two long, white plastic strips, and brought them to Nick. "Why do you carry zip ties in your car?"

He wrapped one around the biker's wrists and pulled it tight. "They can come in handy. You never know when you're going to need one." His actions were smooth and practiced. He'd clearly done this many times before.

"I guess not."

With a grunt, he shoved to his feet and faced her. His jaw was tight, and his dark eyes blazed. "The ambulance will be here any second, but before the cops arrive I want an explanation. What are you doing carrying a gun? You could have killed someone."

Zoë lifted her chin. "I'm licensed, and it's registered —just like yours."

Before he could reply, the ambulance pulled up, followed by a police cruiser.

Nick glanced at the officers getting out of the squad car then back at Zoë. "This isn't finished."

If he thought he could intimidate her, he could think again. She wanted answers, too. She squared her shoulders and met his angry gaze head on. "You're darn right. I have a few questions of my own."

Chapter Nine

A pair of paramedics, one male and one female, unloaded a gurney from the back of the ambulance and wheeled it to the car, followed by the cops. Nick was relieved to see Hugh Swanson, a friend and one of the officers who had taken the report after the most recent break-in at the Prescotts'.

Nick nodded to him. "Hey, Hugh. I'm afraid we've got another mess here."

Hugh raised his brows. "Looks like it." He tipped his head toward his partner, a short, chunky blonde with her hair skinned back in a tight bun. "This is Officer Halliwell. You want to tell us what happened?"

"I will—as soon as the paramedics do their thing."

The heavyset, middle-aged black female paramedic surveyed the scene from the man on the ground to Marian in the back seat of Nick's SUV. "How many patients do we have here?"

"One for sure, possibly two, but take the woman first. She may be in pre-term labor. After you evaluate this one," —Nick toed the man at his feet— "you can decide if he needs a ride to the hospital or the police station."

Zoë stepped forward. "But if he needs medical attention, please call another ambulance. They can't ride together under any circumstances."

The woman eyed her with skepticism. "I'm not going to ask why, but since we're only equipped to transport one patient at a time, that won't be a problem." She turned to her partner, a young man with a tattoo creeping up his neck from the edge of his collar. "Let's get her in the wagon, and you can hook her up and check her vitals while I see to this fellow."

Five minutes later, the young man was tending to Marian in the back of the ambulance with Zoë in attendance, while the others stood over the fallen biker. Nick had rolled the man onto his back and removed his helmet. The man stared up at him with a scowl but remained silent. Something about his boxy face and reddish blond hair seemed familiar, but Nick couldn't place it.

The paramedic squatted beside him. "Why is this man in restraints? Is he under arrest?"

Hugh leaned forward to examine the man more closely. "I could swear I've seen him somewhere before. Halliwell, do you recognize this guy?"

She gave the prisoner a quick once-over. "I don't think so."

Hugh glanced at Nick. "Did you check him for ID?"

"No, I waited for you, but I had the same feeling."

Hugh ignored the downed biker's silent glare while he patted him down and withdrew a wallet from the back pocket of his pants. He flipped it open and studied the man's driver's license.

"Is he one of your usuals?" Nick asked.

His friend shook his head. "No. His ID says his name is Rudolph Gehke."

"That doesn't ring any bells." Nick stared at the man a moment longer. Where had he seen that face before? Then it came to him. "I can't be sure, but I think he was on the news a few nights ago. He looks a lot like the sketch of one of those guys who held up the bank in Evanston."

Hugh's face lit with an excited grin. "You're right. Halliwell, it looks like we've caught a bank robber. I never expected to be able to say that. You'd better go call this in."

Zoë approached from the ambulance and pointed to the alleged thief. "Wait a minute. This guy tried to run us off the road then came after Nick with a tire iron. Why would a bank robber do that?"

Hugh shrugged. "Beats me. Nick, have you got any idea?"

"No, but I'll be very interested to hear what your detectives get out of him."

"Me, too. At least you're on your feet and he's on the ground, so you came out on top." Hugh straightened and turned to the paramedic. "Under the circumstances, we'll need to keep him restrained unless there's a medical emergency."

She nodded and turned back to her patient. "How're you feeling, sir? Do you have any pain?"

He clamped his mouth shut and shook his head.

She unzipped the man's jacket. "I don't see any blood. Of course, he could still have significant internal injuries or a head injury, but at least he was wearing leathers and a helmet." She spoke into her radio and listened to the response. "The second ambulance will be here in five. Then you can cuff him to the gurney so I can do a more thorough evaluation."

When the second ambulance arrived, the paramedics confirmed Rudolph Gehke had no immediate life-threatening injuries. The cops decided Officer Halliwell would accompany him to the hospital for evaluation while Hugh Swanson stayed behind.

As the second ambulance departed, Hugh turned his attention back to Nick and Zoë. "Okay, now take me through exactly what happened here, starting with your first contact with Gehke."

Nick stuffed his chilled hands in his pockets. "Actually, there were—"

"Excuse me," Zoë interrupted, "but can you start without me? I need to check on Mrs. Prescott's condition and notify her husband."

"Sure. Go right ahead."

She hurried off toward the ambulance holding Marian, which was still on site while the young paramedic finished his evaluation and radioed the hospital.

Hugh turned back to Nick. "You were saying…"

"There were two cyclists. I first noticed them about a quarter mile back. They came up behind us fast, way too fast for the conditions."

Hugh made a notation in his notebook. "What would you estimate your rate of speed?"

"Maybe thirty. I was hardly speeding. I was driving a pregnant woman to a doctor's appointment on an icy road."

"Did you give them room to pass?"

Nick shot him a disgusted look.

"What?" Hugh raised his brows. "You know I have to ask these things."

Nick heaved a sigh. "Yeah, I know." Hugh was just doing his job, but the official tone of his questions gave Nick a nasty sense of *déjà vu*.

"So, did you give them room to pass?"

"Of course. Hugh, they targeted us. Trust me — this wasn't an incident of road rage."

"What happened to the second rider?"

"He sped off after the crash."

They were interrupted when Zoë rushed up, her brows pinched in consternation. She let out a breath. "Marian's contractions have calmed down some, but the paramedic wants to take her to the hospital to have her checked out." She paused for a second. "I called Lyman, and he's practically hysterical. If we don't go right home and pick him up, I'm afraid he's going to try to drive himself in the Bentley, and believe me, he's in no condition to do that safely."

Nick glanced at his SUV. The front end had suffered serious damage. He could only hope it wasn't totaled. "I'm afraid my car's not going anywhere except the repair shop. Hugh, can you give us a ride to the Prescotts'? We can finish our statements at the hospital or stop by the station later."

"I guess we can do that. In the meantime, I'll send the Accident Investigation Unit out to take photos and gather evidence."

Twenty minutes later Hugh dropped them at Strathmoor with a promise to meet at the hospital in an hour. Lyman was waiting on the front porch, wearing his hat and coat. He thrust the keys to the Bentley into Nick's hand.

"I called the hospital, and they said she's doing well, but we have to hurry. I have to see her." His hand shook.

Nick palmed the keys. The Bentley was a beautiful automobile, but at this point in its life, it should be the pampered centerpiece of a classic car collection, not the everyday vehicle of a distracted eccentric. One day soon Lyman would need to buy something more practical, assuming the man had remembered to file an insurance claim for his wrecked car.

Zoë placed her hand over his but addressed Lyman. "The roads are horrible. It would be much safer to take my car, and we can make better time."

Lyman's hand fluttered, dismissing her concerns. "Whatever. It doesn't matter. Let's just go."

When she glanced at Nick for support, he nodded. Given the conditions, he'd rather be driving, but the Mini was the best alternative.

She headed down the icy steps, keeping a firm grip on the wrought iron handrail. "Wait here, and I'll be back with the car in two minutes." She took off around the side of the house at a speed that defied the conditions.

As Lyman settled in the back, Nick climbed into the front passenger seat. "Hey, we fit pretty well in this Hot Wheels wannabe."

Zoë put the car in gear. "If a Mini was good enough for Mark Wahlberg and Jason Statham in *The Italian Job*, it's good enough for you."

He decided not to push his luck by mentioning that both actors were several inches shorter than either he or Lyman.

Thirty minutes later they found Marian resting peacefully in a cubicle in the Emergency Room. A young, bespectacled man dressed in a white coat over green scrubs stood beside her bed, reading her chart.

Lyman rushed to her side. "How is she, Dr. Moseby? Is the baby all right?"

The doctor glanced up with a smile. "They're both doing fine. The contractions have stopped. They appear to have been caused by the stress of the accident, not true labor, but I'd like to keep her overnight for observation."

Lyman nodded. "Whatever you think is best." He scooted the side chair close to the bed and sat. "Will I be able to stay with her?"

The doctor flipped the clipboard closed. "That won't be a problem. We'll be moving her to a room as soon as the admission paperwork is finished."

Marian reached for her husband's hand then turned to Nick and Zoë with a grateful smile. "Thank you for bringing him. I would have worried if he'd tried to drive that old relic in this weather."

Nick nodded. "No problem. That's why we're here."

"You two don't need to stay," Lyman said. "There's nothing more you can do tonight."

Zoë glanced at Nick then smiled at Marian. "Okay. You take it easy, and we'll check on you later."

They left the cubicle in search of Hugh Swanson and found him leaning against the admitting desk with a paper cup of coffee in one hand, chatting up a pretty young nurse.

Nick walked up, slapped him on the back, and gave the nurse a wink. "It must be a pretty slow day in the ER if you've got time for this clown."

She laughed. "We're taking a breather before the afternoon rush. In this weather, there will be plenty of accidents as soon as people start getting off work."

"I need to borrow Officer Swanson for a few minutes, if that's all right. Hugh, are you ready to finish our statements?"

Hugh patted his padded uniform jacket. "I've got the paperwork right here. Let's find someplace we can sit." He turned and gave the nurse a wave. "See you, Carla."

She waved back. "Anytime."

As soon as they were out of earshot, Nick nudged his buddy. "Cute girl. Don't you think she's a little young for you?"

Hugh's brows shot up . "Hey, I'm young...at heart."

Nick gave a huff of disbelief. "She could beat you to the blue line wearing snowshoes. Wait until she finds out what a pitiful old wreck you really are." He pointed toward a sign with a red arrow that read *Cafeteria*. "Let's talk while we eat. I'm starving."

He loaded his tray with a burger and fries, while Zoë chose a chef salad, and Hugh stuck with coffee. They headed for a table in the corner, away from the buzz of medical staff on their lunch breaks. While Nick and Zoë dove into their food, Hugh spread photos of the accident scene on the table and took out his notebook.

"Before we start, I've got something to tell you. You're never going to believe who that guy we arrested turned out to be."

Nick paused, burger in hand. "The would-be bank robber, like you suspected."

"Yeah, but he's more than that." Hugh slapped an old mug shot on the table as if it were a royal flush.

Nick picked it up and examined the photo. "So who is he?"

Hugh's smug enthusiasm faded. "I forgot you weren't living here then. About seven years ago, two Chicago cops were convicted of running a drug ring and sentenced to ten years. They were released from Danville six months ago." He tapped the mug shot with his index finger. "Rudy Gehke was one of them."

Nick noticed Zoë had stopped eating, and her face had lost its usual healthy glow. "What about the other?" he asked.

"Jimmy Mahoney—"

Zoë's fork clattered to the table. Color flared in her cheeks as she reached for it. "Excuse me." Fork in hand, she glanced at Hugh. "You were saying?"

Hugh's brows drew together in a little frown as he picked up another paper and scanned it. "Jimmy Mahoney was the name of the other cop. Apparently, no one's seen or heard from him since he got out."

Nick took a bite of his burger and chewed slowly. "I wonder if Mahoney might have been the other biker—the one who sped off."

Zoë choked on her water.

He reached over and slapped her on the back. "Are you okay?"

Her face reddened, and she coughed twice. "Yes. It just went down the wrong way. Sorry."

She closed her eyes and took a deep breath. For a woman who treated an intruder firing a gun in the basement like an everyday occurrence, she seemed to be struggling to hold herself together. Maybe it was the physical shock of plowing into a tree—his face stung, and he knew he was going to have some major aches and pains tomorrow-or maybe the cumulative effect of the happenings of the past few days was getting to her. Either way, the sooner they wrapped up the police interview the better.

He turned his attention to Hugh. "Maybe we ought to get to those questions now. You probably have other things to do this afternoon."

Hugh glanced at his watch. "I need to get back on patrol. In this weather, we're going to have plenty of fender-benders, or worse, before third watch takes over."

Nick and Zoë finished giving their statements then returned to the ER. When they asked about the Prescotts, one of the nurses said Marian had already been admitted. She gave them the room number and directions to the nearest bank of elevators.

They had the car to themselves for the ride to Obstetrics on the third floor. After pressing the button, Nick stepped back and glanced at Zoë. Her normally straight spine had relaxed into an exhausted "S" as she rested her weight against the stainless steel rail that circled the interior of the car, and the heavy fringe of her lashes fanned out across the upper curves of her cheekbones. She was beautiful, but there was something disturbing about seeing her usually animated features in complete repose, as if he were somehow violating her privacy.

Before he could speak, the elevator bell sounded, signaling their floor.

Her eyes popped open. "Huh? What?" She straightened and blinked.

"You fell asleep standing up. I don't think I've ever seen anybody do that before."

Confusion clouded her eyes. "I didn't. I couldn't have."

He steered her out of the elevator. "You could, and you did. Let's go check on Marian and get you home before you pass out and I have to carry you."

She jerked her arm from his grasp. "I am not going to pass out. I was just…resting my eyes."

"Right. That's what they all say." He pointed to a sign on the wall. "Come on. Room three twenty-four is down this hall."

The door was open, but he knocked firmly before they entered. Inside, Marian lay sleeping in the bed, hooked up to a scary number of cords and tubes, while an array of monitors beeped and hummed. The remains of a lunch tray had been shoved to the side, and Lyman sat beside her, holding her hand.

"How's she doing?" Zoë whispered.

Strain had etched fine lines in the skin around Lyman's eyes. "The doctor said she looks fine, but these machines make me nervous."

"Are you planning to sit up with her all night? You'll never get any sleep in that chair."

"The nurse said they can bring in a cot." He glanced at Nick. "You two should go back to the house. I'll call you tomorrow and let you know what time Marian's being discharged so you can pick us up."

Nick nodded. "Will do." While he headed for the door, Zoë lingered at Marian's bedside. "Zoë?"

She turned. "Hmm? What?"

"Are you coming?"

"Oh...yes." She patted Lyman's shoulder as she passed. "Take care of her, and we'll see you tomorrow."

As soon as they were back in the hall, Nick touched her arm. "Are you okay?"

She drew a deep breath then released it slowly. "I'm not sure. My head feels fuzzy—like I'm here, but I'm not—and I'm really tired."

He'd had the same feeling many times after a stressful operation. "It's the post-adrenaline letdown from the accident. You'll feel better after some rest, but maybe I should drive on the way back."

Her back stiffened, and the spark returned to her eyes. "Not on your life. No one drives my car except me. No one." She clutched her purse to her chest as if he had threatened to steal her keys.

He shook his head. She was too stubborn for her own good. "Have it your way, but if you start to nod off, I'm taking over, whether you like it or not."

On the drive back to the Prescott estate, he had to bite his tongue to keep from snickering. Zoë reminded him of a rabid teenage gamer in an arcade as she gripped the steering wheel with single-minded ferocity and kept her gaze trained on the road. As soon as she parked the car, she went straight up to her room without a word.

The last of Nick's energy disappeared when he reached the top of the stairs to his apartment. His head was pounding, and his chest hurt, so he downed a couple of ibuprofens. He'd decided to give her an hour to rest before forcing the confrontation that had been building for days, so to pass the time, he stretched out on the bed and closed his eyes.

He awoke with a start and glanced around the dark room in a disoriented panic. The digital alarm clock on the bedside table glowed seven-zero-five. Impossible. How could he have slept almost three hours? He bolted upright and swung his legs to the floor. His stomach lurched, and his head spun for several seconds before it cleared. He stumbled to the bathroom and flipped the switch. Squinting against the bright light, he glanced in the mirror and winced at his reflection.

He looked like a boxer who had lost the title fight in twelve rounds. Raw, red abrasions streaked his cheeks and forehead. His eyes were bloodshot, and incipient bruises showed beneath them from the force of the airbag deployment. He couldn't have a serious conversation with Zoë, looking like this, but what choice did he have? He wet a washcloth in cold water, wrung it out, and then plastered it across his face.

Yow!

He sucked air in through his teeth. His battered face stung like an army of fire ants had been snacking on it, but as he held the cold cloth in place, the pain gradually lessened. After a couple of minutes, he lowered the cloth and surveyed the damage again. He didn't look any better, but at least it didn't hurt as much. His stomach grumbled, reminding him of the time. He needed to eat. He also needed to sit down with Zoë, no matter how bad he looked.

Even if they both felt like something you scraped off the bottom of your shoe, it was time for the truth.

He found her curled up on the living room sofa, staring at a re-run of an old eighties detective show.

"Have you eaten?"

When she turned her head, surprise registered in her eyes, as if she'd forgotten about him. "You look awful!"

He pressed his lips together. He didn't want his appearance to color their discussion. He raised one shoulder in his best attempt at a nonchalant shrug. "Airbag. It looks worse than it feels."

"I hope so. Otherwise, we need to head straight back to the hospital." She clicked off the television, unwound her legs, and stood. "Maybe you'll feel better if you eat. I'll see what I can pull together."

Her eyes were brighter and no longer dazed with shock and fatigue, but the dark smudges beneath them remained, in stark contrast to her fair skin. According to his sister Angela, Nick was worthless at sensing what women wanted or needed, but even he could tell a little pampering might go a long way right now. "Tell you what—you join me in the kitchen, and I'll cook something for us both."

She frowned in confused suspicion. "I thought you said you couldn't cook."

"I may have exaggerated slightly. Come on." He raised one hand to the small of her back in a gentle nudge.

After parking her at the kitchen table, he poured her a glass of red wine and rummaged through the cabinets for pots.

Zoë sipped her wine and sighed. "This is nice. You don't have to cook, you know. I'm the chef, after all."

He turned with a skillet in one hand. "Are you?"

She glanced away and let his question drop.

Nick let her drink her wine in peace while he hunted for a tall pot and gathered ingredients from the fridge and pantry. Olive oil. Garlic. Cherry tomatoes. Basil. Parmesan cheese. Spaghetti. He hadn't lied completely about his culinary skills. His repertoire consisted of only a handful of dishes, and this specialty of his mother's was one of them. While the pasta cooked, he halved the tomatoes then sautéed them in olive oil with the garlic and basil. A few minutes and a sprinkle of grated parmesan later, dinner was ready. Simple, but satisfying.

He set two steaming plates on the table, poured himself a glass of wine, and settled into the chair across from Zoë. He wanted a straightforward view of her and wanted her to see him just as clearly. Evasion and lying were much more difficult face-to-face. Not that he expected her to pull her arms inside her sweater and stare at the floor when he asked uncomfortable questions like many of the suspects he'd interviewed over the years, but small changes in expression could be just as telling.

She twirled a bite of spaghetti around her fork and popped it into her mouth. Her lips curved in a smile as she chewed and swallowed. "Mmm. This is delicious."

Nick's pulse leapt. She'd just given him the opening he was looking for. "I'll teach you how to make it, if you like."

Hot pink rushed to her cheeks. "Um…thanks."

He laid his fork on his plate and focused his attention on her. "Zoë, after what happened today, we need to be honest with each other. You're not a professional chef, are you?"

She didn't pull her arms into her sweater or stare at the floor. Instead, she met his gaze full-on with challenge flashing in her emerald eyes. "No, I'm not. Any more than you're a chauffeur."

He nodded in acknowledgement. As he'd told her, there was nothing to be gained by hiding the truth at this point. "So why are you here?"

"Lyman hired me to protect Marian. I'm a bodyguard."

A bodyguard. Not what he'd suspected, given her appearance, but then he wasn't sure what he had expected. "So why the pretense of being a personal chef?"

She swirled her wine then took another sip. "My firm specializes in operatives who work undercover, and Lyman didn't want Marian to know he'd hired a bodyguard." She stabbed a tomato. "He was afraid she'd worry if she thought he was worried."

Nick let out a short laugh. "That circular logic sounds familiar."

Zoë tilted her head and assessed him with a cool expression as she finished her tomato. "What about you? You used to be a detective with the Detroit P.D., and now you're a licensed private investigator."

Her statement drew him up short. Had she been a step ahead of him all along? "How do you know that?"

"My employer has an excellent research department."

"I couldn't find anything on you."

"You're not meant to. Because we work undercover, our names don't appear on the company website, and our boss requires no social media footprint as a condition of employment."

She gathered another bite of pasta on her fork. "So, Mr. Private Investigator, what are you doing at Strathmoor, pretending to be a chauffeur?"

"Pretty much the same as you. After Lyman's car accident, Marian was terrified and hired me as a bodyguard for him."

Zoë's eyes sparked with understanding and amusement. "And I bet she didn't want him to know."

"You'd win that bet."

"How did she find you?"

"My brother-in-law was the first officer on the scene of the accident. Afterward, Marian kept calling him at the station, insisting on police protection for her husband. Kenny tried to explain the police don't provide that service, especially not without a direct threat. Finally, she wore him down, and he referred her to me."

Zoë's expression grew thoughtful as she ate another bite. When she finished, she lifted her gaze to meet his. "So we've been dancing around each other for weeks, each pretending to be someone else, like some kind of ridiculous French farce. This situation would be funny if it weren't so serious."

He nodded. "Yeah. I can't be sure about Lyman's original accident, but I'm afraid a gunman in the basement and a pair of homicidal bikers definitely qualify as serious." Without thinking, he cut his spaghetti into short segments with the side of his fork. When he glanced up, Zoë was smiling. "What?"

She raised her brows and pointed at his plate. "My brother does that for his six-year-old."

Heat rose in his cheeks. "Old habits die hard. My mom made me and Angela cut up our spaghetti when we were kids. We preferred the full-strand-suck method, but Mom insisted that left more sauce on our faces than in our stomachs."

"I'm sure she was right. My mother swore my brothers made messy eating into a competition."

They ate in silence for a few minutes before he refilled their glasses. "Since we seem to be working the same case, what do you say we pool our efforts? Do you have any theories about the guy in the basement or the kamikaze cyclists?"

She kept her gaze on the ruby liquid in her glass and took her time answering. "Are you convinced the incidents are connected?"

"Aren't you?"

"I think it's likely, but we shouldn't jump to conclusions. The gunman who demanded the plans to GRAMPA didn't have the same voice or accent as Victor Watanabe. And why would Rudy Gehke, a rogue cop-turned-bank robber, try to run us off the road? It's hard to see a connection."

He'd had the same thought. "So what do you think we should do next?

She pushed back from the table, stood, and began to pace, glass in hand. "Since the Prescotts are the only point of connection, they probably know more than they realize. We need to talk to them."

Nick stacked the dirty plates and carried them to the sink. "I'm not sure how much they could tell us now. They've both been traumatized by the accident today."

Zoë joined him at the sink and set her empty glass on the counter. "I'm afraid we're all a little worse for wear. I'm still shaky, and you look like you're ready to go trick-or-treating."

When she raised a hand to the abrasion over his brow, her touch was cool and gentle. "We'll need to be subtle and go slow."

Warmth suffused his body, and his thoughts blurred. What was she talking about? Oh, yeah. The Prescotts.

"And we can't abandon our covers without permission," she continued.

"Uh...no."

He struggled to follow the conversation as her fingers trailed down the side of his injured face then withdrew. What was wrong with him? Maybe he was suffering the delayed effects of trauma from the airbag. He dumped the rest of his wine, filled the glass with cold water, and downed it in two gulps. As he focused on the concern in her eyes, his head cleared.

"Better?" she asked.

"Yeah."

She turned on the faucet to rinse the dishes. "I think we'd better get you to bed. We can discuss strategy tomorrow before we head back to the hospital."

His brain froze again at *we* and *bed*.

150

She shook her head and wiped her hands on a dishtowel. Taking him firmly by the arms, she steered him toward the back door. "Go. Now. And don't come back for at least ten hours."

When his hand touched the knob, he turned and hesitated, mesmerized by the perfect curve of her upper lip. He couldn't think of anything except how much he wanted to kiss her. No, needed to kiss her. There were probably a dozen excellent reasons he shouldn't, but none came to mind.

He reached for her and slowly closed the space between them, half expecting her to pull away or object. But she didn't. She smiled.

"Go," she murmured. "You too tired to know what you're doing."

She was wrong. He knew exactly what he was doing.

Just before their lips touched, she turned her head, and his mouth brushed her cheek.

She slipped from his hands. "Go." Reaching around him, she opened the door and gently propelled him onto the porch.

He had stumbled half-way across the courtyard to the garage when she called out, "Oh...and thanks for dinner."

Chapter Ten

Daylight glowed orange through Zoë's closed lids, but opening her eyes required more energy than she could muster. When she rolled to her back and stretched, her muscles screamed in protest. She sucked in a breath and waited for the pain to ease. Car accidents—even minor ones—always had the same effect on her body. The next day every square inch hurt as if she'd been beaten with a two-by-four, even if she hadn't been injured.

She rolled back to her side and picked up her phone to check the time. Seven-twenty-two. If she hadn't been too tired to think last night, she would have spent an hour soaking in the old cast iron tub with a handful of Epsom salts before tumbling into bed.

She forced herself out of bed and winced her way to the bathroom. Normally, she was a shower-and-go kind of girl, but this morning the tub beckoned. She ran the water as hot as she could stand, climbed in, and sank down until the steaming water reached her shoulders. The tub was too short to stretch her legs out, but she managed to get enough of her body under the water to get some relief. She dunked a washcloth then draped it over her face and settled back.

While the hot water worked its magic, she chewed on her dilemma. Last night she hadn't told Nick about Jimmy Mahoney. They'd agreed to work together, but she hadn't shared a key piece of information. Why?

Because the only facts she knew for certain were that Jimmy was Marian's ex-husband and he'd come to the house a week ago. His visit had upset Marian, but that didn't necessarily tie him to any crime. His leathers were similar to those of one of the cyclists she'd encountered her first morning at Strathmoor, but that proved nothing.

The gunman in the basement had been masked, and she hadn't noticed anything about the second biker who'd sped off yesterday after running them into the tree. Any connections she tried to make at this point would be pure speculation, and she refused to violate Marian's confidence on speculation. If convincing evidence turned up connecting Jimmy to either crime, she would share it.

Thoughts of Nick inevitably shoved her to the place she'd been avoiding, the place she didn't want to go — their almost-kiss. Last night had changed their relationship, but she wasn't sure how. On the surface, they no longer had reason to distrust each other, but that didn't necessarily mean there was anything between them on a personal level. She had to admit she found his strength and single-minded professionalism sexy. And since he'd tried to kiss her twice, he must be attracted to her, at least some of the time. But as to where that might lead, she hadn't a clue.

Since the whole conundrum gave her a headache, and her bath water was getting cold, it was time to set speculation aside and deal with the business at hand. She pulled the plug, grabbed a towel, and climbed out of the tub.

After a gentle yoga routine, her sore muscles had loosened, and she felt almost human. She dressed and went down to the kitchen, where she found Nick sitting at the kitchen table, reading Lyman's newspaper.

He glanced up when she entered the room. "You look better this morning."

"I feel better." She studied his face. The scattered small cuts had scabbed over, but the bruises under his eyes had blossomed into a stunning mix of purple and green. "You, on the other hand, look like the backside of a June bug."

One side of his mouth curved up. "This is nothing. You should see me after taking a high stick to the face."

"I'll pass, thank you. You made coffee." She crossed to the counter, grabbed a mug from the cupboard, and poured herself a cup.

"Since we've established that you're not a real chef, I figured I could help out in the kitchen."

She carried the pot to the table and refilled his cup. "I appreciate the gesture this morning, but remember— as soon as Marian gets back, I'm in charge of the cooking again."

"For better or worse."

She raised one brow. "I was going to offer to make pancakes, but after that crack, it's plain toast for you, bucko."

When the phone on the wall jangled, Nick jerked around in his chair, sloshed hot coffee on his hand, and swore. Since Zoë was only a couple of steps away, she reached for the receiver. It had better not be that nasty anonymous caller again. She was so not in the mood. "Prescott residence."

The caller was Lyman with the news that Marian was being discharged in a couple of hours. After assuring him she would be there to pick them up, Zoë returned the receiver to its cradle.

"I'll need to leave for the hospital around ten."

Nick folded the paper and set it aside. "If we leave a little early, you can drop me at the car rental agency. My insurance agent has arranged for a loaner while my truck's in the shop. I'll meet you at the hospital and follow you back to the house."

Normally, she would have insisted she could handle the task on her own, but after yesterday, the thought of seeing Nick's face in the rearview mirror brought a welcome reassurance.

At the hospital, the staff insisted on bringing Marian to the curb in a wheelchair. Her hair hung limply across her shoulders, and her face was pale and drawn, but she greeted Zoë with a warm smile. Lyman helped her into the back seat of the Mini then slid in beside her.

After arranging her seatbelt around her belly, Marian settled back with a sigh. "I can't wait to get home." She reached for her husband's hand and gave him a tired smile. "We're both exhausted. I don't know how anyone can sleep in a hospital. People pop in and out of the room all night, and then there are all those tubes and wires and beeping things."

"It's nice and quiet at home," Zoë assured her. "And I've made you a special welcome home lunch. Then you can take a nice nap."

"That sounds like heaven."

Before pulling away from the curb, Zoë glanced back to see Nick idling behind her in a big black Escalade. *That* was his loaner? He must have one heck of a good insurance agent. For a moment she wondered if it would be safer to transfer Marian and Lyman to the Escalade, then she decided she'd prefer to have Nick riding shotgun. If anyone tried to intercept the Mini, he had the weight and power to stop them. He would also have more freedom to take offensive action without passengers in the car.

The drive home was smooth and uneventful, but when they pulled up to the gate, a large brown box sat on the ground next to the intercom. It looked as if the delivery person had abandoned it after failing to find anyone at home.

Zoë glanced back at her passengers. "Is either of you expecting a package?"

Lyman leaned over to peer out the car window. "Not me. Marian, did you order something for the baby?"

"No. We got everything on my list on our shopping trip."

It might be a gift, but it was awfully big. Zoë's stomach twisted and tightened. What if the box contained a bomb? After yesterday, her imagination might be in overdrive, but she pushed the opener and drove through the gate at twice her normal speed, only slowing when she reached the courtyard behind the house.

She met Lyman's gaze in the mirror. "We'll go inside and let Nick take care of the package."

He nodded and helped Marian out of the car and up the back steps, while Zoë waited for Nick to park behind her.

"Did you see that box by the gate?" She kept her voice low because Lyman was still fishing through his pockets for the key to the back door.

Nick nodded. "I stopped to check it. The box is unmarked and the delivery label is torn, so there's no sender's name or address. I assume it's the last remaining piece of inventory from that baby shop downtown."

"No. We didn't order anything, and neither of the Prescotts is expecting a package." She shot a worried glance down the driveway toward the gate. "Do you think we should call the bomb squad?"

"That's kind of a stretch, but I don't think we should take any chances." He pulled out his phone and placed a call to the Lake Forest Police Department. After a quick explanation, he tucked the phone back in his pocket. "They'll be here as soon as they can muster the team and equipment. I'll wait at the gate. You go inside and take care of the Prescotts."

Curiosity and duty grappled for the upper hand. Although she was anxious to find out what was in the box and had never seen a bomb squad in action, responsibility won out. "Okay." After one last glance toward the gate, she hurried up the steps and into the house.

For lunch, she'd made a chicken pot pie. She'd cheated and used frozen vegetables and prepared pastry, betting neither of the Prescotts would know the difference. She was right. For whatever reason—probably sheer exhaustion—they both seemed to have forgotten the box at the gate. They raved about the pot pie and cleaned their plates before Lyman ushered Marian into the elevator and up to their bedroom for some desperately needed sleep.

Zoë tried to settle on the living room sofa with the newspaper but found herself re-reading the same article over and over without absorbing a word. Her mind was on the officers outside. After fifteen minutes she gave up and went to Lyman's office to peer out one of the long front windows. She couldn't see the activity on the other side of the elaborate wrought iron gate clearly, but the suggestion of movement helped calm her nerves.

As time dragged on, she wondered if she should call Nick's cell to ask him for an update. There had been no loud noises, so they hadn't exploded the package. What could be taking so long?

After what seemed like hours, the figure of a man stepped through the gate opening and walked up the driveway toward the house, carrying some kind of contraption. As he drew closer, she recognized Nick's dark hair and long, purposeful stride, although she couldn't yet identify the device in his arms. She rushed to the front door and stepped out onto the porch. Within a minute, the object became clear.

He was carrying a stroller.

He toted it up the steps then set it on the porch at her feet. "I called the bomb squad for a freaking stroller. They brought the sniffer dog and the robot. Those guys are never going to let me live this down."

"You couldn't have known. We had no idea what was in the box. And after yesterday..."

She bent for a closer inspection. The device was incredibly elaborate, much more than a simple stroller. It reminded her of one Marian had seen at the baby shop, but this one was even fancier. Someone had spent a pretty penny on the gift. "Was there a card?"

Nick handed her a small envelope. "This was inside."

She turned the envelope in her hand. It was made from heavy duty, high quality paper stock—the kind often used for wedding invitations—and read *Mrs. Lyman Prescott*. Zoë opened the envelope and slid out a card of the same quality. The front of the card was emblazoned with an elegant monogram—LBE. She recognized it immediately as belonging to Le Bébé Élégant. When she opened the card, it read simply, "So Very Sorry."

She showed it to Nick. "Who's sorry, and for what?"

He examined the card and envelope as if some clue would magically appear. "I have no idea, but I don't like it."

"We'll have to ask Marian. Maybe she told a family member or friend about the accident."

"Maybe, but don't you think someone close to her would have signed their name?"

"I do." She certainly didn't know anyone who would send such an expensive gift anonymously. "Is it safe to bring inside?"

He pressed his lips together and waited a couple of seconds. "Would I have brought it up here if it wasn't?"

Her cheeks warmed. "I guess not." She opened the door and stepped aside as he pushed the stroller into the foyer.

Three hours later Zoë heard the hum and rattle of the elevator from her place on the living room sofa and hurried into the foyer. When the door opened, Lyman and Marian appeared, both looking rested and refreshed.

Marian's face lit with delight when she spied the stroller in the middle of the floor. "What's that?"

"It was in the box at the gate. Apparently, it's a gift for you."

Marian beamed as she ran her fingers over the canopy. "It's The Entourage." She turned to Zoë. "We saw one like it at the baby shop, do you remember? It has so many amazing features. But I couldn't bring myself to buy it."

Lyman wrapped one arm around her middle where her waist used to be. "Why not? I told you to buy everything you wanted."

She turned in his embrace and touched his cheek in a gentle caress before shaking her head with a smile. "Don't be silly. It cost more than my first car. I wasn't about to spend that kind of money on a stroller."

Nick frowned at The Entourage as if it were hiding some malevolent intent. "Do you have any idea who might have sent it?"

Marian hesitated a moment then shook her head. "None at all. No one I know could afford one."

"Maybe it's a group gift from your co-workers," Zoë suggested.

"I'm sure it's not. They gave me a car seat at the shower. Was there a card?"

"Oh...yes." Zoë retrieved it from the hall table. "Here."

Marian read the brief message then showed it to Lyman, who pursed his lips and frowned. Then she handed it back. "That's strange and kind of creepy. What do you think it means?"

Zoë glanced at Nick. "We assumed it referred to the accident yesterday. Did you call any family members or friends from the hospital?"

"No. At first things were too chaotic, and later I was too tired. Besides, I had Lyman with me." She smiled into her husband's eyes. "I honestly didn't think to call anyone else."

Nick glanced from one to the other. "So, as far as you know, no one is aware of the accident except the four of us, the police, and the medical personnel. Is that correct?"

If he'd been standing closer, Zoë would have given him a subtle kick in the shin. How did he expect Lyman to believe he was nothing more than a chauffeur if he couldn't keep the cop out of his voice?

Lyman stiffened and tightened his hold on his wife. "That is correct."

Since the Prescotts clearly couldn't provide any useful information, Zoë decided it was time to puncture the growing bubble of tension in the room. She pasted a bright smile on her face. "Well, it's a fantastic stroller, so you might as well enjoy it, no matter who sent it."

Marian's blue eyes sparked, and the tight lines around them faded. She eased out of her husband's embrace and turned, her face alight with renewed excitement. "The Entourage is much more than just a stroller. I can't wait to show you everything it does. It even comes with this matching diaper bag. Isn't it cute?"

Lyman smiled and nodded. "Absolutely."

Zoë suspected he wasn't referring to the stroller, and her throat tightened. His devotion to his wife was a palpable entity, hovering around him at all times. No man had ever looked at her like that, and she'd pretty much given up hope one ever would.

She blinked a couple of times then caught Nick's attention and signaled for him to follow her to the kitchen. While Marian demonstrated the wonders of The Entourage to her ostensibly captivated spouse, Zoë and Nick left unnoticed.

He poured himself a cup of stale coffee left over from breakfast, but before he could bring it to his lips, she snatched it from his hand and dumped it in the sink.

"Hey! What—"

She rinsed his cup. "You can't drink that stuff—it's foul. I don't know why I didn't throw it out after breakfast. I'll make a fresh pot."

He crossed his arms and studied her as she measured fresh grounds into the filter and placed it back in the machine. His scrutiny made her already jumpy insides leap higher.

She kept her attention on her task as she poured the water into the coffeemaker and set the pot on the warmer. "You're a lousy P.I., you know."

He stiffened. "Where did that come from?"

She wasn't sure. The words had just popped out on their own. "Keep your voice down."

Nick narrowed his eyes and stepped closer. "You're the one who started a conversation we shouldn't be having here."

She eased away from his simmering anger. "We're okay for now. The Prescotts went into the living room. I saw them through the doorway."

He glanced into the foyer, and Zoë picked up faint voices from the television in the living room.

He faced her and crossed his arms. "Fine. So tell me what makes you an expert on private investigators."

"I'm not, but I do know something about working undercover."

"I've worked undercover before." A current of challenge ran through his flat statement.

When pushed, her natural response was to push back, regardless of whether it was the smartest tactic. "I don't see how. Everything about you screams *cop*—the way you look at people, the questions you ask and the way you ask them, even the way you walk."

"What's wrong with the way I walk?" The defensive edge in his voice was sharp enough to slice through granite.

She pictured his strong, confident stride. *Nothing's wrong with your walk – if I'm the only one watching.*

But she wasn't the only one, and that was the problem. "You march into a room like you're in charge."

"So?"

She poured two cups of fresh coffee and handed one to him. "You're supposed to be the chauffeur."

Based on his puzzled expression, he really didn't understand. She elaborated. "You're an employee, not the boss. Why do you think Lyman gives you strange looks and bristles when you speak?"

Nick swirled the coffee in his cup with ominous nonchalance. "I haven't noticed anything like that."

"Then you're not watching closely enough. I thought police detectives were supposed to be trained observers."

"We are, but we're also trained how to ask questions and where to look for answers."

"Well, if you watched the people around you more closely, you'd see that Lyman is developing serious suspicions about you."

He scowled at his coffee before slugging it down in one long, continuous gulp. When he lifted his head, anger snapped in his eyes. "I'll try to be more subservient in the future."

"I didn't mean—"

He brushed past her and stalked out of the kitchen.

She dumped the untouched contents of her cup in the sink. The thought of coffee, which she usually loved, curdled her stomach, along with the dregs of guilt. Her mother was right—sometimes she didn't have the sense

God gave a flea. She could tell herself she was only trying to help, but the truth was she'd been on edge since her close encounter with Nick the night before. Still, she shouldn't have taken it out on him that way.

He was furious, and she couldn't blame him. Nobody liked being told they were bad at their job. Besides, the man was a former police detective, and she was a...what? A novice bodyguard on her first real case. Who was she to criticize his methods?

But yesterday's accident had brought the whole situation to a tipping point, and she didn't know what to do next. She'd been putting off a status update to her boss for days. A glance at her watch told her she had at least an hour before she needed to start dinner. Maybe now was the time to make that call.

Madelyn picked up on the first ring. "Zoë, why haven't you returned my calls? You know company policy. Texts don't cut it. I was nearly ready to drive to Lake Forest to check on you."

Zoë's pulse jumped. Had she put her job in jeopardy by trying to handle such a complex situation on her own? "I know. I'm sorry. But things have been a little crazy here."

"You'd better tell me about it."

Referring to her notes, Zoë filled her boss in on everything that had happened, from the break-in the day before she arrived to the car accident yesterday, including Jimmy Mahoney and his connection to Marian.

"It sounds like you might be in over your head," Madelyn said at the end of the litany. "Maybe I should drive up tomorrow to talk to Mr. Prescott about taking over the case personally."

Calm and confident, Hargrove. Calm and confident. "I'm sure that's not necessary." *At least not yet.* "But I could use some help."

"The full resources of Phoenix, Ltd. are always available to our operatives." Madelyn's words were strictly business, but her voice had softened a degree or two.

"I know, and Risa's been a big help so far. But a strange thing happened this afternoon, and I wondered if she could check it out for me." Zoë detailed the appearance of the pricey stroller and its mysterious card. "Finding out who sent it might help clarify the situation here."

"I'll ask Risa to call the store and try to talk them into giving her the name of the sender."

"If they won't, maybe she could use some of her mad computer skills to find out."

"I am not going to authorize hacking the store's database when the only potential crime we're looking at is someone anonymously sending our client an extravagant baby stroller."

"But—"

"No. And that's final. Additionally, I believe it's time to make some major changes in the way this operation is being handled."

Madelyn's words jolted Zoë as hard as Nick's truck hitting the tree. She closed her eyes and rubbed the back of her neck. The boss was going to replace her. She knew it.

Chapter Eleven

Zoë had failed to protect her client from a possible attempt on her life, and now her boss was going to pull her off the Prescott case, maybe even fire her. Not that she didn't deserve it. She'd accused Nick of being a lousy P.I., but she was an even worse bodyguard. She'd really thought she was ready to handle an assignment on her own.

Impulsive and unprepared, Hargrove.

Why did her inner voice always have to channel her old drill instructor? Why couldn't it choose someone more positive and affirming?

"Zoë? Are you still there?" Madelyn's voice penetrated her veil of self-pity.

"Yes. Yes, of course." She might as well get it over with, take her lumps, and figure out a way to move on.

"Regardless of the nature of the previous incidents," her boss continued in a brisk, professional tone, "the accident yesterday has elevated the threat level. It's time for Mr. Prescott to take his wife into his confidence and share the real purpose of your presence in the house. You will find it much easier to protect her if she's able to cooperate."

Had she heard correctly? Madelyn intended to keep her on the assignment? She wasn't being fired? "I absolutely agree."

"Do you feel comfortable discussing the matter with your client, or would you like me to call him?"

Zoë grinned into the phone, barely able to keep from hooting out loud. Madelyn had called Lyman *your client*, as if she were a full-fledged field agent. She allowed herself a silent fist pump.

Then she remembered how much more was at stake than her professional standing. Yesterday's crash could have seriously injured or even killed one of them. The thought sobered her instantly. "That won't be necessary. I'll talk to him. I have a very good relationship with Mr. Prescott."

"Excellent. Also, you said Mr. Rosetti is working under a similar arrangement with Mrs. Prescott."

"Yes. I'll ask him to have the same conversation with her." *If he's still speaking to me.*

"Very good. Is there anything else you need right now?"

"Not that I can think of. I'll call you in a day or two with an update."

"See that you do."

"And Boss...thanks."

"I'm just doing my job, as I expect you to do yours. And Zoë...don't call me Boss."

Zoë ended the call with a smile.

She would talk to Lyman in the morning. Today, his full attention was where it belonged—on his wife. But first she needed to find Nick and get him on board with the plan. Since he'd probably retreated to his room, she might need a peace offering to persuade him to open the door.

Ten minutes later she stood at the top of the stairs to Nick's garage apartment with a plate of two-day-old chocolate chip cookies in one hand and a travel mug of coffee in the other. She balanced the cookies on top of the mug and knocked. And waited. And knocked again. Where the heck was he? She wasn't interested in roaming the estate with coffee and cookies, calling his name.

She'd turned and started down the steps in disgust when the latch clicked and a hinge creaked behind her.

"What do you want?"

She pivoted, taking care not to tilt the cookie plate and risk dumping her bribe on the driveway. Nick stood in the doorway with the knob firmly in hand. His tousled hair and shadowed jaw accentuated the aggravated animosity in his gaze. Maybe this wasn't the best time to have come calling.

Zoë gave him her best attempt at a friendly smile. "Did I wake you?"

He scrubbed his bristly jaw with one hand. "Yeah."

"I'm sorry. I brought you a snack." She held up the plate and mug. "May I come in?"

His eyes narrowed. "Are those chocolate chip?"

She climbed a couple of steps and waved the plate in front of him. "They sure are."

"Okay." He stepped back and held the door open. "Come on in."

The cushions on the old sofa were askew and flattened in places, and a college football game played on the television. He must have fallen asleep watching the game. He grabbed the remote and clicked it off then straightened the pillows. "I wasn't expecting company."

She set the mug and plate on the coffee table before settling at one end of the couch. "It's been an odd day. I thought you might need a pick-me-up."

Nick plopped down at the other end with a short laugh. "Odd. That's one way to describe it." He chose the biggest cookie and took a bite, washing it down with a slug of coffee. "These are good. Thanks."

She glanced down at her hands in her lap. *Now for the tough part*. Drawing a deep breath, she lifted her chin and met his gaze. "I wanted to apologize for the things I said earlier. I was out of line, and I'm sorry."

"No, you weren't."

She started to protest, but he raised a hand to shush her. "I thought about what you said...a lot...and you were right. I do sound and act too much like a cop." He ran one big hand through his hair, leaving small tufts sticking up here and there. "I guess old habits are hard to break."

"How long were you a police officer?"

"Nearly ten years." Dark pain shadowed his eyes.

"So you haven't been a private investigator long."

He shook his head and grabbed another cookie. "About six months. And Marian is the first client to request any kind of undercover work. I should have been more careful."

"Actually, that's something else I wanted to talk to you about." She leaned forward and picked up the smaller of the two remaining cookies. "I think this chauffeur/cook masquerade has outlived its usefulness."

The corner of his lips tipped up teasingly. "I don't know. You are getting to be a much better cook." He took another bite of his cookie. "I'd hate to go back to frozen dinners and Oreos. Not that I don't love Oreos, but these are better. "

She gave him a quelling look. "I'm glad you like them, but be serious. I'm not proposing we abandon our current duties. The Prescotts obviously need our help."

Nick washed down the last of his cookie with another long swig of coffee before setting mug on the table. "It would be a lot easier to protect Lyman if I didn't have to worry about inventing excuses to stick close to him."

"It would be much easier for both of us to protect the Prescotts if we were able to work together, without all the playacting and subterfuge. In light of what's happened, it's time to persuade Marian to come clean with her husband about hiring you."

"I agree. And you'll do the same with Lyman?"

She nodded. "I think it would be a relief to everyone."

"When do you want to do this?"

"Tomorrow morning. I don't see any reason to wait."

"Neither do I."

She pushed to her feet and headed toward the door. "Good. I'm sorry I woke you. I'll see you at dinner."

Before Zoë's hand touched the knob, Nick slipped between her and the door. She had to pull up short to keep from running face-first into his broad chest. Taking a half step back, she lifted her chin, and sent him a questioning look.

"There's something more I want to say."

His voice rumbled in his chest, it's deep tone sending goosebumps up her arms. Her heart fluttered in her chest. Was he going to try to kiss her again?

"I'm sorry for the way I acted."

Not what she'd expected. Zoë released her breath and relaxed a fraction. "It's my fault. I woke you up."

"Not then... earlier... in the kitchen. When you so graciously pointed out my shortcomings."

She glanced down at the ratty old green shag carpeting. "About that...I probably could have been more...um...diplomatic."

He slipped a forefinger under her chin and tipped it up until she met his gaze. "No, you were right. I've never taken criticism well—just ask my former lieutenant. I overreacted."

"Let's agree we both could have handled the conversation more professionally and leave it at that." She offered her hand. "Deal?"

His hand enveloped hers with heat and strength, squeezing lightly. "Deal."

When she tried to release her grasp, he tightened his hold and gave a little tug, drawing her forward. "I'm wide awake now."

"I can see that."

He pulled her steadily forward until his face loomed above hers and only inches separated their lips. "You could stay a while and keep me company."

"I could, but then you'd get no dinner."

His voice dropped even lower as his head came down and one arm slid behind her back. "Maybe I'm hungry for something besides food."

As his lips drew closer, Zoë's chest tightened, but she fought back, refusing to let the old panic overtake her. Instead, she focused on the solid reality of the man in front of her.

This is Nick. You're safe.

His warm breath fanned her lips, and his strong arm supported her like a branch of her favorite climbing tree back home. She felt nothing but a kindling excitement deep inside. He wasn't holding her too tightly—she knew she could escape if she needed to—but he'd aroused her curiosity, among other things. At the moment all she wanted was to taste him.

Nick's kiss was tentative at first, but as soon as she moved her mouth, his arms tightened around her. As he increased the pressure, Zoë steeled herself against the sense of suffocation, but it never came.

Instead, a warm tingle spread from her lower abdomen to her breasts and down her arms to her fingertips.

He moved one hand up and speared his fingers through her hair, cradling her head and holding it steady while he teased her lips open. She half-expected his other hand to go wandering in search of more titillating destinations, but it remained firmly welded to her back.

After a few minutes that seemed like an eternity, he slowed and ended with one last, lingering kiss before releasing her lips.

She rested her head against his chest and listened to the rhythmic thuds of his heart while she regained her breath. She ran her tongue over her lips, missing the feel of him already. Kissing Nick had been a revelation on many levels. He was unlike any man she'd ever known—certainly unlike any she'd kissed. He hadn't tried to overwhelm or push her. He'd taken his time, leashed his passion. Maybe that was the reason the old fears had lost their teeth.

With a gentle push she slipped out of his arms. There was something oddly endearing about the confused frustration on his face. She smiled and touched his hard jaw. "That was delightful, but I've got to cook dinner. You know the old saying—man cannot live on love alone."

Nick grabbed her wrist and gave her fingers a light nip. "I don't think that's how the quote goes. Besides, who said anything about love?"

Nobody. "You can't live on sex alone, either."

"I'd be willing to give it a try."

"Maybe another time. I've got work to do."

****

Nick stood in the doorway as Zoë crossed the courtyard to the back porch of the main house. He loved the way she moved. Her purposeful, long-legged stride lent just the right amount of motion to her hips to push his personal buttons. Only when she disappeared through the kitchen door did he retreat to his apartment.

Too edgy to settle, he picked up the mug she'd left and took a couple of swallows. Lukewarm. He set the cup back down and returned to the door to stare blindly out the row of small glass panes at the top.

He couldn't get the taste and feel of her out of his mind. She was a paradox—hard, yet soft at the same time. Her finely-tuned body might remind him of velvet over steel, but her emotions were the opposite. That tough-appearing exterior protected an enticingly feminine vulnerability.

When their lips first touched, her body had vibrated, as taut as an over-tightened piano wire. He'd half expected her to break and run or, knowing her, knee him in the groin. But when he'd slowed down, eased off, and let her come to him, she'd relaxed and joined the party with enthusiasm. Too bad it had to stop there.

Under different circumstances, he would have enjoyed taking the time to get to know her better, to let any potential relationship grow naturally. He might have asked her out for pizza and bowling with Angela and Kenny or a trip to the zoo to laugh at the antics of

173

the penguins. But he couldn't do that. They were both working twenty-four/seven, and despite their agreement to coordinate security efforts, they had separate responsibilities and separate priorities. He couldn't afford any relationship that might threaten his commitment to his client's safety, and neither could she.

He'd learned the hard way how lethal that kind of attachment could be. An innocent man would be alive today if he'd done a better job keeping his personal and professional lives separate.

A few hours later he crossed the courtyard to the main house for dinner. Despite having taken a nap, Marian yawned her way through the meal, and she and Lyman retired for the night shortly afterward, leaving Nick and Zoë alone in the kitchen. She studiously avoided his gaze as she rinsed the dishes and washed the big pot she'd used to boil the mostaccioli.

He snagged a dishtowel and reached to take the pot from her hand as she was about to set it in the drainer. "Let me dry that for you."

She held firm to the pot. "I can do it. You go to bed. It's been an eventful day."

"I'm not tired." He twisted the pot away from her and attacked it with the towel. "And we need to talk about one of those events."

"I thought the bomb squad determined the stroller was no threat."

He set the dry pot and towel on the counter. "They did."

She picked up the damp towel and turned to hang it over the oven handle. "Then I don't—"

He laid one hand on her shoulder. "Zoë, look at me."

She turned and met his gaze, daring him to spit the words out.

"It can't happen again."

She didn't ask what he meant. She didn't say anything, just continued to watch him with those big green eyes.

His frustration multiplied with every second she remained silent. He ran one hand through his hair and blew out a breath. "You know what I mean. The kiss. It can't happen again. We can't get involved...in any way."

"If that's what you want." Her words were clipped and tight.

The question she hadn't asked hung in the air like a toxic cloud.

Why do women always insist on explanations?

Nick clenched and released his jaw. "It doesn't matter what I want...or what you want, for that matter. We have an obligation to protect the Prescotts, and I won't risk their lives for a little fun in the sack, no matter how great it might be."

His apprehension grew as a dull red crept up her neck to her cheeks and forehead, until he was afraid steam might come shooting out her ears.

"Fun in the sack?" She advanced toward him, hands balled into fists and eyes flashing. "Fun in the sack!"

He took a step back but bumped into the front of the stove. He'd irritated more than his share of women over the years, but he'd never seen one so enraged. Zoë was madder than Angela with the hemorrhoid cream, and he hadn't thought that possible. Suddenly, her right fist shot out of nowhere and nailed him hard on the cheekbone, beneath his left eye.

His head reeled, and both eyes watered instantly.

Damn. He should have known she wouldn't hit like a girl.

She gasped, and both hands flew up to cover her nose and mouth, her eyes round with horror. He touched his cheek gingerly. It was tender, but the skin seemed to be intact.

She pushed his hand away. "Don't touch that. Let me get you some ice." She tossed a handful of cubes into a plastic bag and pressed it gently against his injured face. "I'm so sorry. I don't know what came over me. And you already have a major shiner under that eye."

His hand covered hers. "I'll live. Besides, I probably deserved it."

"You definitely deserved it, but I'm sorry anyway." She slid her hand out from under his, leaving him holding the ice.

Nick moved his jaw up, down, and around. Everything seemed to be in working order. He tried a small smile. It didn't hurt...too much. "You pack quite a wallop. Are you sure you're not part Italian? I remember once when I was little, my mom chased my pop through the house with a giant zucchini, threatening to smack him like a baseball because he spilled half a gallon of blue paint on her new white carpet."

"And they stayed married?"

"Until the day he died, five years ago."

The humor in her eyes faded. "I'm sorry."

"I'm sorry, too. He was a great guy and a great dad, even if he was a clumsy painter."

Zoë seemed to have made some sort of decision. She reached behind him and grabbed the big pasta pot by one handle. "Time for you to go to bed. Would you like some ice to take with you?"

"Nah, I'm fine. But before I go, I want to make sure you understand what I meant earlier, about the kissing...and any other extracurricular activities."

She straightened, holding the pot in front of her like a shield. "You made yourself perfectly clear. I understand, believe me."

"I don't think you do. I enjoy kissing you—maybe a little too much."

"But...?"

"I won't go into details, but I've learned firsthand the dangers of getting involved with someone I work with."

Two small furrows appeared between her brows. "It's not like you're my boss, or vice versa."

"That's true—our circumstances are much more serious. In a life-or-death situation, I never want to have to choose between the person I've been paid to protect and the person I care about."

She slowly lowered the pot. "I've never looked at it that way."

"I have." *And I never want to face it with you.* "If we'd met under different circumstances, who knows? As things stand, everyone will be safer if we keep our relationship strictly professional."

She was silent for a moment. "Can we at least be friends? Until we wrap this case up, we have to work together and live in the same household. I'll go crazy if I have to tiptoe around you all the time."

What choice did he have? "Friends it is." He held out his hand. When she clasped it, a tiny jolt arced between them, and he released her as if he'd been burned. "I...uh...guess I'll see you tomorrow."

"I'll talk to Lyman in the morning."

He nodded. "It'll be a relief to have everyone on the same page."

The next morning Nick went looking for Marian after breakfast and found her in the soon-to-be nursery, pondering paint chips and fabric samples.

When he entered the room, she glanced up with a sunny smile. "Oh, good, just what I need—another pair of eyes. Which do you like better?" She held up two short lengths of fabric, one with what looked like bunnies wearing vests and the other featuring bright, stylized zoo animals.

Was there a right answer? He had no clue. "Um..."

"They're for the curtains."

Still nothing. "Are we talking boy baby or girl baby?"

She grinned. "We're talking baby baby. Lyman and I wouldn't let the doctor tell us what we're having, so whatever I choose has to work for either."

"I don't think you could go wrong either way." *How's that for a diplomatic answer?*

She draped the fabrics across the rail of the white crib and held up a couple of paint chips. "The pale yellow goes best with the zoo theme, and the light green picks up the tufts of grass with the bunnies." She pursed her lips while she pondered her choices. "I just can't decide."

"Which one does Lyman like best?"

She laughed. "Since I refuse to go with a robot theme, he doesn't care."

"Maybe you should ask Zoë." She might not be an expert on baby décor, but she was bound to know more than he did.

"That's a great idea. She has a good eye for color and fashion."

He turned to leave then remembered his mission. "I'll ask her to come up, but before I go, there's something I need to talk to you about."

"Sure."

Nick laid out the case for sharing his true purpose with Lyman and was pleased when Marian readily agreed.

"At first, I just wanted to protect him." She shook her head. "But after everything that's happened, it's gotten harder and harder to keep the secret. I've felt like I was lying to him."

He took her hand and gave it a squeeze. "You acted out of love. He'll understand. Now, let's go downstairs and see if we can pull him away from GRAMPA for a few minutes."

He escorted Marian to the elevator, and they rode down to Lyman's basement workshop together.

When the elevator came to a stop with a gentle thud and the door started to open, she whispered, "I'm nervous."

He squeezed her shoulder. "You have nothing to worry about. Your husband worships the ground you walk on."

She stepped out into the chilly stone basement, hugged her arms tight across her chest, and glanced around. "Lyman, are you down here?"

The lights in the workshop were on, but GRAMPA stood next to the workbench, alone and forlorn.

"No one's here." Nick frowned. "Let's go back up."

They checked the kitchen and living room but found them empty, too.

Marian shook her head. "I can't imagine where he is. He's always so predictable. Every morning after breakfast he goes downstairs to work on that robot—no exceptions." She tilted her head and paused for a moment. "There's only one other place he might be."

Nick traipsed behind her across the foyer and down the hall to her husband's study, where they found him seated at his desk, deep in conversation with Zoë. When they entered the room, he broke off mid-sentence, rose with a smile, and crossed to greet his wife with a kiss on the cheek.

"Come in, my dear. I have something important to discuss with you."

Marian settled into a plump, upholstered chair next to the desk. "I have something to tell you, too."

Nick glanced at Zoë, who nodded in response to his silent question.

Lyman rolled his chair close to Marian's until they sat face to face, leaned over, and took her hands in his. "I'll go first, if that's all right."

"Okay."

He straightened and released a big breath, as if girding himself for battle. "Zoë is not a chef."

Marian's light laugh held a note of relief. "Don't be so hard on her. I think she's doing fine. She's certainly a better cook than I am."

Her husband pressed his lips together and shook his head. "No, my dear, you misunderstand. I didn't hire her to be a chef. I hired her to protect you. She's a professional bodyguard."

Marian's eyes rounded, and her mouth fell open. "But—"

"I knew you would fuss," Lyman continued, "but after the crash, I'm confident I made the right decision."

Marian glanced at Nick, and a giggle bubbled up and spilled out.

Lyman stared at her as if she'd sprouted a third eye. "My dear, you must take this threat seriously. Those motorcycle maniacs could easily have injured you and the baby."

She sobered and squeezed his hands. "I know. And I am taking the situation seriously. So seriously, in fact, that I hired Nick." She glanced at Nick again then back at her husband. "He isn't here to drive you around because you wrecked your car. Well, he is...but I hired him mainly to watch out for you. He's a bodyguard, too."

When Lyman shot him a glance, Nick raised his brows and shrugged.

Marian framed her husband's face with her hands and gazed into his eyes. "I love you, Lyman Prescott, and I couldn't stand the thought of anything happening to you."

"I love you, too." He planted a tender kiss on her lips then sat back. "I must say this is a relief. You can't imagine how much better I feel not keeping secrets from you."

"I think I can." She glanced around the room from Lyman to Zoë to Nick. "And since we're laying everything out in the open, I have another confession to make."

Chapter Twelve

Another confession?

Zoë's pulse ticked up. She was relieved to be able to give up the chef/chauffeur pretense, but what else had Marian been hiding?

Marian reached for her husband's hand. "It's about Jimmy."

Lyman's naturally pale complexion took on a faint greenish tint, and his Adam's apple bobbed in his throat, but he held firm. "Yes?"

"He came to see me."

"Here?"

Marian nodded and dropped her gaze to their intertwined fingers.

Lyman's head whipped around, and he lashed out at Zoë. "How did you let this happen? You were supposed to be protecting her."

Zoë's throat tightened. What could she say? She'd failed. She'd let her charge meet with a criminal, although she hadn't known it at the time. "I —"

Marian interrupted. "It's not her fault. Jimmy called, and I snuck out to meet him."

"Oh." Lyman's face crumpled before he pulled his hand free and stared out the window to the barren front yard.

"It's not like that," Marian insisted. "It's nothing like that. You have to believe me. All he wanted was money, and I didn't give him a cent."

Before Lyman could respond, Nick stepped forward. "Excuse me, but I think Zoë and I should let you two have the rest of this conversation in private."

"No, sit down." Marian motioned him toward the chair next to Zoë's. "You need to hear everything. I think Jimmy might be responsible for at least some of what's been happening here."

Zoë had had the same fear ever since she'd seen him at the summer house, wearing his leathers.

Nick had reverted to cop mode and was all business. "Who is this Jimmy, and what makes you think he's involved?"

Marian shot a glance at Lyman then closed her eyes and drew a deep breath before releasing it. "Jimmy Mahoney is my ex-husband."

Nick jerked back as if she'd slapped him. "Jimmy Mahoney? The cop who went to prison? The partner of Rudy Gehke, who robbed the bank in Evanston and ran us into a tree? That Jimmy Mahoney?"

Marian nodded miserably.

Zoë pictured him standing in the clearing outside the summer house. "Do you think he could have been the other biker, the one who sped off? He didn't even bother to check on your injuries."

"It might have been him—I was too scared to look closely at the time—but I wasn't injured," Marian insisted.

"Mahoney couldn't have known that." Lyman tapped rhythmically on his desk with a pen clenched in one fist. "The day he was released from prison I warned you he would bring nothing but trouble."

Nick raised a forefinger. "We'll get back to that, but first, Marian, can you think of any reason Jimmy would want to harm you?"

"Honestly, no. I've known him since we were kids. We were high school sweethearts. He was always very protective of me—a little jealous, maybe, but not in a scary way."

"Prison can change a man. What about during his arrest and trial?"

"He was angry, of course, and I'm sure he must have been frightened."

"Did he ever blame you?"

Marian straightened and cocked her head. "Why would he? He got himself into that mess."

"Did you testify against him?"

"I wouldn't put it like that. The detectives asked simple things like was he home on such-and-such a night. Since I didn't know anything about what he and Rudy were doing, there was nothing to tell."

Nick sat back in his chair. "In his mind, your cooperation alone might have been enough. Plus, he's had years to let his suspicions and resentment fester. He may have convinced himself you were at least partially responsible for sending him to prison."

Marian's brow puckered. "I wonder if that's why he demanded money. He kept saying I *owe* him. I didn't know what he was talking about."

Nick's questions had given Zoë a thought. "Marian, have you seen Jimmy at any other point since he was released?"

"No. He called a few times, but that was the only time I agreed to meet him."

Zoë leaned forward, resting one arm on Lyman's desk. "What about the gunman in the basement? Could that have been Jimmy?"

Marian's eyes rounded, and the natural pink faded from her cheeks. "I don't know. I never considered it."

"He had roughly the same build."

"Maybe." Marian shifted her gaze to her husband. "I didn't focus on the intruder. I was only concerned about Lyman."

Nick pushed up from his chair and paced across the room. "I don't like it. This doesn't make sense. The gunman demanded the plans to GRAMPA, right?"

Lyman nodded. "Yes. That's all he wanted."

"What would a rogue cop, who was broke enough to resort to bank robbery, do with the plans to a cooking robot? I doubt he could build one himself."

"I suppose he could try to sell them," Zoë suggested.

Nick halted and faced her with impatience stamped across his hard features. "How would he find a buyer? It's not like trying to fence a stolen TV."

He had her there. "You're right. It doesn't make any sense." She scooted back in her chair. "Sorry. It was a dumb idea."

"Don't apologize. No idea is dumb. At this point, we don't have much to go on. The best thing we can do is toss ideas around, take them apart, and see if any hold up to scrutiny."

Zoë almost smiled. There was nothing funny about the situation with Jimmy Mahoney, but she enjoyed watching Nick in his element. Her first impression of him had been dark and sullen with very little to say, usually lurking around with a suspicious scowl on his face. Since getting to know him better, she'd learned to see past that gruff, laconic exterior. Now, with a case to solve, he exuded a whole new level of energy.

She debated whether now was the time to bring up her encounters with the bikers but decided to take Nick at his word. "There's something else I should probably mention. It might be nothing, but there could be a connection to Jimmy and Rudy."

Nick gave her an encouraging nod. "Go ahead."

"The morning I started this job I had two odd run-ins with a pair of bikers—once in the city on Lake Shore Drive and again outside the front gate of Strathmoor."

"Odd in what way?"

She described both encounters then paused and glanced from Nick to Marian and back. "The bikes were similar to the two that drove us off the road, and one of the riders wore leathers that matched the ones Jimmy wore the day he met Marian. I doubt it's a coincidence."

Nick perched on the corner of Lyman's desk and rubbed both hands down his thighs. "I doubt that, too. But how would Jimmy and Rudy have known who you were? And how could they have known you'd be coming to Strathmoor that day?"

"I have no idea."

When she met his gaze, the same idea seemed to flash between them. They turned to Marian in unison.

She gave her head a vigorous shake. "Oh, no, it wasn't me. I never told Jimmy we were getting a new chef. I never shared any details about our lives with him." She reached for Lyman's hand again, and when she spoke, her voice broke. "I swear. You have to believe me. I felt sorry for him, but our relationship died years ago. I just wanted him to go away and leave me alone."

Lyman squeezed her hand. "Of course, I believe you, my dear. You have never given me reason to doubt.

That man is nothing but trouble." Still clutching his wife's hand like a lifeline, he turned to Nick. "The first order of business is to get Jimmy Mahoney behind bars again as soon as possible."

Nick nodded and rose from the desk. "The police are looking for him now." He glanced at Marian. "If you have any information that might help them locate him you can call Officer Swanson, or I'd be happy to pass it on."

She hesitated with a little frown. "I don't know where he's been staying since his release. The police probably have better information than I do, but if I think of anything, I'll let you know."

"Thanks. In the meantime, the Lake Forest police have promised to do more frequent patrols on this street, and Zoë and I will take care of security on the estate."

Marian turned to Zoë with a hopeful little smile. "I know you'll be busy, but will you still be able to cook? If I try to take over now, I'm afraid we'll all starve."

Zoë returned her smile. Marian was amazingly resilient, but she couldn't imagine what the woman was going through, being eight months pregnant, with a broken arm, and dealing with the threats of a criminal—and possibly crazy—ex-husband. Cooking was the least she could do. "If you're willing to eat what I cook, I'm happy to keep trying."

"We're more than willing, and I'll do my best to help. I'm sure I could learn a thing or two." Marian gave a little laugh. "Maybe you and GRAMPA and I can try a few recipes together."

"It's a deal."

The "big reveal" conversation seemed to have wrapped up, and Zoë had work to do. She started to rise, and Nick had already edged toward the door when Lyman stopped them.

"I have an idea."

Nick turned, and they both waited while he helped Marian from her chair.

"Since Thanksgiving is only a week away, why don't the three of us spend some time experimenting on a few holiday recipes with GRAMPA?"

Marian smiled. "I know I've complained before about him creeping me out, but that actually sounds kind of fun."

"You deserve some fun, my dear. You've had far too many worries lately. It isn't good for you or the baby. We'll continue to be careful, of course, but Zoë will be with us, and I'm confident Dominic and the police can handle security for the house and grounds."

The lines between Nick's brows eased, and his shoulders seemed to relax a fraction. "That's a great idea."

Zoë wasn't sure whether to be insulted or not. Was he relieved to be able to do his job without pretense, or was he happy to have her relegated to the kitchen where she was less likely to interfere?

Whatever Nick's thoughts, he kept them to himself and kept himself largely out of her way for the next several days. He patrolled the grounds and sat in when Sergeant Lewis came to interview Marian about her ex-husband. He also took a couple of mornings to spread two coats of sunny yellow paint on the nursery walls after Zoë helped Marian finalize the decor.

Otherwise, Zoë, Marian, and Lyman spent most of the mornings in the kitchen with GRAMPA. The robot turned out to be a whiz at making breadcrumb stuffing but still struggled with vegetables. Zoë spent one entire afternoon on her hands and knees or on a step stool, sponge in hand, dealing with the aftermath of a serious cranberry incident. Thereafter, she vowed any future sauce would come from a can.

Wednesday afternoon, the day before Thanksgiving, Nick drove the women to the grocery store in the loaner Escalade, which Zoë had nicknamed the Black Beast. The body shop estimated another week before his truck would be ready. Not that she was complaining—the Beast was as heavy and solid as a Sherman tank. With Nick beside her, she knew Marian was safe from any threat.

She and Marian chose a fat fresh turkey and fresh green beans and yams, leaving Nick to trail behind with the cart. They also picked up a sack of potatoes for Lyman and GRAMPA, who were in charge of the mashed potatoes. Since she no longer had to pretend to be a professional chef, Zoë happily snagged a bag of rolls from the bakery department. And for dessert, she had agreed to bake a pumpkin pie, as long as the pumpkin came from a can. By the time they'd added all the other necessary odds and ends, the cart was mounded high, and Nick was grumbling under his breath as he pushed it toward the checkout counter.

Unfortunately, they weren't the only ones who had saved their holiday shopping for the last minute. It took twenty-five minutes to get through the line, check out, and load the bags in the car. By the time they reached Strathmoor, Marian's eyelids were drooping, and she stifled a huge yawn.

Nick parked as close to the back door as possible then turned to Zoë. "I'll take care of the groceries."

"Thanks."

She popped out, opened Marian's door, and helped her step down from the tall vehicle. "Why don't you put your feet up and watch some TV in the living room, and I'll bring you a cup of tea?"

Marian sighed. "That sounds great. Between the cast and the baby, you'd be amazed how tiring it is dragging all this extra weight around."

"At least it won't be much longer."

Zoë punched in the code and unlocked the back door, ushering Marian into the kitchen. She was grateful that since the incident with the armed intruder, Lyman had been much more diligent about the locks and alarms. After settling Marian in front of a re-run of *Castle* with a cup of tea, she returned to the kitchen and found Nick unpacking the groceries.

He hefted the twenty-five pound turkey in both hands as if testing its weight. "This is a mighty big bird for four people."

Zoë opened the refrigerator door for him. "It had the best shape and nice full breasts."

Omigosh. I am such an idiot! Heat rushed to her face, and she fought a sudden urge to tuck her head inside her sweater.

Nick set the turkey on the shelf and straightened. His expression was dead serious, but amusement twinkled in his eyes. "I've always been a leg man, myself."

Zoë almost choked.

She retrieved the carton of whipping cream from the counter, stepped around him, and tucked it into an open space on the inside of the door. "Then you're in luck." She made a show of squeezing one of the drumsticks. "These legs are nice and plump—perfect for a man to sink his teeth into."

A sudden metallic thud sounded behind her, and she jerked up, clipping the handle of the freezer with the top of her head. She sucked in a swift breath and rubbed the sore spot on her scalp, but before she could complain, a can of cranberry sauce rolled across the tile floor toward her feet, immediately followed by a deep, muttered curse.

She bent to pick up the can and offered it to Nick. When he snatched it from her hand with a frown, she had to compress her lips tightly to keep a laugh from bubbling out.

Ha! Gotcha. Score one for the home team.

****

The next morning Zoë woke early with a dull headache. She'd had trouble sleeping because her mind kept running over the food prep schedule for the next day. She might not be a real chef, but she was in charge of Thanksgiving dinner for the first time in her life, and she was anxious to avoid a fiasco.

After a quick shower she poked through the drawer of the battered old dresser, discarding one sweater after another. Boring. Wrong color. Too long. Too short. Nothing she'd brought seemed festive enough for the occasion. When she was growing up, her mother had always insisted the family dress up for holiday meals. Maybe one of her options would look more appealing when it was time to change for dinner. She finally gave up and threw on a plain black turtleneck and stretchy black pants—talk about boring. As a final touch, she slipped into her favorite pair of red ballet flats. At least she could wear fun shoes.

The kitchen was dark and quiet, like the rest of the house. Some people might be spooked by the lonely, pre-dawn stillness in the old mansion, but Zoë had come to appreciate the solitude. It gave her time to gear up for the day ahead. Once the Prescotts awoke, she would be busy every minute until they retired. She brewed a quick cup of coffee and scanned the recipe on the side of the pumpkin pie spice mixture she'd bought instead of a slew of individual bottles neither she nor Marian would probably ever use again. She was amazed to find it barely more complicated than buying the pie from the bakery since she'd had the foresight to purchase a ready-made crust. Ten minutes later the pie was in the oven. Cooking was almost fun if you allowed yourself a few short cuts.

A wave of nostalgia washed over her as she sipped her coffee and smelled the first hints of spice from the baking pie. The aroma brought back vivid memories of her mother and grandmother preparing holiday dinners in the old farmhouse kitchen. Zoë hadn't been home for Thanksgiving in years, and usually tried not to think about it, but maybe she could find a minute to call home later in the afternoon, before dinner.

The pie had been in the oven for half an hour by the time the others straggled into the kitchen. The men were dressed, but Marian still wore her pink-flowered flannel pajamas with a white terry robe cinched just below her breasts and fluffy pink slippers. Her long blond hair hung loose around her shoulders.

"I couldn't even take the time to get dressed." She closed her eyes and sniffed the air. "That smells like heaven. I've never had pumpkin pie for breakfast before, but I want it now."

Zoë chuckled. "I'm afraid it's not quite ready. Why don't I make you some cinnamon toast to go with your eggs? That might make it easier to wait for the pie." She pulled a partial bag of sliced brioche from the old-fashioned bread drawer in one of the lower cabinets.

"Perfect!" Marian beamed. "You're the best."

"That does sound good." Lyman seated his wife at the kitchen table then sat beside her. "I believe I'll have some, too."

Nick helped himself to a mug of coffee. "Make that three."

Zoë eyed the remaining bread. "I'm beginning to think I should have bought another loaf."

Just then, the wall phone jangled. She glanced at the clock on the stove—ten minutes after eight, awfully early for a call on Thanksgiving morning. At the second ring, she sent a questioning look to the Prescotts. "Were you expecting a call, maybe from family?"

Lyman frowned and pushed back from the table. "No. I'd better take it."

He strode to the phone and jerked the receiver from its cradle. "Hello?" As he listened to the voice on the other end, his expression changed from irritation to relief and then to gratitude. "Yes, I understand. Thank you so much for calling." When he hung up and turned, new light shone in his plain brown eyes, turning his nondescript features almost handsome.

"Who was it, dear?"

He crossed to the table and took Marian's hand. "It was Sergeant Lewis with the best possible news. They caught Jimmy Mahoney last night." A slight tremor shook his hand as he clutched hers. "He's in custody at the Cook County Jail."

Marian's back curved, and her shoulders sagged like someone had let the air out of her.

Lyman gently brushed her hair away from her face. "I know you never wanted to believe the worst of him."

Marian leaned her head into his hand. "I know I should feel relieved — and I do — but I'm also a little sad. I've known Jimmy nearly all my life. Now, he'll probably go back to prison." She tipped her face up to meet her husband's gaze. "You never knew him, but he wasn't always a bad person. I still can't believe he wanted to hurt me."

Lyman bent and kissed her forehead. "Sometimes people change. Jimmy made some serious mistakes, and now he has to pay. The important thing is, he'll be behind bars, and you and the baby are safe."

"Does this mean we can finally relax and live like normal people?"

He smiled into her hair. "As close to normal as people like us can get."

Zoë popped slices of bread into the toaster and wondered if this turn of events signaled the end of her assignment with the Prescotts. The twinge of regret surprised her. Every job ended — it was the nature of the work — but she'd grown fond of Lyman's absent-minded brilliance and utter devotion to his wife, as well as Marian's sweet, cheerful disposition. She would miss them when she left Strathmoor.

And then there was Nick. She would have no reason to see him again after this job ended, and whatever was growing between them would wither and die. It was a shock to realize she would miss his crooked nose and suspicious frown. She would even miss his sarcastic comments about her cooking. Maybe it was his physicality, or maybe his self-confidence, but there was something about his mere presence that made a person feel safe.

There you go, jumping the gun again, Hargrove. Before you start sniveling in the scrambled eggs, stop and assess.

As usual, her inner drill instructor made a good point. Lyman seemed convinced Jimmy Mahoney was behind all their problems, but some things still didn't add up.

Nick seemed to have the same idea. He refreshed his coffee and joined the Prescotts at the table. "I'm glad to hear the cops collared Mahoney, but I wouldn't recommend lowering your guard until they get some answers from him."

Lyman tilted his head and frowned. "Such as...?"

"If Mahoney was the gunman in the basement, why did he want the plans for your robot? If he's short of money, why not demand cash?"

Lyman pursed his lips. "That doesn't make much sense."

"And then there's the question of the two bikers who harassed Zoë the day she arrived. If they were Mahoney and Gehke, what were they trying to accomplish, and how did they know she was coming here? Also, who sent that mystery stroller?"

"Those are all good questions, to which I would like to know the answers." Lyman settled into the chair next to his wife and patted her hand. "It appears we can't put the whole business behind us quite yet, my dear. However, with Mahoney safely in jail, I think we deserve a few days to simply enjoy the holiday and each other."

Soft rose bloomed in Marian's cheeks, and she smiled. "Hear, hear."

He lifted his napkin with a flourish and spread it across his lap. "Now, I don't know about the rest of you, but I intend to enjoy my breakfast and later the wonderful Thanksgiving dinner Zoë's preparing. I have a great deal to be thankful for this year."

At that moment, the toaster dinged and the oven timer buzzed simultaneously. Zoë managed to rescue the toast before it burned then grabbed a pair of oven mitts. With a quick prayer, she opened the oven door.

On the center rack sat a shining wonder, a veritable work of art. The crust was a little too brown in a couple of spots, but otherwise the pie was perfect. She reached in and carefully slid it out. It was a miracle. The top was smooth and uncracked. It even had tiny beads of moisture on the surface, just like a bakery pumpkin pie. And she had made it herself. At that moment, she didn't care if the rest of dinner was a disaster. She had done one thing exactly right.

She was sorely tempted to take a picture with her phone and send it to her mother as proof.

A couple of hours later, while the others watched the Bears play the Lions on television, Zoë slipped up to her room to make her call. Her hand shook as she pressed the Send button. How long had it been since she'd spoken to her parents—six months, maybe? Or was it more like nine? She never seemed to know what to say, and besides, she'd been busy.

Her oldest brother, Adam, answered the phone. "Hey, Zoë, how've you been?" Children's voices clamored in the background, then Adam's voice softened, as if he'd put his hand over the phone. "You guys settle down, or no pie for you!"

"I'm fine. I just called to wish everyone a happy Thanksgiving. Is Mom busy?"

"Always, but I know she'll want to talk to you."

A few seconds passed before her mother's flustered voice came on the line. "Zoë, I'm right in the middle of mashing the potatoes."

So much for wanting to talk. "Hi, Mom. I'm sorry to interrupt. I just wanted to wish you a happy Thanksgiving."

"That's sweet of you. I suppose you're eating alone, as usual."

"Actually, I'm on a job, and I'm cooking dinner for my clients."

"You're cooking?" Incredulity rang in her mother's words.

"I baked a pumpkin pie this morning, and it turned out perfect."

The rhythmic metallic ring of an old-fashioned potato masher against a metal bowl sounded in the background. "Pumpkin is the easiest. It's a good thing you didn't try something that takes skill—like mincemeat or lemon meringue."

And there it is. Why do I even try? "You go back to your potatoes. I just wanted to say Hi."

"Call any time, and good luck with the rest of your dinner."

Zoë hung up with the same miserable feeling of inadequacy that usually accompanied conversations with her mother. At almost thirty, she should have learned better by now.

Happily, the rest of dinner was not a disaster. The turkey with its pop-up timer proved to be idiot-proof, and a serious topping of brown sugar disguised any problems with the yams. Only the mashed potatoes were a near miss. Lyman decided to try having GRAMPA add the hot milk, and the result ended up all over the kitchen. A few clumps even decorated the ceiling. In true inventor spirit, he chalked the mishap up to experience and insisted on cleaning up the mess himself.

Since Marian had decided they would eat in the formal dining room, Nick volunteered to retrieve the heavy, gold-edged china and etched crystal stemware from the enormous glass-fronted buffet cabinet. Frankie "No Nose" might have started life in a tenement, but he'd made certain future generations of Prescotts dined like royalty.

Dinner was a resounding success. Lyman and Marian couldn't say enough about the food, and Nick managed to pack away both turkey legs and at least three helpings of everything else. As he wiped the last drop of gravy from his plate with the last bite of turkey, Zoë tapped his shin with her toe under the table.

She raised one brow. "Do you still think the bird was too big?"

Before he could reply, Lyman spoke. "Zoë and Nick, you've done so much for me and Marian. We'd like to do something for you."

Zoë started to object. "But that's —"

He raised one hand and shook his head. "You've worked long hours, day in and day out, for weeks. I want you both to take the rest of the weekend off."

Nick set his fork on his empty plate. "I thought we agreed it was important to remain diligent for the time being."

"And I wouldn't feel comfortable leaving you alone now," Zoë added.

Lyman turned to her. "I spoke to your employer this afternoon, and she agreed you need a break. Your colleague, Ms. Callahan, will be here tomorrow morning at nine o'clock and stay through Sunday evening."

"Casey's terrific, but she's just one person."

"Marian and I plan to spend a quiet weekend at home, so I'm sure one bodyguard will be sufficient for three days. I promise we'll keep the alarm set at all times."

Zoë had to admit the idea of three days off sounded appealing. It would be nice to sleep in her own bed, eat food she didn't cook, and refresh her wardrobe. Since she and Nick had agreed to collaborate on security, she would have liked the chance to confer with him in private, but since that wasn't possible she shot him a quick, questioning glance.

He shrugged, as if to say, "Up to you."

So she gave Lyman a gracious smile. "In that case, thank you very much."

After all, it wasn't like they were leaving the Prescotts on their own. Casey was a perfectly competent agent. And what could happen in three short days?

Chapter Thirteen

The next morning Casey Callahan arrived at eight forty-five with a small overnight bag and her usual sunny smile. Zoë knew the Prescotts would love her. Everyone loved Casey. She was warm and friendly, yet calm and practical—like everyone's favorite babysitter—but her softly rounded curves and honey-blond hair hid a sharp mind and amazing observational skills. Nothing slipped by Casey.

Zoë led her into the foyer. "It's so great to see you. It seems like our paths hardly cross anymore."

Casey unwound her camel cashmere scarf. "It's been at least a month—since the job in Dallas, wasn't it?"

"Um, hm. You can leave your bag by the stairs, and I'll take you to the living room to meet the Prescotts."

As she'd predicted, Lyman and Marian warmed to Casey immediately. If pressed, Zoë would admit to being a little jealous of her friend's natural ability to put people at ease. And it didn't help when Nick ambled into the room and fell all over himself, smiling and offering to carry the newcomer's luggage up the two long flights to the staff quarters. She crossed her arms and watched them make their way upstairs, chatting like old friends.

Hmph. With her he's all smiles, while I get nothing but attitude.

She was shocked when he came back down carrying her rolling suitcase.

"This was sitting in the hall. I assumed you wanted to take it with you."

"Um...yes." She reached for the handle. "I thought I'd switch out a few things and make a quick trip to the dry cleaner."

He kept a firm grip on her bag and headed for the kitchen. "If you're ready to go, I'll take this out for you. It doesn't weigh much. You must be leaving most of your shoes here."

Zoë grabbed her jacket from the closet in the foyer and her purse off the table on her way through the kitchen. "I have plenty more at home." She held the back door open for him then locked it and set the alarm.

Nick headed across the courtyard toward her Mini Cooper. "Casey seems quite competent. She should be able to handle things while we're gone. I think the Prescotts like her already."

"Everyone always does."

"She's very pretty, too."

She raised one brow. "Do you want me to fix you up?"

He laughed. "I was just wondering if all the Phoenix, Ltd. agents are as gorgeous as the two I've met."

Nice save.

He set the suitcase next to her car. "Do you have big plans for your unexpected long weekend?"

She unlocked the doors and opened the back hatch so he could stow her bag. "Not really. Everyone I know is spending the holiday with family. I'll probably water my cactus, do some laundry, and binge-watch a couple of my favorite shows on Netflix."

"You probably have time to make a quick trip home to Iowa."

She thought back to her call with her mother. "I don't think so."

Nick hesitated, as if he'd like to ask more questions, then seemed to decide against it. "Since you're not super busy, how would you like to go to a hockey game tomorrow night?"

His tone was casual, but Zoë noticed a subtle tightness around his mouth.

"Hockey?"

"Yeah. You know, guys with sticks chasing a little black disc around on the ice."

"I know what hockey is, but I thought the Blackhawks were sold out for the season."

"They are, but we're much smaller potatoes."

"You're inviting me to watch you play hockey?"

"Well...yeah. I haven't been able to play since I started this job, but my team has a game Saturday night, and I told the guys I'd play. My brother-in-law plays on the team, and my mom and sister will be there."

He must have sensed she was about to decline his invitation and dangled the perfect bait. How could she pass up a chance to meet the two most important women in his life? In her experience, mothers and sisters were the best sources of information about a man. They knew where all the skeletons were buried and took great pleasure in exposing them. She was bound to pick up an interesting tidbit or two she could tuck away for future use.

"Okay. What time?"

"The game starts at seven. We're playing at the Northland Arena. Let me give you the address." He started to reach into his jacket pocket.

"I'll find it." She turned and rested her hand on the car door handle. "I guess I'll see you then."

"Drive safely." He didn't smile, but something indefinable flashed in his eyes.

"I always do."

He stepped aside but made no move toward his own vehicle. Instead, he stood and watched as she backed up and turned to head down the driveway. When she neared the gate, she glanced in the rearview mirror again. He was still standing in the same place, arms at his sides.

She tried to shake off the unsettled feeling all the way home. Traffic on Lake Shore Drive slowed to a snail's pace, coming to a standstill a couple of times as she neared downtown. Shoppers appeared to be out in droves, snapping up Day-After-Thanksgiving bargains, and she briefly considered joining them. Nordstrom's shoe sale was always worth braving the crowds, but for some reason, she couldn't work up her usual enthusiasm. She let the exit slip by and continued south until she reached the turn-off for her apartment near the Museum of Science and Industry.

She breathed a sigh of relief when she found a space only a half-block from her vintage red-brick building. After hauling her bag up the four flights to her charming-but-compact one bedroom apartment, she threw herself on the bed and stared at the ceiling.

Why had Nick asked her to his hockey game? What did he expect to happen? Their only full-blown kiss had been amazing, but afterward he'd made it clear that wasn't happening again. He had no intention of getting involved with her, even casually. So why would he ask her to spend time with him the minute they had a couple of free days? If he was simply looking for an opportunity to show off his manliness, he could stuff it.

She closed her eyes and rubbed her brow, drained. Her head hurt. Maybe a cup of tea would help.

Tea, a bath, and nine solid hours of sleep revived her, but by the following afternoon, she still hadn't made up her mind about the game.

But you promised.

So what? He'll live with the disappointment. Besides, he'll be busy. He probably won't even see me.

There's always afterwards.

He'll be tired.

But she'd been around enough men to know physical exhaustion was no match for the excess testosterone that flooded their bodies when they banged into each other, sweating and grunting, trying to prove who was fastest or strongest.

What if he wants to burn it off with me?

You are so overthinking this. Just go, you coward.

At six-fifteen she slipped on a pair of cashmere socks under her boots, shrugged into her down parka, grabbed a knit hat, and left. Forty minutes later she pulled into the arena parking lot. The lot was almost full, and small clusters of women with well-bundled children in tow were making their way toward the entrance. When she stepped out of the car, a last-minute urge to turn around and drive home seized her, but she fought it back and followed the steady trickle of fans through the glass-fronted metal doors.

"Zoë, over here!"

Startled, she turned toward the voice and saw a petite, pretty brunette with bright red lipstick on the other side of a swarm of people, waving her arm and smiling. Next to her stood a handsome, middle-aged woman with wavy black hair, whose strong nose and square jaw bore a striking resemblance to Nick's. Zoë wove her way through the crowd until she reached them.

"I knew it was you," the younger woman exclaimed. "Nick described you perfectly." She thrust out her hand. "I'm Angela Zolnicki."

Zoë shook her hand. "It's great to meet you." She turned to the older woman. "And you must be Mrs. Rosetti."

"Teresa. But call me Terry."

Zoë smiled. "Terry."

Terry glanced up at the big clock above the front doors. "We'd better get inside. It's almost time for face-off."

Angela steered Zoë toward the main aisle. "One of the other wives is saving us seats in the family section behind the bench. Nick will walk right past us when the players come up from the locker room."

So much for him not seeing her.

They had barely taken their seats when the army of red-and-white-clad giants lumbered up the rubber-surfaced ramp, sticks in hand. Zoë had seen a couple of hockey games on television, but she'd never been close enough to reach out and touch the players before. Suddenly, a stick banged the plexiglass next to her head, startling her so badly she bumped into Terry's shoulder and almost knocked her off the bleacher bench.

Nick's face, encased in a scarred white helmet, grinned at her from the other side of the glass. "Very funny," she mouthed, knowing he'd never hear her over the din, even if she shouted.

His skates added at least three inches to his already considerable height, and the pads gave the illusion of an additional thirty pounds of muscle. All in all, he was a fearsome sight—kind of like Conan the Barbarian in a red number eighteen jersey. And based on his cocky expression, he knew it.

After the face-off Zoë tried to follow the game the best she could, but the size of the players, the speed of the puck, and her minimal knowledge of the rules worked against her. Besides, Nick's mother was much more interested in chatting about her son than watching him play.

"So, Nick tells me you're a personal chef."

"Um...yes, that's right." She didn't want to spill any beans he hadn't.

"That sounds like a great job." Terry laughed. "I wish I'd been paid for all the meals I've cooked over the years."

Zoë just smiled.

"Do you cook much Italian food?"

"I'm learning." She glanced at the ice. Why couldn't Nick score or something—anything to take his mother's attention off her?

Terry gave a vigorous nod. "That's good. Maureen was a nice girl, but her idea of cooking was pouring cereal from a box."

Zoë straightened and tilted her head. "Maureen?"

Terry didn't seem to notice her sudden interest, but simply nodded. "She's the reason Nick left Detroit. Not that I'm sorry, mind you. I'm glad to have my boy home again."

Hmm. This new tidbit didn't jibe with Risa's research. Maybe she could learn more if she kept her questions casual. "I thought his move was work-related."

"Yes, that too...but Maureen was behind it. Mark my words." Terry shook her forefinger for emphasis. "She was more than his partner, if you get my meaning. And after the shooting," —she shrugged— "well, you know how it is."

Zoë didn't know at all.

She was about to ask another question when Angela jumped up and shouted, "Nick!"

Zoë's gaze darted back to the rink, where players huddled around the prostrate figure of number eighteen. Her chest tightened when she saw the dark pink stain forming on the ice under his head. Someone tossed a towel to one of the players, who knelt and pressed it against his forehead. Terry's hand flew to her mouth, and she began to mutter prayers for her son's safety.

****

Nick blinked and waited a second for the lights to stop spinning. What the hell had happened? One minute he was making a fast break, driving the puck toward the net, and the next he was flat on his back while his brother-in-law tried to suffocate him with a towel. He reached up to push Kenny's hand away.

Kenny pushed back. "Don't move. You're making a mess all over the ice."

"What happened?"

"You took a stick to the face. The cut's not big, but it's bleeding like a sonofabitch."

Nick's stomach lurched then settled, and his vision cleared. He reached for the towel. "I'll hold that." Pulling off his gloves, he pressed the bloody towel against the cut with one hand and reached up with the other. "Okay. I'm ready."

Kenny hauled him to his feet. Cheers and applause erupted when he waved his free hand and slowly made his way to the players' box unassisted. Hugh Swanson hopped over the side and skated out to take his place, while he collapsed on the bench then lowered the towel to check the bleeding.

Jeff Barnes, a sports-loving ER doc who moonlighted as team physician, appeared at his side, black bag in hand. "Let's get that helmet off so I can see what we're dealing with."

Nick eased his helmet off and tipped his head so Jeff could inspect the cut above his right eyebrow.

Jeff poked and prodded, dabbing the edges of the wound with an antiseptic-soaked wipe. "It's only about an inch long. These head wounds usually look worse than they are." He straightened and rummaged in his bag. "Three or four stitches and you'll be good as new. Not as pretty, maybe, but my wife tells me women prefer ruggedly handsome anyway."

Suddenly Nick remembered Zoë. He twisted and found himself staring into three anxious feminine faces on the other side of the glass. He wasn't worried about Angela and Zoë's matching frowns of concern, but his mom's lips were moving, and she was fingering the strap of her purse like a rosary.

He turned to Jeff. "Doc, do I need to go to the hospital?"

"Not unless you want to. If you can stand a little pain, I can fix you up here. All I've got with me is lidocaine."

His mother hadn't witnessed one of his sports injuries since high school, and she didn't seem to be taking it well. A trip to the ER might send her into a Hail

Mary frenzy. It would be better to suck it up and let Jeff do his thing here. "Let's just get it over with."

"Okay, but maybe we should go to the locker room. I think your mom is giving me the stink eye."

"If she's mad at anyone, it's me. Just go ahead. She'll be fine as soon as you're done."

Nick clenched his teeth when Jeff injected the lidocaine, but the actual stitches were a piece of cake. In less than ten minutes, he was sewn up, with a small patch of fresh white gauze covering the stitches.

"Can I go back in the game?"

Jeff frowned then pulled a penlight from his bag and flashed it in Nick's eyes. "How does your head feel?"

Nick stared into the tiny light as Jeff moved it up and down and from side to side. "Okay."

Jeff clicked off the light and returned it to his bag. "I don't see any signs of concussion, but why push your luck?"

Nick glanced at the lighted scoreboard. They were still down a goal. His team hadn't managed to capitalize on the high sticking penalty and score when they were up a man. "I need to get back out there."

Jeff shook his head. "You guys are all the same—hopeless."

Nick wanted the team to win, but more than that, he wanted a goal so bad he could almost feel the solid slap of the puck reverberate against his stick. He tried to tell himself it was because he'd missed a couple of games. The fact that Zoë was in the audience was irrelevant. Right. "Come on, Doc. You know how it is."

"You're lucky I do." Jeff clapped him on the shoulder. "Go ahead, but put your helmet on and keep your face away from hard objects. If you tear those stitches, next time you're going to the hospital, where they'll use staples."

At the next stoppage, Kenny came off and Nick took his place. He skated hard and made a couple of nice passes, but the net eluded him. In the end, it was a young patrolman he barely knew who led the team to victory with the winning goal.

The women were waiting for him when he returned to the lobby from the locker room after a shower and change. His mother rushed to grab his arm and pull him down so she could check his bandage up close. After a thorough examination, she released him. "The cut looks pretty small, but why do you do these things to me?"

"I'm fine. Besides, you should be used to it."

"Hmph. A mother never gets used to seeing her son bruised and bloody."

Angela wore a classic younger-sister smirk. "Better you than Kenny, I always say."

At that moment the man in question appeared. He slid an arm around his wife and gave her a squeeze before planting a kiss on her cheek. "Should my ears be burning?"

Angela snuggled into his embrace. "I was just saying how glad I am your handsome face is still intact, unlike this lunkhead."

Nick grimaced and felt a twinge in his brow. The lidocaine must be wearing off. "That's enough, you two. Get a room, for Pete's sake."

Kenny slung his arm over his wife's shoulders and glanced from Nick to Zoë and back. "Some of us are going out for pizza and beer. You want to come?"

Nick gave Zoë a questioning look. "What do you say?"

She turned to Kenny. "Thanks, but I think I'll take rain check."

Kenny shrugged. "Sure. What about you, Nick?"

He glanced at Zoë. He hadn't even had a chance to talk to her yet. "I think I'll pass. Next time, for sure."

Angela reached in her purse and pulled out a set of car keys. "Suit yourself. We'll drop Mom off on our way." She turned to Zoë. "It was nice to meet you. We'll have to get together someplace quieter where I can spill all my big brother's secrets."

Zoë smiled. "You're on." She made no move to leave when the others headed out the main doors to the parking lot.

Nick cleared his throat. "So, are you hungry? You want to go someplace—just the two of us?"

She tilted her head and regarded his face long enough to make him antsy. "I should probably get going. It's a long drive back to my apartment."

When she started toward the door, he fell in line beside her. "Where do you live?"

"In Hyde Park, a few blocks from the lake."

All the way on the opposite end of the city. He could apologize for asking her to drive so far to watch him play, but he wouldn't mean it. He was glad she'd come. His heart had done a funny little dance when he'd seen her in the bleachers with his mother and sister. "I'll follow you then—just to make sure you get home safely."

He flipped up his collar against the wind and the small, wet flakes that had started to fall sometime during the evening. Patches of white had already gathered in the crevices in the pavement and around the windshield wipers of the vehicles. The roads would be slick soon.

Zoë stopped next to her car and faced him, her expression unreadable in the harsh glare of the overhead light. "That's silly. You're injured, and I'm perfectly capable of getting myself home in one piece." She pushed the Unlock button on the key fob and reached for the door handle.

Nick placed his hand over hers. "I know you are. It's just that I'll feel better if I can see for myself that you're safe. We've been through a lot lately, and it's hard to let my guard down."

Some of the tension left her face, and her lips curved slightly. "Since you put it that way, I guess I can understand. I've been looking for threats around every corner, too." She pulled a small notebook and pen from her purse and scribbled something before tearing off the page and handing it to him. "Here's my address, in case we get separated on the highway. Since it's Saturday night, there's bound to be a lot of traffic on Lake Shore as we pass downtown."

He turned the page to the light and scanned it quickly before tucking it in his pocket. "I'll stick as close as I can. Thanks for humoring me."

"Just doing my part for the walking wounded." She flashed him a quick smile then climbed into the Mini, buckled her seatbelt, and fired it up. He was about to head toward his loaner SUV when she lowered her window a few inches. "There's a good noodle shop a couple of blocks from my apartment. It'll be full of college kids, but we can probably find a table in the corner, if you're interested."

Any food sounded good right now, and he was far from ready to call it a night. "I'm interested. Hang on a second, and I'll be right behind you." Ignoring the slippery surface of the parking lot, he sprinted for the Escalade.

The drive to Zoë's apartment took over an hour, and Nick's stomach was growling by the time she pulled over and parked at the curb. He circled the block and found a spot on the opposite side of the street. It was still snowing lightly, but here in the heart of the city, it hadn't yet started to stick.

He settled his Blackhawks cap on his head, careful to avoid the cut that was beginning to throb, and climbed out of the Escalade to meet her on the wet sidewalk. Tiny droplets spiked her lashes and sparkled on her smooth cap of dark hair. He offered his elbow. "Still hungry?"

She slid her gloved hand into the crook of his arm. "Starving. The restaurant's this way."

Occasional boisterous groups of students reminded him how close they were to the university as they strolled past pre-war brick apartment buildings and Queen Anne-style, shingled Victorian houses. Up ahead, on the corner of a commercial street, a brightly lit storefront with steamy windows and a colorful neon sign enticed chilled diners. "Is that the place?"

Zoë nodded. "It's one of my favorite restaurants in the neighborhood. The food is good and reasonably priced, and it's so busy you never feel lonely."

They pushed through the door past clusters of diners on their way out and joined the groups waiting to be seated. Nick glanced around the room packed with chattering college students and neighborhood families and understood what she meant about the vibe — the cheerful din was irresistible. After a few minutes, the harried hostess ushered them to a tiny table for two next to the front window and handed them menus.

Nick studied the list of Thai-themed dishes while the waitress poured two cups of hot tea. "What's good here?"

Steam rose in front of Zoë's face as she blew on her thimble-sized tea cup. "Pretty much everything. A lot of people like the broad Chow Fun noodles or the Pad Thai, but my favorites are the red and green curries over rice. It depends on how you feel about spice."

"I'll have whatever you're having." He closed his menu.

She ordered one red and one green curry. "We can share. That way you can try both."

The food arrived quickly, and he leaned over the bowl of green curry and took a sniff. A complex aroma of chilies, coconut milk, and lemon grass met his nose. "This smells great."

She scooped up a spoonful of the red and waved it at him. "Just wait 'til you taste it."

He did, and the spicy concoction instantly banished the last hint of chill. Before he knew it, his bowl was half empty. When he glanced up to tell her how much he liked the dish, he found her regarding him with a look of frank assessment. He raised his spoon. "This is great."

She barely blinked. "I'm glad you like it. Now maybe you can tell me what is actually going on here."

Chapter Fourteen

Momentary confusion clouded Nick's eyes, but it cleared quickly. Good. He wasn't going to try to pretend he didn't understand.

"I don't understand."

Or maybe not.

"Why did you invite me to your hockey game? Why did you insist on following me home?"

He shifted his weight in his chair and took a sip of tea. "You said you didn't have plans for the weekend, so I thought you might enjoy the game. I already told you why I followed you home — to make sure you were safe."

"Okay. But why are we sitting here eating dinner together?"

"We were both hungry."

"Stop it." She leaned forward and lowered her voice. "Is this a date?"

"You say that like it would be the end of the world."

She suppressed a smile at the hint of bruised male ego in his tone. "I just want to be clear. After you kissed me, you made a point of telling me you refuse to get involved with work associates."

He dug his spoon into his curry. "We're off-duty. Besides, now that Mahoney's in custody, the Prescott job may not last much longer."

"So this is a date."

"Not exactly. Let's call it a pre-date."

She sat back and raised her brows. "That's a new one."

He muttered something under his breath then popped the spoon into his mouth, but she refused to let him off so easily. "You were saying?"

Nick took his time chewing. When he finished, he washed it down with the remaining tea from his small white cup and looked up to meet her gaze. Tight lines of exasperation bracketed his mouth. "Why do women always insist on defining and categorizing every aspect of a relationship?"

"We like to know where we stand. Are you saying we have a relationship?"

His lips tightened in frustration. "Now who's being dense? Of course we do. We're colleagues, and I thought we'd become friends."

She teased the bits of chicken, rice, and brightly colored vegetables in her bowl with the tip of her spoon. "I think we have, in a way. But I wonder what will happen when this job ends."

"Who knows?"

She stared into his fathomless, coffee-colored eyes, wishing she could read his thoughts. "What would you like to have happen?"

"I thought we might get to know each other better — on a more personal level — and see where it takes us." He reached across the table and covered her hand to still its motion. "What would you like to have happen?"

The dark intensity of his gaze sent tiny flutters zipping through her stomach. "I suppose I might be willing to set aside my feminine need to — what did you call it, 'define and categorize' — for a while."

He dropped her hand abruptly. "Finish your dinner."

"What?"

"The kids are starting to talk." He tipped his head toward a table of four giggly female undergraduates to his left.

Zoë met the gaze of a pretty Asian girl with a wide purple stripe in her straight black hair who mouthed, "Go for it" then grinned. She turned back to Nick. "I agree. We should continue this conversation someplace more private."

The heat in his gaze flared again. "Your apartment's practically around the corner."

"Yes…it is."

Gulp.

They finished quickly, and he motioned for the check. The snow had picked up by the time they left the restaurant, making the walk back to Zoë's apartment more of a challenge. She kept an eye on the growing patches of white on the pavement while maintaining a firm grip on Nick's elbow. As they neared her building, wet strands of hair stuck to her cheeks, and she chastised herself for giving in to vanity by leaving her hat in the car. Hat hair might not be flattering, but it beat the drowned-cat look any day.

She almost lost her footing when Nick stopped suddenly.

He scanned the façade. "Isn't this your building?"

"Yes." She'd been so annoyed about her hair she'd nearly passed it. "Come on." They hurried up the granite steps, and she used her key to let them into the small lobby.

Nick pulled off his cap and slapped it against his thigh, knocking clumps of snow onto the tile floor. "If this keeps up, the roads are going to get ugly."

Zoë brushed snow off her shoulders and resisted the temptation to shake her wet hair like a dog. "I'm glad I don't have to go out again."

He glanced back through the beveled glass panes at the fat white clumps plummeting through the cone of light cast by the fixture above the door. "I'm not looking forward to driving all the way back in this."

She started up the stairs but paused on the second step. Nick was hard to read sometimes, but that almost sounded like he was hoping to wrangle an invitation to spend the night, which was way outside her comfort zone for a relationship he'd just described as being in the "pre-date" stage.

She turned and almost bumped into him. "Don't get any big ideas. This invitation is for talk and maybe a cup of coffee. Period."

Her favorite dimple appeared in his cheek, and he raised his hands in surrender. "No ideas here. No, ma'am. Not a one."

"Good."

When they passed the third floor landing, he slowed and glanced up the stairwell. "You're on the top floor?"

"Yep."

"That must be what keeps your legs in such great shape."

Her insides kicked into a mindless little victory dance until her brain shut the music down. Over the past fifteen years or so, she'd received more than her share of easy compliments and knew better than to put much store in them. "I don't mind the exercise…and thanks, but you're still not spending the night."

His expression was all innocence as he stood beside her in the hall outside her door. "It was just a simple observation."

She rolled her eyes and stuck the key in her lock. "Yeah, and I'm Julia Child."

He laughed and followed her into her apartment.

She flipped on the lights and pointed to the small dining set in one corner. "You can hang your coat over one of those chairs. It should dry pretty quickly. I'm going to deal with my hair."

A few minutes later she returned—fluffed, smoothed, and ready. Well, maybe not completely ready. She found Nick standing in the living room, studying her collection of framed travel photographs.

He turned. "Did you take these?"

"Um, hm."

He leaned closer to examine her favorite picture of a Parisian street market. "I've always wanted to see Europe. When did you go?"

"While I was stationed in Germany, I spent every free weekend traveling."

He straightened and regarded her with a mixture of surprise and respect. "You never told me you were in the service."

She nodded. "Army Military Police. Eight years."

"That explains a lot."

"It was a good way to get out of Iowa and see the world. What about you?"

"Marines. Two tours. Unfortunately, they didn't send me anyplace as scenic as Paris."

"I bet not. Would you like some coffee?"

"Sure." He followed her into the kitchen. "Your first day on the job you said your specialty was German food. Did you do much cooking in Germany?"

"No, but I did a lot of eating."

He laughed. "That sounds like my kind of posting. MREs with a little sand mixed in for texture get old fast."

"I can imagine." She'd heard stories from fellow MPs who had served in the Middle East.

The coffeemaker signaled it was ready, so she took a pair of cheery red mugs from the cupboard and filled them. When she turned to hand one to Nick, the coffee sloshed dangerously close to the rim as she nearly hit him in the chest. He'd snuck up behind her again. It seemed to be one of his favorite moves.

Without stepping back, he took the mug from her hand. He took one long, appreciative sip then set it on the counter. Resting his hands lightly on her upper arms, he caught her gaze. "I was just teasing, you know. About not wanting to drive home in the snow."

A tiny shiver zipped up Zoë's spine. He might be telling the truth, but she couldn't be sure. She edged back until her hips pressed against the counter.

"I guessed that." She'd meant to sound confident, but the waver in her voice betrayed her nerves. Nick unsettled her. Whenever she thought she understood him, he surprised her.

He took a half-step forward until only a couple of inches separated them and tightened his hold on her arms almost imperceptibly. "I promised not to get any big ideas, but I might have a smaller one."

"And what's that?" Part of her wanted whatever he was offering, but her inner voice warned her to be careful.

"Since this is a pre-date, we could try a pre-date kiss, just to make sure we like it." He bent his head towards hers.

On cue, the old anxiety tightened her stomach.

He drew back, keeping his hands in place but loosening his grip. Concern creased his brow. "Are you okay?"

She hesitated. Was she? As she gazed into his worried dark eyes, the niggling remnant of fear dissolved. She was okay. In fact, she was much better than okay. "Yes."

"You'd tell me if you weren't."

"Yes."

He reached up and tucked one side of her hair behind her ear. "I know I'm not the smoothest guy in town, but I don't like to think I could scare a woman, especially you."

His fingers brushed her cheek with a touch so gentle she couldn't be afraid. "It's not you. It's something...old."

"Zoë, did someone hurt you?"

She dropped her gaze to the hollow at the base of his throat. "He tried."

"But you fought back."

Nick made it sound so purposeful. At eighteen, she'd just thrashed out wildly, fueled by anger and fear, and gotten lucky. "Yes, I fought back."

"Can you tell me about it?"

"There isn't much to tell. The night of my high school graduation, my best friend had a party at her house. Her brother was home from college. He was bigger, stronger, and very determined." She couldn't suppress a shudder at the memory of bruising hands and crushing weight.

"Did you manage to subdue him?"

"I'd like to say yes, but the truth wasn't nearly that neat and pretty. I was terrified. I screamed and hit and kicked. I might have even bitten him. I guess I surprised him because he backed off long enough for me to get away."

"Is that part of what made you join the Army?"

She nodded. "I wanted to get as far away as I could, as fast as I could." She dropped her voice to a near-whisper. "My mother never understood."

"Did you tell her?"

"No, I couldn't. I've never told anyone…until now."

"I hope I don't remind you of him."

She lifted her head and met his gaze. "No. You don't use your strength to restrain and overpower." She shuddered and glanced away again. "He was like a wild animal."

Nick hesitated, as if weighing what she'd told him, then dropped his hands. "I should go."

She knew then she didn't want him to leave. He was so big and solid. So safe. "No, stay."

"Are you sure?"

She nodded and reached for his hands, placing them on her waist.

His touch remained light, almost reluctant. "I guess we could go into the living room and watch TV if you want."

"I don't want to watch TV." She leaned forward and lifted her face.

"No?"

"No."

His hands slid behind her back and pulled her against his chest as his mouth descended. Gone was the tentative, gentle lover who'd touched her cheek so softly only moments before. In his place was a powerful, hungry man, eager to taste all she was willing to give.

Zoë could do little more than hold on while his lips forged a hot trail down the side of her face, past her ear, and along her jaw before settling firmly on her mouth. Her brain switched to auto-pilot, and sensation took over. Like a match to kindling, tiny flames of desire spread until they threatened to envelop her. After a few minutes—or hours—Nick ended the kiss with a series of seductive little nips that did nothing to cool her off.

If that was a pre-date kiss, she might incinerate if they ever went on an *official* date.

When he loosened his grip, she eased back until she could see his face. A pair of deep lines creased his brow and disappeared beneath his bandage. He looked worried. Or angry. Not exactly the reaction a woman wanted from a man who had just singed every nerve ending in her body.

She crossed her arms in front of her chest, putting a few more inches between them. "Don't tell me how we're not going to do this again. That line's getting old."

He pulled her back into his arms and dropped a quick kiss on her forehead. "I wasn't going to. I was going to say we'd better wrap this case up fast, because I don't know how I'm going to survive until we do."

"Good." Her voice was muffled against his chest.

His laugh rumbled in her ear. "You want to see me suffer?"

"Yes."

"I should have known. Bloodthirsty as well as beautiful." When he shook his head, his chin brushed the top of her hair. Keeping one arm around her shoulders, he turned and steered her to the living room sofa.

He sat far enough away to look her square in the face. "Since you're so quick to jump to conclusions, I'll spell it out. I enjoy kissing you. I'd like to kiss you again. I'd like to do a whole lot more than just kiss you. Is that clear enough?"

Heat rose in Zoë's face. She appreciated plain speaking, but his blunt words merely served to underline her own desires. "Perfectly."

He settled back against a pile of blue and white striped throw pillows in the corner of the sofa. "Good. I'm glad we understand each other. That being said, I still think we should hold off taking our relationship any further while we're working together."

While she considered her response, one of Terry's comments at the hockey game about Nick's former partner elbowed its way to the front of her mind. She wasn't sure how he would react to being questioned, but since he'd dragged out one of her most difficult memories, turnabout was fair play. "Does your decision have anything to do with Maureen?"

He stiffened. "How do you know about Maureen?"

"Your mother mentioned her earlier tonight."

"I should have known." He shook his head. "What did she say?" He managed to sound both defensive and aggressive in the same breath.

Zoë refused to be put off. "Not much. Just that Maureen was your partner in Detroit and had something to do with you leaving the force and moving back to Chicago."

He huffed out a breath and absently rubbed his forehead. But the second his fingers touched the stitches, he winced and dropped them.

She reached over to gently smooth the bandage, as if the gesture could take away his pain. "I'm not trying to pry—well, I am, but only because I want to understand. You kiss me like a starving man who's been given a nice, juicy porterhouse steak and then tell me you'll only take one bite." When an indecipherable look shadowed his eyes, she hesitated. "Don't get me wrong, I'm not looking to hop into bed with you this minute, but I'd like to know what's going on in your head."

He grimaced. "No, you wouldn't."

"Yes, I really would."

He stared into her eyes for a long moment. "Okay, since it affects you, I guess you have a right to know."

She turned slightly, tucked her legs up under her, and waited for him to continue.

"What Mom told you was true. Maureen was my partner, and she's part of the reason I left the department and the city. But Mom doesn't know the whole story. "

"I want to know."

"You told me you'd read some of the newspaper stories your company researcher turned up, so you know the basics."

She nodded. "You were involved in a shootout with a drug dealer, and an innocent bystander ended up dead."

He closed his eyes and tipped his head back, as if replaying the whole scene in his mind.

When he didn't speak, she reached for his hand. "You don't have to tell me if it's too painful."

"No, I'm okay. Except for the department investigator, I've never told anyone the whole story. I want you to hear it."

Zoë's heart swelled. She hardly knew what to say in response to his trust. "Thank you."

"Maureen and I were more than partners. We were lovers. We'd even talked about getting married. But we had to keep the relationship completely under wraps."

Not a surprise, but not exactly what she wanted to hear, either. "That must have been difficult, especially since you worked out of the same precinct house."

"I'm sure some of our co-workers guessed, but no one said anything. At any rate, one night about a year ago, we were investigating a shooting at a rundown apartment complex that resulted from a dope deal gone bad. While Maureen and I were questioning the suspect's mother about his whereabouts, the guy jumped out a second story window and tried to make a run for it. We chased him down an alley then split up. While I continued the pursuit, Maureen circled the block and came up behind him." He paused and closed his eyes, his throat working.

Zoë gave his knee a short, reassuring squeeze. "Why don't I freshen the coffee and bring the cups in here?"

By the time she returned with the pair of steaming mugs, Nick appeared back in control.

"Sorry," he said.

She handed him a cup. "Take your time."

He took a couple of sips then set the mug on a coaster on the coffee table. "I need to get it out. I want to get it out."

She settled back against the sofa cushions and blew across her mug. "I'm listening."

He leaned forward and rested his elbows on his knees. "So, it's raining, and we're in this dark alley littered with trashcans and dumpsters—most of the light is coming from streetlights on the cross street. I'm running flat out and yelling at the guy to halt when Maureen rounds the corner. He sees her and stops. We're both ordering him to drop his gun, but he just keeps looking back and forth between us as we advance with our weapons drawn. Finally, as Maureen approaches, he sticks his hands in the air, but he's still got the gun. When she reaches up to grab it and cuff him, he spins and somehow gets her in a headlock and rams the barrel of the gun against her temple." Fear mixed with anger in his eyes at the memory.

"That must have been terrifying."

"I keep seeing the whole thing play out in slow motion, but it only took a split second. I'll never forget the sight of them, silhouetted against the light from the street behind. The kid is screaming at me to get back or he'll blow her head off, while she's struggling to find an angle to take him down."

"What did you do?"

"I froze. I was close enough. I had a shot, but I couldn't take it. I couldn't risk hitting Maureen."

"So what happened? Did she manage to break free?"

Nick shook his head. "I was only about five yards away, with my pistol pointed at the suspect's head. I couldn't see his face clearly, but I could tell he was scared. The arm around Maureen's neck was shaking, and he couldn't hold the gun steady against her head. Suddenly, he shoved her to the ground, pointed his gun at me, and fired."

Her heart thudded in her chest. "Were you hit? The news article didn't mention that."

"A split second after I heard the bang and saw the muzzle flare, the bullet whizzed past my ear."

"You were lucky."

"Luckier than the owner of the convenience store who'd stepped outside to dump his trash in the alley behind me."

"Was he hit?" She already knew the answer.

"Square in the chest—never had a chance."

"I'm so sorry."

"If I'd shot the perp when I should have, that store owner would still be alive. The man lost his life because I hesitated. It never should have happened—none of it.

And it wouldn't have if I hadn't gotten involved with my partner."

"You can't know that."

"The odds would have been greatly reduced."

She sensed there was more to the story. "Your mom also suggested Maureen had something to do with you leaving Detroit. What happened after the shooting?"

"My captain and the rest of the precinct—including Maureen—tried to convince me it wasn't my fault, but I knew better. I became more and more angry and bitter, drank too much, and was a general, all-around jerk. I basically pushed her away until she called it quits."

"What about your job?"

"I didn't have the stomach to go back on the streets, and without Maureen, I had no reason to stay in Detroit. I shoved it all and came home."

She raised her hand to his cheek with a gentle touch. "I know your family's glad to have you back."

He nodded then reached for her arm and tugged her toward him until she settled against his chest with his cheek resting against her hair. "Now do you understand why we can't take what's happening between us to the next level until we're off this case?"

She nodded. "You don't want to be responsible for anyone else getting hurt."

"This time it could be Lyman or Marian, or even you, and I couldn't live with that."

Zoë twisted and leaned her head against his arm, tilting back until she could see his face. "I don't want you to get hurt, either. Tonight, when I saw you lying on the ice bleeding, I felt like I was the one who'd been flattened by two hundred and twenty pounds of charging winger."

He touched the bandage on his forehead. "I'd almost forgotten about that. It's just a little cut. Head wounds bleed a lot."

"That didn't make it easier to watch."

A smile tickled the corners of his mouth then spread. "So, you were worried about me?"

He was teasing her. She frowned and gave his chest a shove. "Yes, you big oaf. The ice turned red, and you didn't move."

"I'd just had my bell rung. It wasn't the first time. Probably won't be the last."

She rolled her eyes. "Brain damage. That answers so many questions."

"I'm sorry you were worried." He tugged her closer to his mouth. "But I kind of like it, too."

When she started to protest, he silenced her with his lips. Without thinking, she allowed her arms to twine around his neck. He held her head in place with one big hand while the other found its way under her sweater to the bare skin of her lower back.

Zoë shivered at the touch. When she sought deeper contact with his mouth, he groaned and obliged. She squirmed against him, the intensity of his kiss threatening to ignite every molecule in her body.

She might not be the most experienced woman in the world, but she knew where this was leading. And it wasn't to a platonic working relationship. She drew back. "I thought you just said our relationship couldn't go any further while we're working together."

He nuzzled her neck. "That doesn't mean we can't enjoy ourselves in the meantime."

His warm lips on her neck must be interfering with her brain waves. She couldn't think. But something deep inside told her it was important to get this right, so she pulled herself back from the brink. "Enjoy ourselves?"

"Think of it as a little pre-date exploration. Don't worry. I won't let things go too far."

He might have confidence in his self-control, but she had serious doubts about her own. After only a few minutes, her normally vigilant sense of caution was about to throw back its head and scream, "Yes, yes, yes!" When he shifted one hand to cup her breast, all pretense of sanity flew out the window.

She was in the process of unbuttoning his shirt when a persistent sound distracted her. She paused for a second to identify it. Her phone. It was buzzing on the kitchen counter where she'd left it.

"Let it go," Nick murmured against her lips.

It buzzed, and buzzed, and buzzed.

Reluctantly, she broke contact and drew away. "I should get it. It might be important."

She dragged herself from the sofa, ran quick fingers through her hair to return it to some semblance of order, and crossed the room. Glancing at the screen, she saw the caller was Casey Callahan and frowned. "Hi, Casey. What's up?"

She listened for a moment, her anxiety rising with each word. "Got it. We'll be there in an hour." When she disconnected and glanced up, Nick stood before her with his shirt half untucked and concern in his eyes.

"Who was that?"

"Casey." She was still trying to digest the implications of her friend's call.

"You look worried. What did she want?"

"The police just called. Jimmy Mahoney has escaped."

Chapter Fifteen

Nick's mind clicked into high gear. He and Zoë had to get back to Lake Forest, and fast. Casey Callahan was alone at Strathmoor with Lyman and Marian. If Mahoney had half a brain, he'd be headed out of state as fast as his bike would take him, but that was a big "if." His motivation for coming after the Prescotts, whatever it was, must be strong because of the risks he'd already taken. There was no way to predict what the man might do next.

Nick stuffed his shirttail back in his pants and grabbed his jacket from the back of the chair where he'd dumped it. "Nobody escapes from the Cook County Jail. He must have had inside help."

Zoë headed toward the bedroom. "Since he's a former cop, maybe he still has friends in the department."

"Not unless they're dirty, too. The rank and file hates dirty cops. They make everybody look bad."

She emerged with her small suitcase, shrugged into her coat, and grabbed her purse. "Do you need to stop by your apartment on the way to pick up your bag?"

"I can manage for a day or two. I'll get it later."

They stepped into the hall, and Zoë locked the door behind them. When they reached the street, she headed toward her car, key in hand. "I'll follow you."

Nick snugged his hat on his head and flipped his collar up. A couple inches of wet, heavy snow blanketed the sidewalk and parked cars, and it was still coming down. The street was a mess of deeply-rutted, rapidly-freezing slush. Given Zoë's Mini Cooper's low ground clearance, she would be lucky to make it out of her block, much less all the way to the Prescotts' house. "I'd feel better if I followed you, in case you get stuck."

Her lips thinned in exasperation. "I won't get stuck."

"Humor me."

She hesitated a second. "Okay, but let's get going. It's going to be a long trip in this weather."

She was right. The normally heavy, Saturday late-night traffic clogged Lake Shore Drive and didn't thin out until they passed Glenview. By the time he pulled into the driveway at Strathmoor behind her, it was past midnight. The new exterior lights were on, but the windows were dark, so he assumed the Prescotts had gone to bed.

Casey Callahan met them at the kitchen door. "I'm glad you came. After the police called, I wasn't sure what to expect, and this is a big house."

Zoë rolled her bag into the house ahead of him. "You seem to have everything under control."

"The place is locked up tight, and as far as I can tell, the alarm system is functioning properly, but I haven't been outside."

"Any phone calls?" Nick asked.

"No, all quiet."

Zoë pulled off her gloves and unzipped her coat. "How did the Prescotts take the news about Jimmy?"

"Lyman got agitated, and Marian seemed more concerned about him than about her ex."

Nick nodded. "That sounds like Marian. I still don't' think she believes Mahoney would do anything to hurt her, despite the evidence to the contrary."

Casey crossed to the stove, where a saucepan simmered over a low flame. "I fixed them some cocoa before they went to bed." She lifted the pan and gave it a couple of swirls. "Would you like some? I've got plenty left."

"I'll take a cup." Nick took a mug from the upper cabinet and handed it to her. "I think I'll stay up and keep an eye on things. You two get some sleep. I'll call Kenny first thing in the morning for an update on the search for Mahoney."

"You can't stay up all night," Zoë protested. "You played hockey for two hours and had your head stitched up. You must be dead on your feet. If anyone's going to stand guard tonight, it should be me."

"I want to scout around outside."

Her eyes rounded, and her brows shot up. "Are you nuts? It's practically a blizzard out there. There's no way Jimmy would be lurking around the grounds tonight. But what if he is?" She reached over and tapped Nick's forehead with one finger. "You might as well wear a sign saying, 'Go ahead. Hit me on the head. I'm already brain-damaged'."

He smiled at her indignation then bent and planted a swift kiss on her hair. When Casey's brows shot up, he gave her a wink. "I'll be fine. Thanks to the security lights and the snow, it's so bright I won't even need a flashlight. I just want to make a quick check for tire tracks or footprints. You two go to bed, and I'll see you in the morning." He downed his cocoa in a couple of swallows, set the mug on the counter, and headed for the back door.

Zoë followed. "I'd better not find your frozen corpse on the back steps, or you'll be sorry."

He stepped outside and shot a glance skyward. Snowflakes swirled and danced in the wide beam of light cast by the new floodlight above the door. "I'll be back in less than an hour. Lock the door behind me, and don't forget to re-set the alarm." Then he swooped in for one last kiss before closing the door in her startled face.

Forty-five minutes later, he was back — cold, soggy, and generally uncomfortable. The heavy, wet snow had the consistency of a half-melted Slurpee and could chill a man to the bone in a matter of minutes. Nick had tried to brush the snow off his cap and jacket on the back porch, but most of it had already melted and soaked in.

"Did you find anything?"

He glanced up and found Zoë standing in the kitchen, wearing an oversized University of Iowa sweatshirt and matching pants with a gold Hawkeye emblem on one leg.

"No. There's no sign anyone's been out there tonight. Why aren't you in bed?"

She gave him a men-are-such-morons look. "You didn't seriously expect me to sleep while you roamed around outside in a snowstorm, did you?"

"I guess not, but there's nothing stopping you now."

She hugged her arms to her chest. "I can't relax — there's too much running around in my head."

"I know what you mean."

She wandered over to the counter. "It's too late for coffee, but I can make us some fresh cocoa if you like."

She lifted a small, square baking pan and peeled back the foil cover. "It looks like Casey made some of her famous killer brownies."

When she waved the pan under Nick's nose, the rich chocolate aroma made his mouth water. The curry they'd eaten earlier was great, but dinner seemed like ages ago. "I wouldn't say no to either."

"Casey also started a fire in the fireplace in the living room. Why don't you go warm up, and I'll be in shortly."

He tugged off his wet boots and left them on the mat by the door before padding across the dark foyer to the living room. Lit only by the glow from the fireplace, the room seemed to have shrunk to half its size and felt much cozier. He stood in front of the fire and allowed his chilled body to soak up the warmth.

"Here we go." Zoë entered and set a plate of brownies and two mugs on the coffee table.

He sat beside her and grabbed a brownie in one hand and a mug of cocoa in the other. The first bite sent him straight to chocolate heaven. He closed his eyes and concentrated on the combination of not-too-sweet dark chocolate frosting and moist, chewy cake. A tiny groan might have slipped out when he wasn't paying attention.

"I know. It's perfect, right?" Zoë took a sip from her mug then set it down. "Casey is soft, pretty, and feminine, in addition to being a fantastic baker and cook and pretty much everything—my mother's idea of the ideal daughter."

"Everyone's got their own talents, and besides, your cooking is improving every day."

Her lips tightened in annoyance at his effort to lighten her mood. "My mother always tells me—and anyone else who will listen—that I'm a 'work in progress,' and she's right. For years I've been trying to figure out where I fit, but I keep missing the mark."

Something twisted in his chest at the barely-disguised hurt in her voice. "Hey, come here." He gently pulled her into his arms.

She settled against him, tucking her head under his chin to keep her gaze on the fire.

Nick nuzzled her hair. "Casey seems very competent, but she's got nothing on you. You're bright, beautiful, and strong, and I'm sure your mother is very proud of you."

Zoë shook her head against his chest. "She had five boys because she wanted a girl so badly, then she got me. I tried to be girlie—I really did—but I never seemed to be able get it right."

With a short laugh, he tightened his hold. "If you were any more of a girl, I might burst into flames right here on this couch."

She wriggled in protest and jabbed him in the ribs with her elbow. "Stop it. Here I am, baring my soul, and you're making fun of me. I'm too tall, and only a blind man would describe me as voluptuous."

She had to be kidding. Her body was long and elegant, with perfect curves in all the right places. If they weren't on duty in a client's house, waiting for a dangerous fugitive to strike, he would gladly demonstrate the effect she had on him.

But they were, and he couldn't.

"We are not getting into a discussion about your desirability." He shifted her position across his lap a few inches to make his point.

Zoë sucked in a quick breath and scooted back to more neutral territory before twisting to face him. "I should probably go upstairs."

"That's up to you. I just want you to know where things stand."

She scampered off the sofa. "Message received, loud and clear. I think it would be safest if I went to bed." Her eyes twinkled in the firelight. "A goodnight kiss is probably out of the question."

"A man can only be expected to resist so much temptation in one night."

She nodded. "True." But as she passed, she dropped a quick peck on his forehead above the bandage. "See you in a few hours." Then she slipped away into the darkness.

Nick leaned back and listened for her steps on the stairs, but the house was silent except for an occasional pop from the burning logs in the fireplace. He closed his eyes—just for a second. It had been a hell of a day.

The next thing he knew, a hand was shaking his shoulder. He jerked upright and blinked, trying to clear his head. The fire had burned out, and pale, watery light filtered through the curtains. How long had he been asleep?

"Time for breakfast." Zoë waved a cup of coffee under his nose.

He accepted it and drank half the cup before setting it back on the saucer. "Thanks."

She stepped back and regarded him with a judgmental frown that reminded him way too much of his mother. "Did you stay up all night? You look awful."

He scrubbed a hand over his bristly face. "I need to shower and shave before anyone else sees me."

"You'd better hurry. Casey got up early to make a blueberry streusel coffee cake, and it's going fast."

Twenty minutes later he joined the others at the breakfast table, feeling cleaner and more alert, but inside, his nerves still crackled like crumpled cellophane.

Marian's eyes rounded when she saw him. "What happened to your head?"

He touched the bandage. "It's nothing—just a little cut."

Zoë set a plate with a big hunk of coffee cake in front of him. "His head got in the way of another player's hockey stick."

"That's awful," Marian exclaimed. "Did you see a doctor?"

Nick shrugged. "It's all stitched up—probably won't even leave much of a scar."

Marian sent her husband a determined look. "If we have a son, he can play something safe like golf...or tennis...or better yet, chess. But he is not playing hockey."

Lyman laughed. "Given the power of genetics, do you think any son of mine is likely to take up a sport like hockey?"

"Hmph." Marian appeared unconvinced. "You never know, and I don't want to spend the rest of my life in the emergency room."

Nick grinned. "My mom got used to it. You will, too."

"Never."

After breakfast Casey packed up, said her goodbyes, and left. Nick called Kenny and learned the Indiana state police had reported a possible sighting of Jimmy Mahoney's motorcycle traveling south on I-65 just outside Lafayette. They had initiated pursuit, and Kenny was awaiting confirmation of apprehension. That was good news. Maybe.

Nick knew he should take a deep breath and relax. He wanted to believe Mahoney was on his way to Louisville, but instinct told him otherwise. The man wanted something from the Prescotts, and wanted it so badly he'd been willing to risk Marian's life by running their car off the road. He was clearly desperate, and desperation drove smarter men than Jimmy Mahoney to take terrible risks. For that reason, Nick decided not to share Kenny's news until he had something more definitive to report.

His apprehension seemed to have spread to Marian, who moved from room to room all morning, picking up and then discarding one project after another. After lunch, she went upstairs for her usual rest but showed up again in the kitchen at two-thirty.

Nick and Zoë were in the middle of a conversation about how to handle Mahoney in the event he eluded capture and showed up at the house, but dropped it the minute Marian appeared in the doorway.

Zoë smiled and reached for the polished chrome knob on the overhead cabinet next to the sink. "Can I get you something? Maybe a cup of tea or some cookies?"

Marian rubbed her lower back with her left hand. "I'd love a cup of that gingerbread-flavored herbal tea we bought. But that's not why I'm here. I've decided what I'd like to do with the rest of the day."

Nick hoped it was something like a rousing game of pinochle in the living room. The last thing they needed to worry about right now was how to protect the Prescotts outside the gates of the estate.

Marian's laugh told him his expression had given away his thoughts.

"Don't worry. I'm in no condition to go ice skating downtown or caroling through the neighborhood." She tipped her chin up and squared her shoulders. "I'm tired of worrying about what Jimmy might do. That just makes me sad. I want to start decorating for Christmas. It always makes me happy, and we could use some cheering up."

Zoë popped a mug of water for Marian's tea into the microwave and pushed the buttons. "That sounds like fun. I haven't decorated for the holidays since I left home."

Nick pictured the enormous windows and stone crenellations of the old mansion and swallowed hard. He'd never been fond of working on a ladder, especially outside in the winter. "I don't suppose you like to hang outdoor lights, do you?"

Marian's blue eyes twinkled. "Lucky for you, no. Just a tree and some wreaths and candles—things like that."

He smiled. "My knees and I thank you. In that case, I'll be happy to carry the boxes. Just point me in the right direction."

"Everything, including the tree, is in a storage room over the garage, next to your apartment. I told Lyman I want a real tree next year, but under the circumstances, we can use the fake one again this year. I'll show you where it is."

The microwave dinged, and Zoë removed the mug and dunked a teabag into the steaming water. "Does Lyman like to help, or should we leave him happily in his workshop?"

"Oh, we don't want to bother him. Lyman enjoys the end result of my fussing and puttering, but the only part of decorating he's good at is getting all the bulbs to light once the tree is in place."

After Marian finished her tea, they headed outside. Nick was glad he'd taken the time to shovel the overnight accumulation of snow from the back porch, courtyard, and steps after breakfast. As it was, he kept a firm grip on Marian to make sure she remained upright. When they reached the bottom of the outside staircase, he handed Zoë his key. She headed up the steps and opened the door while he helped Marian.

The door to the storage room opened off the apartment's living room. Inside, boxes of varying sizes were stacked haphazardly under the sloping roof. Marian pointed to a big rectangular box about six feet long. "There's the tree. We should probably take it down first."

Nick corrected her. "*We* aren't going to take anything down. You are going to point out the boxes you need then Zoë and I will carry them into the house."

"Yes, sir." Marian gave him a jaunty salute and started poking around the boxes, checking the descriptions written on the outside in bold black marker and opening a few to confirm the contents.

Nick tested the weight of the box holding the tree then hefted it under one arm. It wasn't too heavy, but it was awkward. He had a sudden image of stepping through the outside doorway and a gust of wind striking the box, sending him reeling like a drunken lumberjack. "Marian, if you'll open the door and help guide me, we'll take the tree first. It's the biggest and heaviest."

"Absolutely." She stepped in front of him and reached for the knob. "I'm so excited. The house is beautiful, but it can be a little...I don't know...somber at times. Wait 'til you see how cheerful it is with reindeer and angels and elves everywhere."

When she opened the door, his prediction came true as a blast of frigid air hit the tree box. He tightened his grip, lowered his head, and tucked his chin against his chest. "I'll go down first. Marian, you follow, but be sure hold tight to the railing. This wind might knock you off your feet."

"I doubt that. I'm pretty solid these days." She patted her tummy. "But I don't want to slip. It might take a crane to get me back on my feet."

He started down the stairs, placing one foot carefully in front of the other. When the box started to swing sideways, he adjusted his grip. "When we get to the house, you can open the door."

Zoë stood in the doorway as they picked their way down the staircase. "I'll organize the rest of these boxes then start carrying them down."

Nick turned his head but tried to keep the box straight so it didn't smack Marian. "Wait until I get back before you lift anything. Some of those boxes are heavy, and you don't want another twisted ankle."

"What?" Marian turned to Zoë. "You twisted your ankle? When?"

Zoë shot Nick a fierce glare before shifting her gaze to Marian. "It's nothing. I'm fine." She raised her leg and twirled her foot. "See. No problem. You go on in the house and get out of this weather." She disappeared back inside and closed the door.

When Nick and Marian reached the house, she opened the back door and stepped aside, holding it wide while he maneuvered through the opening and into the kitchen. "Where do you want this?"

"In the living room, next to the fireplace."

He toted the box through the foyer and set it down where she directed.

Marian pulled off her gloves and unzipped her parka. "Thanks so much for carrying this. You should have seen me and Lyman trying to do it ourselves last year. It's a miracle we didn't both end up in traction. I can't wait to see how we do with a live one next year."

"I'm sure this will look great when you're finished."

Her face brightened. "Oh, it will. The first year we were married, I bought tons of ornaments."

He couldn't help but smile at her enthusiasm. Marian Prescott was one of the most warm-hearted, optimistic women he'd ever met. She looked for joy and found it in the smallest things. She didn't deserve to have her life turned upside down by a low-life ex-husband. For the first time in months, Nick missed wearing a badge. It would be so satisfying to be able to go after Mahoney personally and put him back behind bars. He hated being forced to wait for someone else to do the job.

He smiled at Marian. "I'd better go help Zoë with the rest of the boxes. You can wait in the kitchen and open the door for us."

She followed him, chatting happily about her holiday decorations and where they would go in the house, until they reached the back door. As soon as Nick pulled it open, he caught a strong whiff of acrid smoke. When he glanced across the courtyard, his heart froze.

Oh, dear God, no!

Flames licked at the staircase and door to his apartment. The garage was on fire.

"Call nine-one-one," he shouted to Marian then rushed outside.

Chapter Sixteen

Zoë was bent over, trying to read the label on one of the boxes when a faint shout from outside caught her attention. She straightened too quickly and hit her head on one of the rafters of the storage room. As she rubbed her injured scalp, another shout followed the first. Then another. Someone was calling her name.

What the…?

Had she accidentally locked Nick out?

"I'm coming," she yelled.

As she wound her way through the boxes of holiday decorations, she sniffed. What was that smell? Sharp, oily, and caustic — like gasoline.

She rushed to the door but released the handle the moment her hand touched the metal. It was hot enough to sear bare flesh in seconds. Shaking her hand, she peered through the glass panes at the top. Yellow and blue flames flared on the steps and slithered up the wooden handrails of the outside staircase like fiery snakes. The exterior of the door itself must be on fire, too. Even if she managed to get it open, she would never be able to make it down the stairs unscathed.

Smoke was starting to pour in around the leaky old door, filling the air with a toxic haze. She ran to the bathroom and grabbed a hand towel, dunked it under the faucet then wrung it out and covered her mouth and nose. Although her eyes still watered and stung, the damp cloth cut the smoke and cooled the air coming into her lungs. She took a couple of deep breaths and tried to beat back the rising tide of panic.

How long had Nick and Marian been in the house, maybe ten minutes? How much longer before someone looked out and saw the fire?

Her breath came in rapid pants, sucking the wet towel in an out against her mouth as she searched for a possible exit. A small, arched dormer window behind the living room sofa appeared to offer the only potential escape route, but it was so tiny Zoë wasn't sure she could shimmy through the opening.

She climbed onto the sofa and knelt against the back, trying to get enough leverage to shove the old window open, but she kept losing her footing on the soft cushions. The window had probably been painted shut half a dozen times over the years and refused to budge

Her eyes and nose were streaming, and a deep, barking cough racked her body every few seconds. If she didn't get fresh air into her lungs soon, she would pass out before the flames reached her. Her oxygen-deprived brain grasped for an alternative, and then she noticed the brass lamp on the small table beside the sofa.

She reached down, yanked off the shade, and grasped it by the base. Wielding it like a broadsword, she smashed the glass of the window. Shards of glass clattered onto the tile roof of the garage.

Smoke rushed past her head and out through the opening, as if it sought the crisp, fresh outside air as desperately as she did. She sputtered and coughed, but kept bashing the wood trim and remaining pieces of broken glass until she could stick her head through without danger of decapitation.

She took a huge gulp of air and screamed. "Help!"

Nick's voice rose above the roar of the flames. "Zoë, hang on!"

She forced her eyes open and tried to focus through her tears. He stood directly below her in the courtyard.

He cupped his hands to his mouth. "The fire department's on the way!"

"I can't get out!"

Multiple sirens howled in the distance, their wails growing steadily louder until two fire trucks and a pair of ambulances roared up the driveway and screeched to a halt in front of the garage. Yellow-clad firefighters poured from the vehicles and began readying various pieces of equipment.

A firefighter propped a ladder against the gutter below her window and climbed toward her. Half-way up, he raised his head and yelled, "Can you climb out onto the roof?"

Zoë curled her shoulders forward and tried to angle her body to fit through the opening, but the wooden frame bit into the flesh of her upper arms. She eased back until only her head remained outside. "No. The window's too small."

As soon as the words left her mouth, another spasm of coughing seized her and wouldn't let go. Each time she gasped between coughs, smoke filled her lungs. She tried holding her breath, but she couldn't fight her body's automatic response. Her head swam, and the tips of her fingers began to tingle from lack of oxygen. Panic gripped her. She couldn't move forward, and she couldn't go back. The heat in the room had grown almost unbearable.

Suddenly a big hand cupped the back of her head and another slapped a mask across her mouth and nose. "Breathe," the fireman shouted.

She obeyed automatically. Despite her continued coughing, he held the mask firmly against her face. After a few breaths, her vision cleared enough for her to raise her head and meet his gaze.

"We're going to get you out of there. Take two more breaths then close your eyes, cover your face, and step back from the window." He raised an axe in one hand. "I'm going to break the frame out to give you enough room. Got it?"

She nodded then followed his instructions. With her eyes closed, she concentrated on the crashing sounds of the axe splintering the old window frame.

After four or five solid hits, he reached in, grabbed her arm and pulled. "Come on. Now!"

Two minutes later she was sitting in the back of an ambulance, shivering inside a reflective blanket and sucking oxygen from a mask. Nick sat beside her, clutching her hand as if someone might snatch her away. Shouts, thumps, and bangs outside told her the firefighters were working to extinguish the blaze.

The paramedic was the same skinny young man with the neck tattoo who had attended Marian after the car accident. After pushing Zoë's sleeve up, he slipped a blood pressure cuff on her arm and pressed his stethoscope against the inside of her elbow. Seemingly satisfied, he released the pressure and moved the cold metal disc to her back and chest, instructing her to take several deep breaths before draping the stethoscope around his neck.

"I'd say you're pretty lucky. Your blood pressure is normal, and I only hear a slight wheeze in your lungs. How do you feel?"

Zoë lifted the oxygen mask. "My throat's a little raw, and I may never be warm again, but otherwise I'm okay." Her voice sounded raspy to her own ears, but her head was clear and her chest didn't hurt. If only the hard shivers would stop.

"I still think we should take you to the hospital and let a doctor check you out."

"That's not necessary." She turned to Nick. "I'll be fine, and I'm needed here."

Lines of worry creased his brow. "Are you sure? I can probably get Kenny or Hugh to stick around until you're discharged."

She shook her head and squeezed his hand. "They've got their own jobs to do, and I'm sure they're even busier now that this has happened."

The paramedic checked the monitor hooked to the plastic clip attached to her finger. "Your O2 sat is ninety-eight percent, and I can't force you to go to the hospital, so I guess you're good to go." He removed the mask and clip. "At least you're in much better shape than the other guy."

Zoë tightened her grip on Nick's hand. "What other guy? There wasn't anyone else in the garage, was there?"

"Not inside, no."

Before he could continue, Kenny popped his head into the back of the ambulance. "Nick, they've got Watanabe stabilized and ready for transport in the second ambulance. Should I call you when he regains consciousness? You might want to be present when we question him."

"Absolutely. Thanks."

Kenny flashed Zoë a quick smile. "You look a lot better." He ducked around the side of the door.

She stared at Nick. Had she heard correctly? Maybe she needed another hit off the oxygen. "Victor Watanabe is here?"

Nick nodded. "We found him outside near the stairs. He was unconscious and had second degree burns on his hands, arms, and face."

She struggled to make sense of this strange twist of events. "So he set the fire?"

"That's what it looks like at this point. We'll know more when we question him." He scooted closer and wrapped one arm around her.

The warmth of his body helped calm her shivers, but it didn't banish the chill of knowing someone had tried to kill her. "I don't understand. Why would he do it? Why would he want to kill me?"

Nick stroked her hair. "We don't know that he was trying to harm anyone. He might have seen me and Marian go into the house and thought the garage was empty."

"I suppose," she agreed, slightly mollified. "But why set the fire at all?"

"Who knows? Maybe to create more stress for Lyman."

"I don't see how that would make him want to sell GRAMPA."

"Neither do I, but I gave up trying to figure out how some people think a long time ago." He straightened and dropped his arm from her shoulder to her waist. "Time to get you inside out of the cold."

He held her tight and helped her ease down from the back of the ambulance to the cobblestone courtyard. Firemen still swarmed the garage, but they appeared to be mopping up the blaze, hitting the remaining hot spots with the hose. The roof had collapsed, reducing the charming old structure to a pile of blackened timbers and scattered red tiles. In the middle of the mess sat the twisted skeleton of Lyman's beloved Bentley, along with a smaller car, which must have been Marian's.

Zoë blinked back a couple of tears. Now that the physical shock of her ordeal had begun to recede, the reality of the situation was starting to sink in. "Lyman will be so upset. I know how much he loved that car."

Nick turned her away from the scene of destruction. "He'll be happier to see you in one piece. Come on. The Prescotts are waiting in the kitchen, and Marian's a wreck."

They found Lyman hovering over his wife, who sat with her left elbow on the table, her head down, and her fingers speared into her hair. When Nick and Zoë entered, Lyman turned and Marian straightened and looked up.

With her blotchy face and puffy red eyes, Zoë barely recognized the same woman who had been so bubbly and excited a few hours earlier. Mascara smudges gave Marian the appearance of a grief-stricken raccoon. Her lovely blond hair hung around her shoulders in lank disarray, but her countenance brightened the moment she saw Zoë.

She pushed up from the table and rushed to enfold her in as big a hug as she could manage, given the firm protuberance of her belly. "You're all right! I'm so relieved!"

Zoë hugged her back. "I had a couple of scary moments, but I'm fine." She released Marian and turned to Lyman. "I'm sorry—your car is a total loss."

He waved one hand in dismissal. "Don't give it a second thought. The Bentley served this family well for seventy years. Besides, I need something safer and more modern to drive Marian and the baby." He tipped his head in Nick's direction. "We won't always have a chauffeur."

Marian took Zoë's hand and pulled her toward the table. "Come sit down, and Lyman will get you a glass of water. Won't you, dear?"

"Of course." He headed for the cupboard where the glasses were kept.

"How about I fix you both a cup of tea?" Nick suggested. "Zoë's still chilled, and you look like you could use a pick-me-up."

Marian settled back into her chair with a sigh. "That sounds wonderful. Are you sure?"

"Trust me. I can nuke water with the best of them."

Five minutes later he set a pair of steaming mugs in front of Zoë and Marian then joined them and Lyman at the table.

Lyman leaned back in his chair and tapped his finger against his upper lip. "Officer Zolnicki said they found Mr. Watanabe near the garage and believe he started the fire."

"That's the working theory. We'll know more as soon as he's recovered sufficiently to answer questions."

Marian looked up from her cup. "I never liked that man, but I can't imagine why he would do such a thing." She sighed. "At least it wasn't Jimmy."

Lyman squeezed his wife's hand but kept his attention on Nick. "I won't be able to relax until I know he's been apprehended. I don't suppose you know if the police have any new information as to his whereabouts."

"Not since a possible sighting in Indiana this morning."

Lyman sighed. "At least that's away from here. I wish I could believe he'll keep heading south."

Zoë's hand shook as another chill struck her. She set her empty cup on the table. Despite the blanket and hot tea, she couldn't seem to get warm. She pushed back from the table. "I think I'll go take a shower. I need to get the smell of smoke off me and out of my hair." Her voice wavered, and when she tried to smile, the skin around her mouth felt like it might crack.

Nick rose quickly. "I'll help you up the stairs."

"That's not necessary. I'll be fine." She didn't want help. She wanted to curl up and close her eyes until the memory of being trapped in choking smoke faded.

"I'll help you up the stairs," he repeated, slowing the words for emphasis.

Her legs wobbled like strands of cooked spaghetti — if she didn't get to her room soon, she might not make it. She didn't want to waste what little energy she had arguing with him. "Fine."

He wrapped an arm around her waist, and she allowed herself to lean against his solid heat. Together they trudged up the stairs to the staff quarters in the attic.

When they reached her room, he sat her on the bed and squatted to pull off her shoes. After tossing them aside, he cradled her feet in his hands then glanced up. "Your feet are like ice."

She tried to smile. "No worse than the rest of me."

He released her feet and straightened. "We've got to get you warmed up. I'll start the shower while you undress."

She wanted to protest. He shouldn't be taking care of her this way. They weren't lovers, at least not yet. She wanted to maintain some measure of modesty, of mystery. She didn't want him to see her like this — weak, pitiful, and broken.

Somewhere she found the strength to pull her sweater over her head and dropped it on the floor, followed by the rest of her clothes, then slipped into the old blue terry robe she'd tossed into her suitcase as an afterthought. Instead of offering comfort, the rough fabric was cold against her skin. She wrapped her arms around herself and shivered.

Nick stuck his head into the room. "The water's hot. Are you ready?"

She nodded, and he stepped back into the hall to allow her access to the steamy bathroom.

He stroked the side of her cheek then tucked a lock of hair behind her ear. "I'll wait out here in case you need anything. Call me if you start to feel weak or have a problem. Okay?"

She nodded again. "Thank you."

After he shut the door, she dropped her robe, stepped over the side of the old cast iron tub, and turned her face to the spray from the wall-mounted shower head. Hot water streamed down her body like liquid sunshine, washing away the charred remains of her fear along with the stench of the smoke. By the time the water cooled, she was refreshed but wobbly with fatigue.

She stepped out of the shower and smiled at the clean, long-sleeved pink T-shirt and loose gray exercise pants folded on the seat of the toilet. Nick. He might claim to be baffled by the fairer sex, but the man understood a woman's needs better than he realized. She had pulled on the top and started to rub her hair with a towel when a knock sounded.

"Are you doing okay in there?"

She opened the bathroom door. "I'm nearly finished. Thanks for the clothes."

"I wanted you to be warm." His serious expression eased, and a hint of dimple appeared in his cheek as his gaze drifted over the soft curves of her unrestrained breasts. "You look...uh...more comfortable. And pink is my favorite color on you."

Certain the color of her cheeks now matched her top, she turned her attention back to drying her hair.

Nick seemed reluctant to leave. He leaned against the doorframe and watched her in the mirror. "Do you want to come downstairs for dinner? Lyman and Marian are making soup with a little help from GRAMPA."

"As much as I'd like to see that, I think I'll pass. I'm so tired, I'm quivering." She held out her hand to demonstrate.

"Post adrenaline-rush shakes." Nick took her hand and pressed a kiss on the back. "Let's get you to bed."

He drew the blanket and sheet back and held them while she climbed in, then nudged her over and sat on the edge of the bed. Pulling the covers up under her chin, he leaned close, until his warm breath brushed her cheeks. "You scared the hell out of me, you know."

As the low, intimate tone of his voice caressed her, Zoë's world shrank until it held only the two of them.

"You can't imagine what I felt when I looked out and saw the stairs and door in flames."

His words drifted above her consciousness, but the movements of his mouth mesmerized her. As it drew closer, she closed her eyes and waited.

Nick's lips touched hers, light as a feather at first. Then the pressure increased until she reached up and clasped his shoulders, trying to pull him closer.

When his phone jangled in his pocket, they jerked apart. He sat back and pulled it out. "Hello."

He listened for a minute. "I'll be there as soon as I can. Thanks for the heads-up."

As he tucked the phone back in his pocket, Zoë sent him a questioning look.

"That was Kenny. Watanabe has regained consciousness, and the doctors say he's well enough to be questioned."

She rested one hand on his shoulder. "Go. I'm ready for this to be over."

"Me, too." He pressed a quick kiss on her lips and rose. "You get some rest. I'll fill you in when I get back."

He closed the door with a soft click, and she sank back against the thin mattress and allowed her muscles to relax. With her eyes closed, her mind seemed to float in space, barely tethered to her body. Her limbs felt leaden and weightless at the same time. Seconds later, her last remnant of thought faded into oblivion.

****

Nick kept one eye on the speedometer, easing his foot off the accelerator when necessary, all the way to the hospital. The last thing he needed was a ticket or another accident, but if he could have teleported, he would have. He reminded himself this wasn't his interrogation—he could only observe while the Lake Forest officers questioned Victor Watanabe—but it was hard to suppress his impatience. Like Zoë, he was ready to wrap this case up, give the Prescotts their lives back, and move on with his own. He wasn't sure which direction he might go from here, but he was beginning to get a few ideas.

At the hospital the receptionist directed him to the burn unit, where he had to suit up in a sterile gown, mask, and booties before being allowed into Watanabe's room. Inside he found Kenny and Sergeant Lewis, similarly attired and standing next to the bed. Watanabe's hands and arms were swathed in gauze, and his face coated in antibiotic salve. A pair of IV bags hung from a pole, and a slew of machines monitored his vitals.

Kenny acknowledged Nick's arrival with a nod. "Pull up a chair. We were just about to get started."

Nick snagged a metal chair with a molded plastic back and seat and settled into a position where he had a clear view of their suspect's face as Sergeant Lewis flipped open his notebook and began the questioning.

"Mr. Watanabe, I understand you have visited the home of Lyman Prescott several times on behalf of your employer in an attempt to purchase the rights to one of his inventions. Is that correct?"

"Yes, that is correct."

"And Mr. Prescott rejected those offers and told you not to return."

Watanabe gave a brisk nod. "Yes."

"So what were you doing there this evening behind the garage?"

The man dropped his gaze to his burned hands and seemed to weigh his response.

"Mr. Watanabe." Lewis's voice had a sharper edge now. "Did you set that fire?"

Watanabe sighed and regarded all three men. "It is a complicated story. If you will allow me to explain..."

"Go ahead."

"As you said, I was employed by Ichiro Electronics to negotiate for the rights to Mr. Prescott's meal preparation robot. As I usually do prior to contacting a potential business partner, I researched Mr. Prescott and his wife, looking for information that would allow me to tailor my sales approach for the greatest probability of success. Since Mr. Prescott is something of a recluse, I found no useful contacts there. Mrs. Prescott, however, has a number of family and friends."

Nick's gut tightened. He had an inkling where this was going, and he didn't like it.

Sergeant Lewis glanced up from his notes. "Go ahead."

Watanabe nodded and continued. "When Mr. Prescott rebuffed my first two offers, I contacted Mrs. Prescott's former husband and asked him to use any influence he might have to persuade her to speak to Mr. Prescott on our behalf."

"Wait a minute," Nick interrupted. "You asked Mahoney to help you?"

"Perhaps it would be more accurate to say I employed Mr. Mahoney to assist me."

Sergeant Lewis shot Nick a warning glance then turned back to Watanabe. "Were you aware of his background?"

"Of course. As an ex-convict, the man was desperate for money. I hoped it would help motivate him."

"And what exactly did Mahoney do for you?"

"As soon as I learned Mr. Prescott had hired a personal protection agent to work in his household in the guise of a chef, I asked Mr. Mahoney and an associate to check the woman out and perhaps discourage her from accepting the position."

Nick clenched and unclenched his fists. Damn. Mahoney and Gehke were definitely the bikers Zoë had encountered on her way to Strathmoor.

"And how did you make this discovery?"

Watanabe bowed his head. "I am ashamed to admit I asked Mr. Mahoney to install a listening device in Mr. Prescott's office."

Lewis turned to Kenny. "That must have been the break-in I investigated where nothing was stolen."

"Yes." Watanabe nodded again.

"Okay. Go on."

"Later, Mr. Mahoney met with Mrs. Prescott but reported that she refused to cooperate. At that point, I am afraid he decided to take matters into his own hands."

"He ran us off the road, didn't he?" Nick's blood pounded in his ears at the memory.

A deep sadness overlaid Watanabe's somber expression. "I most sincerely regret his actions. I am very grateful no one in your vehicle was seriously injured. I hoped Mrs. Prescott would accept my humble gift as my way of expressing my deepest apologies."

"You sent the stroller?" Nick asked.

"I did. The sales associate at the store assured me it was the one she had admired."

Nick sensed a brief twinge of relief. Another mystery solved.

Sergeant Lewis steered the conversation back to the main point. "You still haven't told us what you were doing at the Prescott's house tonight."

"I came to stop Mr. Mahoney."

Nick cursed under his breath. His instinct had been right. Mahoney hadn't left the area. He'd headed straight back to Strathmoor.

Watanabe shot him a quick glance then continued. "When I terminated his employment after the car accident, he was furious. But then he called earlier today, raving about something he planned to do tonight that would make me sorry and get him what he wanted. I couldn't make sense of it, but I convinced him to meet me this afternoon. He gave me directions to a small house at the back of the Prescott's property. I was to leave my car on the street and come on foot."

Lewis glanced up from his notebook. "And you did as he asked?"

"I did. We met, and I tried to reason with him. But that seemed to enrage him further. He shoved me down in the snow and ran toward the house, carrying a gasoline can. I followed, but by the time I reached the garage, he had set the building on fire." He raised his bandaged hands. "I tried to put out the flames with my coat, but as you know, I failed. I am so very sorry."

"Were you aware someone was in the garage?"

Watanabe's eyes widened. "No, I was not."

"Where did Mahoney go after he set the fire?"

"I did not see. I was too busy." He dropped his chin. "Again, I am sorry."

Nick couldn't wait for Lewis to wrap up his questioning. He had to get back. Mahoney could be anywhere. No one was looking for him. He could be hiding in the woods, waiting for the firemen to leave to make his move—whatever that was.

Nick jumped up, knocking his chair over backwards in the process. "I've got to go. I left Zoë asleep, and the Prescotts think Mahoney's half-way to Mexico by now." Without waiting for a response, he raced out of the room and down the hall, leaving a trail of discarded blue protective garments on the floor behind him.

Chapter Seventeen

Zoë's eyelids fluttered when a board creaked somewhere in the hall outside her bedroom door, but her body and brain felt mired in molasses. She blinked several times as she fought to drag herself into consciousness. How long had she slept? The room was so dark she could barely distinguish the outline of the small dresser on the opposite wall.

The creak sounded again, then the slow click of her doorknob turning. She froze.

"Zoë," a low voice whispered. "It's me."

She recognized Nick's husky baritone. The knob turned further, and the door pushed open a few inches.

"Are you awake?"

"Barely. Come in." She scooted into an upright position and reached to turn on the lamp on the small bedside table. "What time is it?"

He stepped into the room, closing the door behind him. "A little before midnight."

She shivered and pulled the blanket up to her chin. "You've been gone for hours. Have the police been interviewing Victor Watanabe all this time?"

He crossed the small room and sat on the edge of the bed. "No. Kenny, Hugh, and I—along with a couple of others—have been outside, combing the grounds for any sign of Jimmy Mahoney."

Her heartbeat surged, waking her fully. "Jimmy? I thought he was supposed to be in Indiana, or points south."

"That turned out to be a false sighting. He's here—or at least he was earlier today. According to Watanabe, Mahoney set the fire."

The fire. Zoë crossed her arms and hugged herself —partly to ward off the chill in the room and partly as a reminder that she'd come through the ordeal whole and unscathed. She'd known the fire was deliberately set, but that was a more abstract concept than hearing the identity of the arsonist. Jimmy Mahoney had tried to kill her. The words rattled around in her brain without grabbing hold. "But why? Did he know I was in the storeroom?"

"Watanabe wasn't able to provide a motive. Apparently, Mahoney wasn't making much sense."

She tilted her head and frowned. "I don't understand. If Jimmy set the fire, what was Victor Watanabe doing at Strathmoor this afternoon?"

"He said he was trying to stop Mahoney. Watanabe claimed he was burned trying to put out the fire."

"Do you believe him?"

"The police are still investigating, but my gut says he was telling the truth."

"Poor Marian. She's going to be so upset when she finds out." Zoë shook her head. "That Jimmy Mahoney is the ex-husband from hell, a nightmare that won't stop." She dropped her hands from her arms. "You don't think he's still somewhere on the estate do you?"

He moved toward her, placed big, warm hands on her shoulders, and met her gaze with determined assurance. "Don't worry. We searched every inch and found no sign of him. You can sleep easy. Mahoney's gone. At least for now."

The taut muscles in her shoulders eased slightly, but an internal tension still thrummed through her body. "I doubt I'll sleep again tonight. You should try to get some rest, though." She touched the side of his face. His formerly white bandage was now gray and streaked with soot, and his eyelids drooped with fatigue. "You're starting to look a little too much like an extra from *The Walking Dead*."

He dropped his hands from her shoulders then scrubbed a hand across his jaw and grimaced. "I need a shower first. I can't smell myself anymore, but I'm sure I reek."

She smiled. "You do have a certain eau-de-Smokey-the-Bear aroma." Suddenly, she remembered what the fire meant to him. "I almost forgot! The apartment. Your clothes. The fire destroyed everything!"

He shrugged. "I'll swing by my apartment to pick up what I need in the morning. For now, I just want to wash off the grime and lie down for an hour or two."

"You can use the bathroom up here. There's soap and shampoo in the shower, and I'll get you a couple of clean towels. You can use my razor, too, if you're desperate."

His dark eyes sparked, and the dimple in his cheek reappeared. "Thanks, but I think I'll stick with the bristles tonight. I try to limit myself to one facial laceration per week."

She pressed her lips together and nodded sagely. "Good policy."

When Zoë shoved back the covers, cold penetrated her thin top, setting her nipples on instant alert. Nick's gaze bounced down to her chest and back up almost before she had time to register it. Almost. She gave him a tight-lipped smile. "The plumbing up here is ancient. Behave yourself, or I'll flush the toilet while you're in the shower."

He snorted and got out of her way while she retrieved her ratty blue robe and shoved her feet into the red ballet flats sitting on the floor in front of the dresser, and then he followed her into the tiny bathroom.

As she handed him a pair of clean towels from the cabinet, she glanced from the top of his head to the ceiling. It would be close. The bathroom had been built a century earlier, probably with petite parlor maids in mind—not hulking, hockey-playing, pseudo-chauffeurs. "Watch your head. I don't have a needle and thread to stitch you up if you have a close encounter with the shower head."

"I promise." He surprised her with a quick kiss then took the towels in one hand, guided her out with the other, and shut the door.

Zoë waited until the water had run for several minutes before she pushed the door open a crack and peeked through with one eye. The coast was clear. He had folded his dirty clothes in a neat pile on the floor and set his pistol in its holster on top. She tiptoed in, gathered the pile in her arms, and snuck back out, closing the door with a soft click. She gently set the Ruger on the dresser in her bedroom then grabbed her own smoky clothes from the back of the chair and headed downstairs.

She had a dresser full of clean laundry, but Nick had nothing. Since she was wide awake and likely to stay that way, the least she could do was give his clothes a quick wash. He had to be exhausted, so it shouldn't be hard to persuade him to take a nap in her bed while she found some way to occupy herself. At least when he woke, his clothes wouldn't remind him of the fire with every breath. He'd been such a rock through the whole ordeal; it was the least she could do.

In deference to the hour, she tried to be quiet on the stairs, although a tap dancing dinosaur probably wouldn't wake Lyman and Marian tonight. The stress and shock of the fire had hit them hard, reminding them how vulnerable they still were.

Despite Zoë's efforts to tread lightly, each step resounded through the dark emptiness of the expansive foyer, prompting her to whisper an apology to the oversized portrait of Frankie "No Nose" hanging above the stairs.

The laundry room off the kitchen had been converted from a service porch sometime in the forties or fifties, but at least the machines were newer. Determined to eradicate every last hint of smoke, she tossed everything in together with a splash of detergent and set the water temperature to hot. As soon as the water started, a loud *thunk* sounded below the floor. Adrenaline flooded her veins with a jolt.

She gripped the front of the washer, dropped her head, and drew a deep breath before releasing it slowly. *There's no bogeyman. It's just an old house with old pipes.* She waited for the wash cycle to begin then made her way to the relative comfort of the living room. She picked up one of Marian's favorite celebrity gossip magazines, but the photos of beautiful movie stars taking their adorable children to the beach did nothing to banish her edginess.

As soon as she heard the faint *ding* from the washer, she returned and moved the clothes to the dryer. It would be another thirty minutes before the laundry would be dry, but she didn't want to spend the time waiting alone downstairs. The house was too big, too dark, and too silent. She decided to go back to her room and check on Nick.

When she reached the third floor hall, no comforting light greeted her. The bathroom door stood open, but the room was dark and empty. Where was he? He couldn't have gone far wrapped in nothing but a towel, and the beds in the other two rooms sported only bare mattresses—not particularly welcoming on a chilly November night. That left her room.

She squinted as she stepped into the darkened room. A white rectangle draped over the back of the chair glowed softly in the faint moonlight coming through the small window. His towel. Her eyes skittered to the bed, where she could just make out the contours of a human form under her covers.

"You took my clothes." His voice leapt from the shadows.

Although she knew he was there, her pulse jumped at the sudden sound. "They were filthy. I'm washing them."

"I guessed that, but you left me no option except the shelter of your bed."

Was he teasing her...or something more? Since his voice was barely above a whisper, it was hard to tell. She wished she could see his face. "Actually, I stayed downstairs hoping you would sleep. I was wide awake, and I was sure you'd be exhausted."

"I am, but I can't seem to relax. Maybe I'm too cold." His outstretched hand and bare arm, pale in the moonlight, reached toward her from the gloom. "Come here. You can warm me up."

"I don't think that's such a good idea."

"It sounds like genius to me."

His deep voice flowed over her like melted caramel. Her pulse beat strong in her throat, and a sudden heat rushed upward from her core, suffusing her chest, neck, and face. She longed to say yes. She craved the comfort he offered. In the aftermath of fear, she didn't want to be alone. But she also didn't want to be left with a pile of regrets in the morning. "We both know what will happen if I do."

"Um, hm."

"What about your vow to avoid relationships with work colleagues?"

"You're more than a work colleague. I let you meet my mom. That's serious stuff."

The voice of caution in the back of her head refused to give up. "What about Maureen? She was much more, too. You planned to marry her."

"I don't want to talk about Maureen. She has nothing to do with us." His voice had a rough, almost raw, edge.

"But you said—"

"Zoë, come here." Then his insistent tone softened. "Please. We need each other tonight."

The plea in his voice nearly pushed her over the edge. "I want to—I do—but..."

The covers rustled, and he stood before her. With the only source of light coming from behind him, she couldn't see his face clearly—only the silhouette of his head. Faint, silvery moonlight defined and softened the muscular contours of his shoulders as he drew her into his arms. She went willingly and rested her face against the hard comfort of his chest. Without conscious direction, her arms slid around to caress the smooth, warm skin of his back.

He tightened his grasp and pressed a kiss against her hair.

"I don't want to be sorry," she murmured against his skin. "And I don't want you to be sorry."

"Life doesn't come with guarantees." He eased her back and tilted his head. "Sometimes you have to take a chance. There are worse things than being sorry. Only you can decide if what we might have together is worth the risk."

"What about you?"

"I've already decided."

Then he crushed her to him and kissed her with a hopeful desperation that made her decision easy. They came together as if they had known each other a lifetime, rather than mere weeks. Their bodies joined easily and joyfully, without a glimpse of fear. Zoë's last conscious thought was that she'd never felt so cherished.

She had no idea what time it was when she stirred in Nick's arms, but the sliver of indigo sky showing through the small window above the bed told her dawn was still hours away. She should go downstairs and retrieve their clothes from the dryer, but there was plenty of time. The Prescotts wouldn't be awake for hours. When Nick mumbled something unintelligible and tightened his grip, she sighed and nestled back against his chest, comforted by the heat radiating from his body and the weight of his arm across her back. Even in sleep, his strength protected her. Her lips curved in a smile of wonder.

Because of the emotional shield she'd raised to protect herself, she hadn't had many relationships, but she'd thought she was going into this one with her eyes wide open. She'd thought she understood the risks and accepted the possibility of regrets. She'd thought she knew what she was doing. Instead, he'd shown her how little she really knew.

Dominic Rosetti was unlike any man she'd ever known. Making love with him had lifted her to a place she'd never been—a place of soaring triumph and aching vulnerability—and she had no idea what to expect next. What would he say to her? What did he want? She had no idea.

Those thoughts bubbled in her mind until fatigue won out, and she dozed for a while. When she woke again, pale light washed the room in watery shades of gray. Taking care not to disturb Nick, she slipped from the bed, pulled on her robe, and tiptoed down to the laundry room. When she returned with an armful of folded clothes, he lay propped against the headboard with one arm behind his head. His rumpled hair and heavy, dark stubble—not to mention the stitches in his forehead—gave him a piratical air. He was the most delicious thing Zoë had ever seen.

Heat flared in his eyes, and his dimple appeared. "Good morning."

"Hi." Warmth rose to her cheeks, and she quickly turned to set the folded stack on the dresser.

"Thanks for washing my clothes."

She turned back and met his gaze. "I threw mine in, too. I figured we didn't need a reminder of…yesterday."

"Come here." He stretched out a hand.

Butterflies danced in her stomach as she complied. He took her hand and drew her closer until she stood beside him. Keeping his gaze locked on hers, he untied her robe and smoothed it down her shoulders. His face was inches from her breasts.

"You're the most beautiful woman I've ever seen."

The butterflies launched into a Macarena, and she gave a jittery laugh. "You don't get out much, do you?"

"Stop it." His expression was deadly serious. "This is not the time for false modesty."

She met his gaze. "Sorry. My mother always warned me about my smart mouth, and when I'm nervous, I make jokes."

"Do I make you nervous?"

"I'd be lying if I said no."

"Let's see what we can do about that." He tugged her toward him and lifted the covers then proceeded to work his magic on every nerve in her body.

The room was much brighter the next time Zoë surfaced. When she rolled toward Nick, she found him staring at her, as if he'd been waiting for her to wake.

The expression on his handsome face could only be described as self-satisfied when he leaned down and kissed her. "Feeling better?"

She scooted backward toward the wall until several inches separated them and shivered when the cold, unoccupied sheets touched her sleep-warmed skin. "Why did we do that?"

He stilled, and worry with a touch of panic entered his eyes. "I admit I'm not the best at reading women's signals, but you seemed willing. Did I misunderstand? Tell me the truth."

She stroked his battered brow and down the side of his face. "No, you didn't misunderstand. I was more than willing. If I'd wanted you to stop, I would have made sure you stopped."

"Then what?"

"I want to know why we made love, when the day before yesterday you told me you would never get involved with me as long as this case lasted. Why now? What made you change your mind? I need to know. I deserve to know." She poked him in the chest with her forefinger to make her point. "And don't try to tell me you don't know or you don't want to talk about it. Those typical male excuses aren't going to cut it."

The tension left his shoulders, and he smiled. "You're one tough cookie."

She refused to be mollified. "I know. So...?"

"The answer is easy. I almost lost you last night."

She gazed into his eyes, trying to read the truth in the early morning light.

He rested a hand on her shoulder but didn't try to pull her close. "Do you have any idea how I felt when I saw flames marching up the steps toward you? Saw them devouring the door? Saw smoke pouring out from under the roof? My heart almost stopped."

Zoë closed her eyes as the terrifying scene played back in her head, but this time from her vantage point inside the building. "It wasn't much fun for me, either." She rolled into his arms and nuzzled her face against his warm chest.

Nick gathered her to him and kissed her hair. "I felt so helpless. Until the firefighters arrived with their equipment, there was nothing I could do." He tipped his head back until he could see her face. "I realized I wasn't ready to lose you. I don't think I'll ever be ready."

It wasn't a declaration of love, but she didn't need one. She wasn't ready to hear those words yet. What they had was still too new to categorize or define. "I feel the same way." And for now, it was enough.

"Good." The single word reverberated with all the passion and relief he poured into the kiss that followed.

"The case isn't over," she reminded him when they finally fell back against the pillows, breathless. "Jimmy Mahoney is still loose and has proved he's as foolhardy as he is unpredictable."

Nick shifted to his back, tucked one arm behind his head, and held her close with the other. "I've been lying here, thinking about it while you slept. This place is built like a fortress and shouldn't be hard to defend if we stay vigilant. No one goes anywhere alone. We'll each do our job—I'll watch out for Lyman, and you take care of Marian. Mahoney shouldn't be able to take anyone by surprise again."

"Until he's found, I don't know what else we can do." She pushed up and leaned across his chest to snag her phone from the nightstand and check the time. "Uh, oh. It's already after eight-thirty." She threw off the covers and clambered over him, ignoring the slap of cold air against her bed-warmed skin. "Lyman and Marian are probably already up. I've got to get downstairs."

Nick caught her hand. "Relax. Everyone knows you're not really here to cook. It won't kill them to make their own toast one morning."

She jerked her hand from his grasp. "Yes, everyone knows I'm not here to cook, but they also know why I am here—to provide bodyguard services—which I'm not doing at the moment." She grabbed clean underwear, jeans, and a sweatshirt from the dresser. "It's all well and good for us to lie around talking about our strategy to protect the Prescotts, but they're downstairs alone, up to who knows what. You know Lyman—he could easily be out nosing around the smoking ruins of the garage, looking for anything he can salvage, with the door unlocked and the alarm off."

"You're right." Nick jumped up and reached for the plaid flannel shirt she'd laundered the night before.

She spared a quick second to admire his body as she pulled on her socks. Earlier, she'd had neither the time nor sufficient light to indulge her curiosity. He wasn't fat by any means, but the thick muscles of his legs, chest, and arms suggested weight and strength. Nick Rosetti was no narcissistic gym rat or waxed pretty boy, but she'd known that. He was a man in every sense of the word. He reminded her of a gladiator whose body told his story through its battle scars.

They took turns in the bathroom, and by the time she'd had a quick wash-up and run a brush through her hair, he was fully dressed and had dragged the covers back up over the bed. In the brighter light, the black thread of his stitches stood out in sharp contrast to the skin of his forehead.

Zoë reached a hand behind his head and tipped it down so she could examine his injury. "You really should cover those. The cut has barely started to heal, and they make you look a bit like Frankenstein's monster. I'll ask Marian if she has any gauze and tape."

He dipped his head for a quick kiss. "Whatever you say. Come on. Let's go."

She caught her lower lip between her teeth. "Do you think Lyman and Marian will be able to tell things have changed between us?"

He shrugged. "I suppose that depends on us. Marian might pick up on something, but if Lyman's mind is on GRAMPA, he wouldn't notice if we shaved our heads. Besides, I wasn't planning to walk into the kitchen and announce, 'Hey, guess what? I slept with Zoë last night'."

"Ha, ha."

He pulled her into his arms and kissed the tip of her nose. "I know our relationship is new, and you're sensitive about it, but I think they'd be happy for us, don't you?"

"I guess so." She slipped out of his embrace. "But we've still got a job to do, so let's go do it."

He grinned. "I believe I already suggested that."

She rolled her eyes then turned and headed down the stairs.

As Zoë had suspected, Marian was already in the kitchen, fully dressed. She was struggling to grasp the rim of a small metal bowl with the tips the fingers on her right hand and whip something with a fork held in her left. Butter sizzled in an empty cast iron skillet on the stove. As soon as they walked in, she stopped mid-whip and turned with a look of mild disappointment. "Oh, you're up. After your ordeal last night, I was hoping you'd sleep in. I wanted to surprise you." She glanced at the bowl. "I'm trying to make an omelet, but it isn't easy when you've only got one good hand."

Zoë smiled. "That's sweet of you, but I couldn't sleep any longer—too keyed up, I guess."

Marian heaved a sigh and nodded. "I understand. I was awake half the night. This old house can be so spooky sometimes. I kept thinking I heard strange noises from every corner."

"That was probably me. I couldn't sleep, and the smell of smoky clothes was driving me crazy, so I did a load of laundry in the middle of the night."

Marian gave a little laugh. "I'm glad to know it wasn't my imagination. What with squeaks on the stairs and pipes rattling in the basement, I was beginning to think I was losing my mind."

Zoë pulled a loaf of seven grain bread from the drawer. "Why don't I take over breakfast? We'll all feel better after we've eaten."

Nick reached above her to open the overhead cabinet. "In the interest of efficiency, I'll set the table. It's going to be a busy day. I expect the fire chief and Sergeant Lewis to stop by this morning with updates. And Lyman will want to contact your insurance company." He shot a quick glance around the room. "Is he still in bed?"

"Oh, no. He's been up for ages. He went down to the basement a few minutes ago. He said he'd had an idea in the night for some new modification to GRAMPA."

The words had barely left her mouth when footsteps sounded on the basement stairs, and her husband appeared in the doorway with his hands raised in the air and a look of helpless apology on his face. He stepped into the kitchen, immediately followed by Jimmy Mahoney, who was holding an ugly black semi-automatic pistol pointed directly at Lyman's back.

Chapter Eighteen

Every nerve in Nick's body jolted into full fight mode. What the hell was Jimmy Mahoney doing in the house?

He shifted his weight until he felt the comforting jab of his Ruger in the small of his back. Thank God, he'd slipped it on with the rest of his clothes out of habit.

Mahoney shoved Lyman farther into the room and waved his gun at the others, who stood together in the area between the sink and stove. "Everybody over there." He motioned toward the breakfast alcove on the opposite side of the kitchen. "And get your hands in the air."

Nick raised his hands and began walking. He wanted to put as much distance as possible between himself and the women. If Mahoney forced him to draw his weapon, he needed Marian and Zoë out of the way.

Zoë, however, ignored Jimmy's instructions, grabbed a dish towel, and reached for the handle of the frying pan, where the melted butter had started to smoke. "I'll just take care of this before we have another fire."

Mahoney acknowledged her with a dismissive grunt then turned to face Marian, but Nick's gaze darted between Zoë and the gunman. Something furtive about her body language caught his attention. Instead of setting the skillet on a cool burner or in the sink, she slowly lowered the heavy pan to her side, keeping a firm grip on the handle. When she glanced across Marian's shoulder at Nick, she dipped her chin in a tiny nod.

Jimmy's anxious gaze bounced from one to the next before settling on Marian. Anger tinged with fear distorted his fox-like features as he waved the gun at her again. "Get over there. Move. Now." For emphasis, he poked Lyman in the back, causing him to stumble.

Marian had been standing frozen, bowl and fork forgotten, staring at her ex-husband. When he pushed Lyman, she came to life and advanced toward him with the fork clutched in her left hand and fury radiating from her petite, rounded figure. "I'll do no such thing, Jimmy Mahoney. Don't you try to order me around. You should have run as far as you could when you had the chance."

"I'm here to get what's mine."

Marian scowled without a hint of fear. "Nothing here belongs to you. Have you completely lost your mind? Put that gun down."

"He set the fire," Nick said.

Lyman dropped his hands in surprise. "I thought Victor Watanabe set the fire."

Nick stared into Mahoney's eyes and saw burgeoning panic. "No. Mahoney set the fire. Watanabe was trying to put it out."

Lyman turned his head with a confused frown. "But why? And what do you want from us now?"

Mahoney gave him a vicious jab in the ribs with the pistol. "Turn around and get your hands up."

Lyman obeyed grudgingly. "I don't understand. What could you hope to gain by setting the garage on fire?"

"It was a diversion to get into the house, and it worked. At the first sign of flames, everybody ran outside." Mahoney's sharp features twisted into a parody of a condescending smile. "Not one of you noticed when I snuck around the side of the house and came in through the unlocked kitchen door."

"Why didn't you take what you wanted and get out while everyone was distracted?"

Mahoney's smile faded. "I couldn't find what I was looking for. You really hid them good after I was here before."

"That was you in the cellar with the gun, wasn't it?" Marian's eyes narrowed. "I suspected as much, but I couldn't bring myself to believe it."

"Believe it." Jimmy's mouth turned down in disgust. "I've spent way too much time in that moldy cave. I searched half the night for those damned plans, and I've been sitting down there for hours, twiddling my thumbs, waiting for your fool of a husband to show up."

Lyman's brow furrowed, but he maintained his position with his back to his captor. "You were still after the plans for GRAMPA? What good would they do you now? Ichiro Electronics dropped their bid after my final refusal."

"If they won't buy the plans, I'll sell them to someone else." Mahoney's words were tight and rushed. "Or better yet, you can just give me the money. I lost everything when I went to prison." He turned on Marian with a snarl. "You owe me...big time."

She pressed her lips together and brandished the fork as if it were a sword. "I don't know what you're talking about. You've been terrorizing my family for weeks. You've tried to kill both Lyman and me with your stupid motorcycle, and yesterday you nearly burned Zoë to death. I don't owe you a thing."

"It's your fault I went to prison."

"That was your own fault, yours and Rudy's," she shot back.

"You turned me in."

She glared at him and aimed the fork at his face. A couple of feet closer, and she could have poked him in the eye. "I did no such thing. Although I would have if I'd known what you were up to."

"You were my wife. You testified against me at the trial."

"I told them what I knew, which wasn't much."

"You could have refused to talk. They couldn't make you. We were married."

"Maybe I could have refused, but by that time I was completely disgusted by what you'd done and wanted you out of my life. I still do."

Mahoney gave his ex a swift, assessing glance and dropped the threat from his voice. "I did it for you, baby...for us. I just wanted to give you the best of everything. That's all I ever wanted."

Marian stiffened her back. "Do you honestly think for one minute that pathetic, wheedling tone will get you anywhere?"

His upper lip curled. "I know you can't love this spineless pansy." He poked Lyman again for emphasis. "There's got to be a pot full of money somewhere in this creepy old dump. If you get it, we'll run away together, and I'll remind you what a real man is like."

She gaped at him as if he'd suggested they hop a rocket ship to Mars. "I'm eight-and-a-half months pregnant, you idiot! Besides, I wouldn't walk across the street with you."

Mahoney dropped all pretense of persuasion and scowled. "If you want to keep your precious husband alive, you'll do what I say."

A cold fist squeezed Nick's heart when Marian marched forward, elbowing Lyman out of the way, and forced herself between her husband and Mahoney's gun.

Lyman's eyes rounded in horror, and he reached for her arm "Marian, what are you—?"

She jerked it from his grasp. "Don't worry. He's not going to shoot me. Are you, Jimmy?"

"I will if you make me." But he eased back a half step.

Nick moved his right hand to the small of his back, pushed his shirt up, and rested his fingers on the butt of his weapon. At the same time, Zoë inched toward Jimmy until she stopped about three feet behind him, still grasping the handle of the heavy cast iron skillet.

She was in the perfect position to attack from behind. She was also much too close to Nick's line of fire. Suddenly, he was back in the alley in Detroit with Maureen's pale face staring at him in the darkness. Sweat broke across his upper lip.

Don't go there. It will only mess with your head. Just concentrate. Everything will be okay.

He took a deep breath, focused his gaze, and flexed his right hand to relax the tight muscles.

Lyman grabbed his wife's shoulders. "Marian, stop!"

She ignored him and pinned Jimmy with a furious glare. "I've had it up to here with you." She tapped cast against her forehead. "I'm sick to death of worrying about what you might do next. You are going to walk out the door this minute and never come back. Go as far away as you can. I never want to see your face or hear your name again. Do you understand?"

Jimmy brandished his gun with a smirk. "Do you think I'm afraid of you? I'm not leaving this house without every damned cent you've got."

Marian narrowed her eyes. "That does it."

She drew her foot back and kicked him in the shin just above the top of his boot with enough force to knock them both off balance. Lyman's arms flew around her to keep her from falling, while Mahoney flung his arms wide as he struggled to regain his footing.

Nick rushed forward, drawing his weapon. But before he reached his target, Zoë raised the skillet with both hands and swung it into Mahoney's wrist. The nauseating sound of iron hitting bone reverberated through the room. Jimmy screamed, dropped his gun, and crumpled to the floor. Before he could grab his weapon again, she spun it out of reach with the toe of her boot.

Nick was on him in a flash, shoving Mahoney onto his face and pinning him to the floor with a knee in the middle of his back. Mahoney groaned and thrashed, but Nick grabbed both his arms and jerked them behind him.

Jimmy let loose a blood-curdling scream. "My wrist!"

Nick adjusted his grip from the man's wrist to his forearm but didn't loosen his hold. He glanced up at Lyman, who had his arms wrapped protectively around Marian. "I don't suppose you have any zip ties in your workshop."

Lyman shook his head. "There might have been some in the garage with the gardening supplies, but I'm sure they melted in the fire."

Zoë returned the frying pan to the stove and bent down to pick up Jimmy's gun. "I've got a set of cuffs in my purse." She skirted the felon sprawled on the floor and retrieved her bag from the kitchen table, where she'd left it the night before.

Marian's eyes rounded. "You keep handcuffs in your purse?"

Nick wondered if she was surprised or impressed— probably a little of both.

Zoë produced the cuffs. "You never know when you're going to need them."

She handed them to him, and he snapped them around Mahoney's wrists. "If you don't want these to hurt like hell," he told the man, "I suggest you remain still."

"I need a doctor." Jimmy turned his head to glare at Zoë. "She broke my freaking wrist."

"Shut up." Nick pushed to his feet. "You're lucky she didn't break your freaking head." He pulled his phone from his back pocket and glanced from Lyman, to Marian, to Zoë. "Is everyone okay? Anyone besides this moron need medical attention?"

Zoë shook her head. "I'm good."

Lyman kept his death grip on his wife. "We're fine."

Nick called nine-one-one, described the situation, and requested police and an ambulance. When he finished, he slid his phone back in his pocket. "They're on the way. It shouldn't be long."

Zoë slipped her arm around his waist and gave it a quick squeeze. "I don't know about anyone else, but I could use some coffee."

Marian sighed. "That sounds like heaven. Count me in."

Before the coffee was ready, the ambulance driver buzzed from the front gate speaker. Lyman let them in and went to unlock the front door. He returned to the kitchen, followed by the two paramedics, Kenny Zolnicki, and Sergeant Lewis.

The senior paramedic greeted the gathering in the kitchen with a big smile. "You folks are getting to be regulars. I'm glad to see none of you needs our help today." She approached Jimmy and squatted beside his head. "Can you walk, son, or do we need the gurney?"

"I can walk," he gritted out between clenched teeth. "Just get me up. But be careful—she broke my freaking wrist."

The woman glanced at Marian in surprise. "You did that, hon?"

Zoë stepped forward. "No. That would be me."

The paramedic nodded then signaled to her partner, and the two hoisted Jimmy to his feet, keeping a strong grip on each arm but taking care not to move his right wrist.

Kenny stepped forward and took the woman's place, wrapping his fingers tightly around Mahoney's left biceps. "This man is under arrest. I'll accompany him to the hospital."

She nodded. "Fine with me. Let's go." She led the way, followed by Kenny and her partner, half-dragging Mahoney between them.

Sergeant Lewis pulled off his gloves and unbuttoned his overcoat. "Mr. Prescott, I'm sure this has been quite a shock, but I'd like to ask each of you some questions while the incident is still fresh in your minds."

Lyman nodded. "Of course."

Marian extricated herself from his grasp and gestured to the kitchen table. "Please sit down. We were about to have coffee. Would you like a cup?"

Lewis smiled and pulled his notebook and pen from his inside jacket pocket. "Thanks. I missed my second cup. We don't often get armed break-ins this early."

Marian eased her bulk into her usual seat. "Technically, it wasn't a break-in. According to Jimmy, he snuck in through an unlocked door during the fire and spent the night in the basement."

The sergeant settled beside her as Nick and Lyman took their seats, and Zoë poured coffee into five cups. "Why don't we start at the beginning with the fire yesterday afternoon?"

He questioned each in turn until he seemed satisfied he had all the facts then closed his notebook and rose to button his coat. "Thank you for your help. I'll be in touch if we have any further questions."

Lyman pushed back from the table. "Sergeant, do you think this nightmare is finally over? Can we go back to our normal lives?"

"I hesitate to answer until we've completed our investigation, but barring any surprises, we appear to have all the potential culprits in custody." Lewis turned to Marian. "And I want to assure you we'll take extra precautions to keep them there."

She gave him a weary smile. "Thank you. I'm pretty tired of all this excitement."

He pulled on his gloves. "So are we, Mrs. Prescott. So are we."

Lyman saw him out then returned to the kitchen. Zoë had topped off their coffee cups and was pouring fresh egg mixture into a clean skillet. He walked up behind his wife's chair, leaned over to wrap his arms around her, and nuzzled her hair. "You're one of a kind, Marian Prescott. Do you know that? You scared me to death this morning, but you were magnificent."

"I was, wasn't I?" She grinned. "Well, we all have our limits, and Jimmy finally pushed me over mine."

Lyman chuckled. "Remind me never to do that."

He moved his hands to Marian's shoulders, and she placed her own over them with a reassuring pat. "Don't worry. You're in no danger. You're the sweetest, most considerate man I've ever known. Now sit down, and let's eat. I'm starving."

On cue, Zoë appeared at the table with a steaming plate in each hand. "Not for long." She set a plate in front of each of the Prescotts then returned with two more.

Nick surveyed the whole wheat toast with jam and a cheese omelet in front of him, surprised at his sudden hunger. Food had been the last thing on his mind for...what? He glanced at the clock on the stove. Had it really been only two hours since he'd been snuggling naked in bed with Zoë?

There was still too much cop in him to relax completely until Mahoney was safely locked away in a federal prison, but that could take months—or even years. In the meantime, he needed to make some changes. No matter what excuses he'd tried to make about coming home and starting over, it was time to admit he'd spent a large part of the past year hiding— mostly from himself. Now he needed to move forward, get a handle on his life, and start living again.

He allowed his gaze to linger over Zoë until she glanced up from her breakfast and smiled. Yes, she was a beautiful woman, but she was so much more. Clever, funny, and resourceful, she challenged him and lifted his spirits when people or situations got him down. On top of that, she was well on her way to becoming a halfway decent cook—and his mom liked her. He didn't know what the future might hold for them, but he couldn't wait to find out.

When everyone had finished eating, Zoë cleared the table. Marian rose with her cup in her hand. "I know I can't have more coffee, but I think I'd like a cup of lemon ginger herbal tea to settle my stomach." She winced and rubbed her belly. "The omelet was delicious, but I'm not sure it agreed with me."

Zoë took her cup. "I'll get it for you. Frankly, I'm not surprised you don't feel well. If subduing your armed ex-husband in the kitchen before breakfast doesn't upset your stomach, I don't know what would."

Suddenly, Marian froze and dropped her gaze to a growing puddle of liquid around her feet. When she raised her face, her eyes were round with amazement.

Lyman regarded her with a furrowed brow. "Is it time? Are you sure?"

She smiled. "Very sure. The baby's coming."

Chapter Nineteen

The baby is coming.

Zoë dumped the dirty breakfast dishes in the sink. She would deal with them later. The baby was coming!

The next half hour passed in a blur. Within minutes of her water breaking, Marian's contractions began in earnest. Since Lyman was fluttering around like a one-winged moth, Zoë helped Marian to the elevator and rode with her to the second floor so she could clean up and change clothes. She also retrieved the overnight bag Marian had packed a week earlier and the baby car seat she insisted on bringing, "so we don't forget it." Nick went outside to warm up the Black Beast. He had it ready and waiting at the bottom of the front steps by the time the women returned to the foyer.

When the elevator door opened, Lyman rushed forward and embraced Marian, leaving Zoë to wrangle both the suitcase and the car seat. His tall, gangly frame shook like a stork in a gale force wind. "It's really happening? We're going to be parents soon?"

Marian's lips turned up in a rueful smile. "Yes, but I'm not sure how soon, so try to relax. According to the doctor, I'll probably be in labor for hours."

"I'm so excited I don't know what to do!"

"You don't have to do anything except hold my hand. The doctor and I will do the rest." As she reached for his hand, her eyes widened then pinched shut, and she grimaced in pain. A few seconds later, her expression eased and she opened her eyes. "That was a strong one. Maybe we ought to get going. This might not take as long as I thought."

Zoë followed them out the door and down the steps, pausing only to lock the door and set the alarm. In the back seat, Lyman and Marian were in a world of their own, murmuring softly with their heads together like a pair of lovebirds.

After a few minutes of awkward silence, she glanced at Nick's tight-lipped profile. "How are the roads this morning?"

"Fine." His white-knuckled grip on the wheel told a different story.

She tried to lighten the mood. "Never been on stork duty before?"

"No."

O-kay.

After that, she kept quiet and watched the landscape roll by while Nick made the drive to the hospital in half the normal time, despite slowing several times to avoid bumps or sudden stops.

When they reached the main Admissions entrance, Zoë hopped out and ran in to find a wheelchair for Marian while Lyman took charge of his wife and her bag and Nick parked the car. Since Marian had already pre-registered, Lyman wheeled her off to Labor and Delivery.

This was Zoë's first experience with childbirth, and ignorance only increased her anxiety. She had been overseas when her two oldest brothers' children had been born, and Marian was the first of her friends to become a mother. As soon as the thought crossed her mind, she was surprised to realize that over the past few weeks, Marian had indeed become a friend, as well as a client.

After several minutes Nick came strolling toward her down the hall, carrying the baby seat as if he didn't have a care in the world. The idiot. Didn't he know what was happening upstairs? She raced to him and grabbed his arm. "Come one. We have to hurry. Marian's already gone to Delivery."

He laughed. "Relax. We've done our part. We got her here safe and sound. There's nothing left to do but wait, and it will probably take hours."

"But what if it doesn't? She was having hard contractions when Lyman wheeled her away." She started dragging him toward the hallway the Prescotts had taken.

"That doesn't mean much. This is her first baby. Trust me—it could take hours."

"Oh? And what makes you such an expert?" A sudden chilling thought stopped her short. "You don't have any children, do you?"

Amusement sparked in his dark eyes, and his lips twitched. "Not yet, but when Angela had her first, I sat with Kenny and my mom for fourteen hours before the real action started."

Fourteen hours? Her mother claimed Zoë was almost born on the kitchen floor. But then, she had been the sixth. "I guess we don't have to run."

After winding their way down several hallways and taking the elevator up two floors, they arrived at Labor and Delivery and were allowed to see Marian.

She greeted them with crossed arms and a moue of disgust. "The doctor said I'm just getting started, and the baby won't arrive before tonight—or maybe even tomorrow. Can you believe it?"

Nick bit back a smile and shot Zoë an I-told-you-so glance.

"And it's a good thing we had breakfast first," Marian continued, "because they won't let me eat until it's all over."

From his seat beside the head of the bed, Lyman leaned over and patted his wife's blanket-covered knee then glanced at Zoë. "You might as well go home and relax." He switched his gaze to Marian. "It's possible Marian may get a little...um...fussy before this is all over, and I'm not sure she'd want you see her in that state."

Marian's brows shot up. "Fussy? You think I might get a little fussy?" She grabbed his hand and slapped it on her belly. "Feel that contraction? I'd like to see how *fussy* you'd get if that happened to you."

"I'm sure I'd be screaming like a scalded cat, my dear." He glanced back at Zoë with a see-what-I-mean expression. "I'll call you as soon as the baby's born, and you can come back."

Nick slid his arm around her waist. "That sounds fine. We'll wait to hear from you. I hope everything goes smoothly."

Zoë gave Marian a sympathetic frown. "I'm sure you're uncomfortable."

Marian snorted and rolled her eyes.

"The baby will be here before you know it." It was a stupid platitude, but she didn't know what else to way.

"I hope you're right." Marian turned to Lyman. "I can't believe this is about to happen. I'm going to be a mother...and you're going to be a father."

Before he could reply, a wave of pain washed over her face. She closed her eyes, gritted her teeth, and released a stream of the most colorful language Zoë had heard since leaving the army. She shot a glance at Nick, he nodded, and they quickly said their goodbyes before escaping to the relative peace of the corridor outside.

As soon as the door closed behind them, he shook his head. "Whew. Marian is always so sweet. Who would have guessed she knew words like that. I'm glad I stayed in the waiting room while Angela was in labor. I don't know how Kenny held up for fourteen hours."

Zoë blew out her breath in a scornful huff. "Weenie. If you think it's tough to listen to, imagine what Marian's going through."

"I don't even want to try." He reached for her hand. "Let's go home. It's already been a hell of a day."

He was right.

Thirty minutes later, they pulled into the driveway. Nick parked in front and followed her up the steps.

When she stepped into the foyer, the big grandfather clock caught her eye. "It's already one o'clock. I guess I should see what I can pull together for lunch."

He unzipped his jacket. "I can think of something I need more than food."

She turned and raised one brow. "Oh?"

"Yeah. A nap. Want to join me?"

"That doesn't sound half-bad."

In fact, it sounded like heaven. Her adrenaline high had crashed and burned an hour ago. Her back ached, and each foot weighed at least fifty pounds. She could hardly believe only four hours had passed since Jimmy first appeared in the kitchen, holding Lyman at gunpoint. The whole scene had taken on a surreal quality in her exhausted mind. Had she really brought down an escaped criminal with a skillet? A bubble of hysterical laugher rose in her throat, threatening to escape until she tamped it down.

A nap was definitely in order.

She remembered the elevator half-way up the second flight of stairs on the way to the attic and sighed. *Too late now.* Against all sense and the dictates of her body, she forced herself to keep climbing.

When they reached her room, Nick headed straight for the bed and stretched out, fully clothed. He patted the covers beside him. "Grab an extra blanket on your way, would you?"

She pulled an old quilt from the shelf in the miniscule closet and climbed onto the bed next to him. "I hope you don't have any ulterior motives. I'm too tired to be much fun right now."

"Plenty of time for fun later." His words were low and indistinct.

He raised one arm, and she slid underneath, dragging the quilt over them. With her head pillowed on the solid warmth of his chest, the slow, steady beat of his heart lulled her to sleep in seconds.

Only a hint of moonlight lit the room when Zoë opened her eyes. She froze and concentrated on the darkness, listening for the smallest sound. Something had disturbed her, but what? Nick mumbled and shifted to his side, tightening his hold.

A faint buzz reverberated from the bedside table. Her phone. She untangled from Nick's sleepy embrace and switched on the lamp before picking up the phone. It was Lyman.

"Hello."

"He's here. William Francis Prescott." Lyman's voice had risen a couple of tones in pitch and trembled with emotion.

"Hmph?" Nick mumbled louder.

Zoë cupped her hand over the bottom of the phone. "Shhh. It's Lyman. Marian's had the baby." Then she removed her hand. "That's wonderful! Are mother and baby doing well?"

"Marian's tired and sore, but they're perfect. They're both perfect." Reverence and relief mixed in his voice. Faint voices sounded in the background before he came back on the line. "Marian says she's not up to seeing visitors this evening. She thinks it would be best if you waited until tomorrow to come over. The doctor told us he plans to discharge them around ten o'clock. You can pick us up then."

"No problem. We'll see you both a little before ten. Give my love to Marian, and give William a kiss from me."

"I will. And Zoë, thanks for everything...from the bottom of my heart."

His words softened the sharp edge of guilt that had been gnawing at her all day. If she'd investigated the noises in the basement the night before, she could have dealt with Jimmy then instead of giving him the opportunity to hold her employer at gunpoint. Only a seriously incompetent bodyguard allowed a thing like that to happen to a client. Happily, Lyman didn't seem to blame her.

"You're very welcome, but I just did the job you hired me to do."

His gratitude came through in every word. "You did so much more, and you know it. But we can discuss that tomorrow."

"Take care of your new family and try to get some rest. We'll see you in the morning."

Nick shoved up onto one elbow. "What time is it?"

Zoë glanced at the time on her phone. Six twenty-two. Had they really slept more than five hours? "After six. Marian and baby William are doing well, but she's too tired for visitors tonight. They expect to be discharged in the morning, so we'll see them then."

He rubbed a hand over his stubbled jaw then tossed the quilt back. "It's probably just as well. I'm sure I'd scare the baby."

She leaned over and gave him a quick kiss. "You look fine. I don't mind a little scruff now and then. It gives your face character."

"Really?" He raised his brows suggestively, and his dimple appeared amid the short black bristles.

"Really." She clambered out of bed. "But put that thought on hold. I'm starving."

Nick slung his legs over the side of the bed and stood. "Me, too. How about we order a couple of pizzas? You deserve a night off."

"You won't get any argument here."

When the pizzas arrived, Zoë poured herself a glass of wine, grabbed a beer from the fridge for Nick, and followed him into the living room. He set the boxes on the coffee table and lit a fire, and they sat side-by-side on the floor, leaning back against the sofa. The atmosphere was intimate and cozy and perfect.

After finishing her third slice, she downed the last of her wine and set her glass on the table. "Do you know what I think we should do now?"

Nick's mouth stretched into a slow smile. "I know what I think we should do, but why don't you go first?"

She shot him a sideways glance. "There's plenty of time for that—the night is still young." After untangling her legs, she pushed up from the floor and walked over to examine the big box in the corner. "Right now, I think we should set up this tree then go buy some ornaments and decorate it."

He tipped his head and scratched his jaw. "Not where I was going, but I guess we could do that."

Inspired by the brilliance of her plan, she began gathering up the remains of their dinner. "It's the least we can do. Think of everything the Prescotts have gone though in the past few weeks. I know they're clients, and this is supposed to be a business relationship, but wouldn't you like to do something nice for them?"

Nick rose and picked up his bottle and her glass. "I would. If we'd stopped Mahoney the first time he showed up, none of the rest would have happened."

"I feel bad about that, too. And yesterday Marian was so excited to decorate the house for the holidays. Now she's lost all her ornaments in the fire. And once she gets home, she'll be too tired and busy with baby William to decorate. I'd love for her to be able to come home to a beautiful Christmas tree."

"There's a big box store out by the interstate. They'll be open, and you should be able to get everything you want."

She slid the boxes with the leftover pizza into the fridge and closed the door "Great. Let's go."

An hour later, they were back with three huge bags of goodies.

"This is going to be so much fun." She carried the smallest bag into the foyer and held the door for Nick, whose hands were full with the other two.

"You don't think you might have gotten a little carried away?"

She carried her bag into the living room and set it on the sofa. "Don't be a humbug. You can never have too much Christmas."

It was ten o'clock by the time the tree was up and fully decorated. Zoë had assigned Nick the task of lightmaster and complimented him on a job well done when all six strands lit on the first try. Because she'd seen some of Marian's ornaments while sorting boxes in the garage, she had decided against the sophisticated maroon and silver theme featured in the store and opted instead for a colorful mix she dubbed *fancifully eclectic*. The red and white glass mittens, embroidered felt birds, and resin gingerbread men added a whimsical touch she hoped would appeal to Marian. She'd also picked up a trio of adorable, fluffy polar bears for the mantle.

After hanging the last shiny red ball, she stepped back and presented the finished tree with a flourish. "All done. What do you think?"

Nick wrapped both arms around her and snugged her back against the solid warmth of his chest. "Gorgeous."

"I hope Marian likes it."

"I'm sure she'll be thrilled." He turned her in his arms. "Now I think it's time for bed."

"But I slept all afternoon. I'm not sure I'm tired enough to sleep."

"Neither am I."

Ah. A flutter of nerves spread out from her stomach. She shouldn't be nervous—they'd made love before—

but for some reason, this felt more deliberate. Maybe it was the determination in Nick's gaze. He looked like he'd made a decision of some kind, but she had no idea what it was. When he held out his hand, she slid hers into it and smiled at his reassuring squeeze.

The several minutes it took to walk the three flights to her room did nothing to banish her butterflies. When he tugged her sweater over her head then ran one finger lightly under the top edge of her bra, they began to beat their wings frantically. And when he unzipped her jeans and used the same blunt finger to draw a sexy little line from the top of her panties to her navel, the whole swarm took flight.

Moments later, they faced each other stark naked, and Zoë shivered.

Nick stroked her bare arm with one warm hand, sending another ripple through her body. "You're cold."

"No." Weak at the knees, she backed up until her legs met the rough blanket on the edge of the bed.

He leaned over and whipped back the covers. "Get in. I'll warm you up."

Her skin tightened into fierce goosebumps the instant she touched the cold sheets, then his warmth surrounded and enfolded her, and she relaxed.

"Better?" he murmured against the tender skin of her neck.

"Um, hm." She closed her eyes to concentrate on the feel of him.

He shifted position. "How about this?"

"Mmm. Even better."

He moved lower. "And this?"

By then she was beyond words.

He took his time, exploring her body at a leisurely pace that slowly pushed her closer and closer to the edge. With the final leap inevitable, she clasped him tight, called out his name, and pulled him with her.

Several hours later, she was awakened by the opening guitar riff from George Thorogood's *Bad to the Bone* coming from Nick's jeans, which hung from the back of the chair. She would get it for him, but she couldn't seem to make herself get out of bed. The room was so cold, and she was so warm.

She nudged his shoulder. "Your pants are ringing."

"Hmph?" He opened one eye.

"Your phone...in your pants."

"Oh." He sat up and ran a hand through his rumpled hair. "I should probably get that. It might be Kenny or Lewis with news about Mahoney." He rolled over and climbed out of bed.

As he crossed the room, she settled back against the pillow to admire the view. She'd never considered herself a true connoisseur of the male posterior, but he did have a fine pair of glutes. He fished his phone out of the pocket of his jeans, took one look at the name, and frowned. Instead of answering, he tapped the red circle to decline the call and returned it to his pants.

"Not the police?" Zoë asked as he returned to bed.

"No." Nothing more.

She checked the time on her phone on the nightstand. "We should probably get up. Lyman is expecting us at the hospital by ten."

He pulled her back into his arms and nipped her earlobe. "It's early. Besides, the way I feel right now, I can make this quick."

"Not too quick, I hope."

"Never."

One thing led to another, and they barely made it to the hospital on time. When they walked into Marian's room, they found the whole Prescott family.

"Good morning. Look what the doctor did for me!" Marian waved her right arm, now free of its cast.

"I think she's more excited about that than the baby." Lyman sent her a teasing smile.

"I am not. " Marian gave him a playful shove with her newly liberated appendage. "But it's going to be so much easier to take care of William with two hands. Would you like to see him?"

Zoë grinned. "Absolutely."

After suitable oohing and aahing over the baby, Zoë asked, "Are you ready to go home?"

Marian walked gingerly to the closet and retrieved her coat. "We're just waiting for the nurse with the wheelchair. They won't let me walk out of here on my own. Hospital rules, apparently."

Zoë noticed a large teddy bear with a big red bow sitting in one of the chairs. She walked over and picked him up. "This is adorable." She glanced at the baby, asleep in his car seat and ready to go. "Even though it's bigger than William at the moment."

"It's a gift from Victor Watanabe."

Marian's matter-of-fact tone made the statement all the more startling. Zoë snapped her head around. "What?"

Lyman nodded. "Yes. His condition has improved enough that the staff allowed him to visit this morning."

"That must have been uncomfortable."

"You would think so," Marian said. "But he was really very nice. He seemed quite remorseful for everything Jimmy did."

Lyman cleared his throat. "So remorseful, in fact, that I've decided not to press charges against him. He also made me a new offer—a very attractive one—and this time I accepted."

Zoë stared at him as if antlers had suddenly sprung from his head. "I can't believe it. After everything you've been through, you're going to sell GRAMPA?"

"Not exactly. Ichiro Electronics has agreed to bankroll the manufacturing process and handle marketing in exchange for a portion of the profits. I will retain majority control and full ownership of the patents."

"That's wonderful...I guess."

Lyman beamed. "It truly is. I'm the first one to admit I'm not much of a salesman, and now I'll be able to concentrate on doing what I love without having to worry about trying to sell anything. But most importantly, GRAMPA will still be mine."

Marian took his hand and smiled. "It's a blessing."

A knock sounded at the door, and a smiling young orderly appeared, pushing a wheelchair. "Ready to go, folks?"

Marian took the seat of honor, and Lyman picked up the car seat with the still-slumbering William. While Nick went to retrieve the car and bring it around to the front entrance, Zoë strolled next to Lyman, carrying Mr. Watanabe's bear and Marian's bag. She stole periodic peeks at the tiny hero of the moment, whose round face was topped by a blue knitted cap. An unexpected spark of pride and accomplishment kindled in her heart at the sight of his perfect little nose and rosebud mouth. She knew it was unreasonable. She'd had no part in the creation of this wondrous new being—he was all Lyman and Marian's doing. But she liked to think she'd played a small part in his safe arrival.

Marian let Zoë hold William while Nick and Lyman worked to install the car seat according to the instruction manual. When he started to fuss, she took him back and bounced him on her shoulder in a time-honored mommy dance.

"Hurry up, you two," she called into the back seat. "Someone's getting hungry." Then she turned to Zoë. "You'd think two men who could repair an elevator and build a robot would be able to install a simple car seat."

Nick popped his head out from the back seat. "All done."

Marian handed the baby to Lyman, who strapped him in, then settled beside him. Lyman sat next to her with his arm draped over the back of the seat, and Zoë and Nick climbed in front. Traffic was heavier on the way back to Strathmoor, and by the time they arrived, William was howling. Marian tried her best to soothe him, but he wanted what he wanted, and no pacifier was going to take its place. Lyman shepherded them up the front step and into the house, leaving Zoë to bring the bear and Marian's tote while Nick parked the car.

Marian carried William straight upstairs to feed him, and Zoë followed. When she came back down, she found Lyman and Nick waiting in the foyer.

Lyman's red-rimmed eyes and pale complexion betrayed his exhaustion, but his smile radiated elation. "I'd like to speak to you both in my office."

Zoë raised her brows and glanced at Nick, who replied with a shrug. Whatever Lyman had to say couldn't be bad—he looked too happy. They followed him into his office and sat in the pair of chairs facing the desk.

Once they were all seated, Lyman withdrew two envelopes from the top drawer and handed one to each. "Marian and I want to give you a little something extra for all you've done for us over the past several weeks."

A pair of lines appeared between Nick's brows as he regarded the envelope, and Zoë started to object, but Lyman cut her off. "No, no, we insist. We feel bad about forcing you to work at cross purposes for so long and exposing you to risks no one could have anticipated."

"But we're bodyguards. That's our job," she protested.

He nodded. "True, but as of today, those jobs are complete. Final payments will be sent to your offices as per the contracts."

As his words sank in, the energy seeped from her like air from a deflating balloon. "You're letting us go?"

He crossed his hands on the desk and beamed. "Exactly."

Chapter Twenty

It was over.

She remembered the dejection of being fired her from her first after-school job at the diner for breaking too many dishes. This time she hadn't done anything wrong, but Lyman's words still brought a sense of loss. She'd known her time with the Prescotts would come to an end. Every bodyguard job was temporary—that was the nature of the work—but this felt different.

"I know Marian will want to thank you and say goodbye when she comes down, but you might as well start gathering your things now." Lyman smiled with the pride of a schoolboy who had just won first prize in a spelling bee.

"Are you sure you don't want to wait a little longer?" Worry lines creased Nick's brow. "Mahoney may be in custody, but he's escaped before."

"Sergeant Lewis assured us the police would take extra precautions, and I have decided to take him at his word. Marian and I are tired of worrying about Jimmy Mahoney."

"I hope you're right." Nick didn't look convinced.

"We're more than ready to get our lives back to normal. Marian is thrilled to have her cast off and be able to take care of William and do her own shopping again."

Lyman glanced at Zoë with a twinkle in his eye. "And she says you've inspired her to learn to cook."

She smiled. "If I can learn, anyone can."

Lyman rose and walked around his desk. "The deal with Ichiro Electronics will allow me to take care of my family the way I want to, and Marian will be able to stay home with the baby until she feels ready to go back to work."

He turned his attention to Nick. "Despite what she may have told you, I'm not a bad driver, and it's time I got back to it. I've ordered two new cars which will be delivered tomorrow — one for each of us."

Zoë thought of Marian's impatience with her temporary disability. "That's wonderful. I know she'll be excited to have her independence back."

"You've got that right."

They turned as Marian appeared in the doorway wearing a big smile. She walked up to her husband and put her arms around his waist. "William is asleep again. I know it probably won't last, but so far, he's a perfect angel."

Lyman hugged her close and kissed the tip of her nose. "Two Christmas angels. I'm a lucky man."

Marian freed herself from his embrace and turned to Zoë. "I saw the tree when I passed the living room." Her blue eyes sparkled with unshed tears as she took Zoë's hands. "It's beautiful. Thank you so much for doing that."

Zoë tried to banish the lump in her throat before she spoke but failed. "I wanted to make the holidays a little cheerier for you after the fire."

"You've done so much." Marian threw her arms around Zoë and engulfed her in a big hug. When she drew back, she glanced from Zoë to Nick. "Did Lyman tell you about our decision?"

Nick nodded. "Are you sure you'll be okay?"

"Absolutely. We've taken every minute of your time for weeks. We want you to be free to spend the holidays with your families."

Zoë's stomach tightened. She'd been counting on using work as an excuse to stay in Chicago again this year. It wasn't that she dreaded going home... exactly...but it had been so long. Things had changed. She'd changed. And she wasn't sure what kind of reception she'd receive.

Marian shooed them toward the foyer. "Zoë, go on up and get your bags. And Nick, be sure to send me a list of everything you lost in the fire. I'll include it in the insurance claim."

Nick walked beside Zoë toward the stairs. "I'll carry your luggage for you."

Her brain still felt fuzzy as she tried to process the sudden wrap-up of the case. "You don't have to do that."

He touched her shoulder then smoothed his hand down the curve of her spine. "I know, but I want to."

She nodded.

When they reached her room, Nick pulled her bags from under the bed and spread them on top for easy access. Since her clothes in the dresser were already folded, she had everything packed in a matter of minutes.

She surveyed the room then did one last check of the bathroom. "I guess that's it."

He hefted her suitcases, trying to balance the weight, and gestured toward the stairs with his chin. "Lead the way."

Downstairs, Lyman and Marian were waiting, and after a flurry of handshakes, hugs, and promises to keep in touch, Zoë and Nick walked out together. When they reached their cars, she unlocked the Mini, and he started loading her luggage. Just as he slung the heaviest bag—the one with her shoes and books—into the back, his phone sang in his back pocket. *Ba-da-da-da-da.*

Half-in and half-out of the car, he twisted his head. "Can you get that for me? I'm expecting a call from the garage. My truck's supposed to be ready tomorrow."

Zoë wiggled the phone out of his pocket and glanced at the screen. It read "Maureen" and a number. A fist squeezed her heart.

He backed out of the car and straightened. "Who is it?"

She held the phone up facing him. His mouth tightened into a straight line as he reached for it. "I need to take this."

Talking in low tones, he walked around to the other side of the Black Beast. Zoë waited for a moment, then loaded the last two bags, and shut the hatch with a loud, metallic thud. She had just opened the driver's door when Nick appeared at her side. They stared at each other for a long moment without speaking.

How hard can it be to say goodbye? It's just one simple word, two syllables. Good...bye.

She opened her mouth, but he beat her to the punch. "I've got some things I have to take care of, but we need to talk. I'll call you. Soon."

Wow. That's all he's got to say after everything we've been through? A declaration of undying devotion might be overkill, but really? How lame can you get?

"Sure." She flashed him a tight smile then climbed into her car and slammed the door.

When she glanced in the rear view mirror, she thought she saw him mouth the words "drive safely".

Jerk.

She drove home, muttering all the way.

After a miserable, mostly sleepless night, Zoë spent the following two days moving back into her apartment, mentally and physically. She cleaned, did laundry, picked up her mail, and restocked the refrigerator. As she pushed her cart down the frozen foods aisle at the grocery store, she caught herself reaching for frozen dinners, but before she succumbed to bad habits and self-pity, she slammed the freezer door and moved on. Over the past couple of months, she'd learned to enjoy cooking...mostly. The fact she no longer had anyone else to cook for didn't mean she had to abandon the progress she'd made.

By eight o'clock the second night, she'd nearly worn herself out trying to ignore the newly oppressive solitude of the apartment she'd loved since the day she moved in. She'd been happy to have quiet and her own private space after years of communal military living, but now the silence weighed on her. At Strathmoor, someone was always around. She'd grown used to Marian's humming or the muted sounds of her television shows. Even memories of Lyman's occasional prissiness and GRAMPA's messy malfunctions brought a smile to her lips.

And then there was Nick. They'd grown so close in such a short time. At least she thought they had. Maybe she'd read too much into his protective behavior and tender caresses. She tried to tell herself their situation was a lot like being in combat, and stress often led to short, intense relationships, but her heart wasn't buying it. She missed his gruff manner, his direct, no-nonsense approach to problems, even his glass-half-empty, semi-suspicious outlook on life. But she also missed his unquestionable integrity, his prickly sense of humor, and that damned dimple.

After pouring a glass of Pinot noir, she snuggled up on the sofa with an afghan and a pile of holiday catalogues that had accumulated in her absence, and flipped on the television to one of her favorite old Christmas movies, the original black-and-white version of *The Bishop's Wife*. The first time the doorbell sounded she thought it was the movie. After the second ring she realized it was her door.

Who could that be at this hour? And how did they get into the building without buzzing?

She set her glass on the coffee table and went to peer through the peek hole in the door. The convex glass of the tiny lens distorted Nick's features as he leaned one eye close to peer back at her. Even looking like an image from a carnival funhouse, he sent her pulse skittering.

She took a deep breath and released it before opening the door. "Hi. I wasn't expecting to see you. How did you get in?"

He grimaced and rubbed the back of his neck with one hand before meeting her gaze. "I piggy-backed on one of your neighbors. The building manager should probably send out a reminder about that." At least he had the grace to look embarrassed. "I thought about calling first, but I wasn't sure how you'd react. Can I come in?"

She stepped back and pushed the door wide. "Sure."

After draping his coat over a dining chair, she led the way to the kitchen. "Can I get you something to drink?"

He glanced at the open wine bottle on the counter. "If that's what you're having, I wouldn't mind a glass."

She poured then handed it to him, and he followed her into the living room. After settling on the couch, she turned off the television, picked up her glass, and faced him. "You said you had things to do, so I assume you've been keeping busy the last couple of days."

He nodded. "I turned in the Beast and got my truck back." He took a long sip from his glass. "I also put out some feelers about a new job."

Her brows shot up. "Really? Doing what?"

"I decided you were right. I'm a lousy private investigator."

She sucked in a sudden breath through her teeth. She'd never intended to suggest he quit his job altogether. "I didn't mean—"

"No, no." He shook his head. "I wasn't any good because my heart wasn't in it. This case showed me how much I miss real police work. I've started talking to several suburban departments about a position as a detective."

"That's wonderful!" She meant it. "Watching you work, I could tell that's the best place for you."

"That's not all." He glanced down at his hands then back at her. "I...uh...also had some other personal things to attend to the last couple of days."

For two days the memory of his call their last morning at Strathmoor had been circling her brain like a hawk eyeing a field mouse. And like any determined raptor, it had refused to give up and fly away.

"Like Maureen?" she blurted out.

Rats.

She'd sworn she wouldn't bring up his old girlfriend. When would her mouth learn to take orders from her brain?

His dark eyes pinned her with a penetrating gaze. "For one, yes. She was in town and wanted to get together."

Double rats.

Zoë was sure she didn't want to hear what was coming next.

"She's getting married next summer. She wanted to tell me in person."

Aah.

Her tension eased, but only a fraction. Should she say, "That's great" or "I'm sorry?" His expression told her nothing. What if he was heartbroken and trying to appear stoic?

He seemed to sense her dilemma, because his lips tipped up and crinkles appeared around his eyes. "It's okay. In fact, it's good. I'm happy for her."

She smiled in response before she remembered Maureen was only one of many unanswered questions between them. Settling back against the pillows, she tucked one leg beneath her. "So what brings you here?"

Nick set his glass on the table and leaned forward, resting his forearms on his knees and clasping his hands. "I've got a proposition for you."

A proposition? That could mean anything from an offer to change the oil in her car to an invitation to jet off to Paris for the weekend. She took a sip of her wine. "O-kay."

"We want you to come for Christmas."

Her brows shot up, and her jaw dropped. He was chock-full of surprises today.

He rubbed the knuckle of one thumb with the other. "Since you said you weren't going home for Christmas, Mom wants you to spend the day at her house. The whole family will be there—Mom, Angela, Kenny, and the kids."

"And you."

"Yeah. And me. How about it? Mom's a great cook, and you won't have to lift a finger."

She pictured the cheerful chaos of the holiday on the farm, with her brothers racing noisily through the house, while her mother and grandmother worked their magic in the kitchen. It might be fun to be around children at Christmas again. She'd been feeling sorry for herself, sitting alone in her apartment. She liked Terry and Angela. And Nick would be there.

"That would be nice. Thank your mom for me."

The tight lines around his mouth eased, as if there had been more at stake in his mind than a simple holiday meal. "Good. But that's only half the proposition."

She narrowed her eyes. Christmas with his family was a big step. What else did he have in mind?

"If you spend Christmas with my family, I'll spend New Year's with yours."

"What?" His first offer had surprised her, but it was nothing compared to the shock of the second. Outrage bubbled up inside her. How dare he try to manipulate her that way? "What makes you—?"

He raised a hand to stem the tide of angry words. "Zoë, listen to me. You wouldn't go home for a short visit at Thanksgiving, even though there was time. You said you haven't spent the holidays with your family in years. I understand you have issues with your mom, but they're not going to magically disappear. You need to go home. You need to see your family." He lowered his chin and gave her a hard stare. "You know I'm right."

As she met his unyielding gaze, the fight drained out of her. He was right. She did know. That was the hell of it.

He picked up her phone from the coffee table and held it out to her. "Call your mother."

She took the phone and stared at it. What should she say? What could she say? Their last conversation had left her hurt and frustrated, as usual. How did she overcome that?

"It's simple." Nick's voice was low and calm. "Tell her you want to come home."

"It's late," she said, stalling. "She's probably already in bed."

"It's never too late. She's your mother."

Zoë swallowed hard then scrolled until she found the number and pressed Call. Her father answered on the third ring.

"Hi, Dad."

"Zoë, is that you? Is everything all right? Where are you?" His voice held the mix of surprise and worry she knew so well. Some things never changed. Once a dad, always a dad.

"Everything's fine. I'm in Chicago. Can I talk to Mom?"

Moments later her mother came on the line. "Zoë?"

"Hi, Mom. I know it's short notice, but I was thinking about coming home for a few days at New Year's."

When only the sound of soft sobbing greeted her ears, her eyes began to sting. "Mom, are you okay?"

"Yes, yes. I'm fine." Her mother stopped to blow her nose. "I'm just so glad to hear from you. I'm sorry I was short with you the last time you called. Adam's boys were chasing the cat, trying to tie a bow around his tail. Of course, you know you can come home any time."

Zoë dashed an errant tear from her cheek. "Um...would it be all right if I brought a friend?"

"This wouldn't by any chance be a male friend, would it?" Her mother's voice had regained most of its usual vigor.

Zoë glanced at Nick, who hadn't taken his gaze off her. "Yes, very."

"Oh, thank God."

Well.

They talked a couple more minutes before she said goodbye and ended the call.

"What did she say?"

One side of her mouth tipped up in a rueful smile. "Apparently, my mother has been waiting for years for me to bring a young man home."

His dimple appeared. "Well, at least I qualify on one count."

She set the phone back on the table. "I feel better, lighter." She turned and searched his eyes. "How did you know?"

His expression sobered. He reached for her and pulled her into his arms, resting his chin on her head. "I knew because I know you. You need harmony. You need things to be right. And you'll never be happy if you're emotionally separated from the people you love."

She felt like he'd ripped back a protective veil and seen straight to her core—exposed, yet liberated at the same time.

She twisted until she could see his face. "We've only known each other a few weeks. How could you possibly know that about me?"

He shrugged. "Because I pay attention…and because I care about you."

She must have looked as surprised as she felt, because he smiled and tugged her close, until only a whisper separated their mouths. "Don't tell me you didn't know. Women are always bragging about their infallible intuition."

She shook her head. "Not me."

His breath warmed her lips. "Don't feel bad. I just recently figured it out myself." Then he closed the gap with a kiss that seared her to the center of her soul.

When he finally eased back, she rested her cheek against his. "I care about you, too, you know."

He shifted her in his arms until he could see her face. "Really?"

"Really." She nodded. "I just figured it out recently, too."

"Then I guess we'll have to decide what to do about it."

"I guess we will."

He brushed his lips lightly across hers. "I know a good place to start."

She smiled against his mouth. "And where would that be?"

"Right here."

His kiss spoke of promises and possibilities, better than any words. And he was right. It was the perfect place to start.

About the Author

I write romance because that's what I like to read. The world provides more than enough drama and tragedy. I want to give my readers the happily-ever-after we all crave.

I haven't always been a writer, but I have always embraced creativity and relished new experiences. By the time I was twenty-one I had traveled the world from Tunisia to Japan. Little did I suspect I was collecting material for future characters and stories along the way.

I've been married to my personal hero for more than thirty years. After decades of living in the Midwest, we heeded the siren call of sun and sea and moved to the most breathtakingly beautiful place imaginable - the gorgeous central coast of California. I look forward to bringing you all the new stories this place inspires.

Alison

For details about my other books and news about new releases, I invite you to visit my website at **www.alisonhenderson.com**.